"STAND BY THE GUNS!"

It was utterly dark, but against the glow of dying flames to the east, Patrick Dalton could make out the dim silhouettes of two pursuing warships closing in on either side. *Faith* slowed and settled as she moved between them.

"Fire as they bear!" Dalton called.

The range was so close he could hear splintering wood to port as the four-pounder roared. Then the starboard gun spoke. Moments later, *Faith* came out of the lee, her sails filling. But on both sides of her, overhead, batteries of heavy guns began to fire broadsides.

"Rig for running wing and wing!" Dalton shouted while thunder and chaos echoed on either side. Then *Faith's* rudder bit water and she rode a crest heading north into darkness.

"Lord a'mercy!" Clarence Kilreagh announced. "They just shot hell out of each other!"

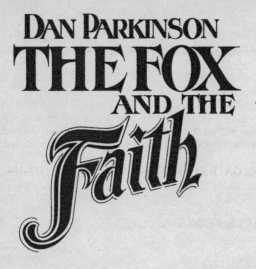

DAN PARKINSON
THE FOX
AND THE
Faith

PINNACLE BOOKS
WINDSOR PUBLISHING CORP.

PINNACLE BOOKS

are published by

Windsor Publishing Corp.
475 Park Avenue South
New York, NY 10016

First printing: April, 1989

Printed in the United States of America

PROLOGUE

She was laid to scale in the mould loft of Point Furness Yards according to the designs of Pietre Van Doorn, who thus paid for his fare to America. Master shipwrights scaled up the plans and drew them full size on the loft floor, then sent their timber crews beyond Chesapeake to find the great live oaks from which they would shape timbers.

Her curving keel was trimmed and set on blocks in the fall of 1773. Stout framing timbers were cut, adze-hewn, and set in place upon the keel. The heavy mallets of muscled men drove great treenails into place to secure the sturdy timber knees and shaped ribwork that must support the weight and tensions of a working ship. Strong stern post was set in place, and stanchions to support tall masts and sturdy deck. She lay then through the winter, fine-curing in the sheltered air below the loft.

With spring they were at work again, dressing timber beams and the broad planks which would enclose the hull—three inches thick for siding strakes, five

5

inches for the spaced wales that must support the stress of rigging. Shipwrights and carpenters assembled upon the cured keel a complex skeleton of curved and tapered timbers. Two thousand mature trees were felled to produce her substance. Live oaks became her timbers, yellow pines her masts and spars, pit-sawn cypress the thick skin of her hull, and white oak from the forests of New England her rails and decking.

Bow and stern they shaped with careful eye for great strength and gliding grace, and the skeleton became a sleek hull, long wales curved into place and the siding strakes below them, each by number. Caulked and tarred she slid downways and her deep keel took first water. "See how she schoons," they said, and were pleased.

From the mast pond they selected tall, straight trunks, seventy-seven feet in length for mainmast, the foremast sixty-nine. Working from a floating stage they stepped these into place. Shorter topmasts were bound atop them, using iron hoops, and high topgallants above these. Wide spars were cleated in on tops and gallants, and from each prime mast swung long mainsail arms—top gaff only for the spencer foresail, rising gaff and bottom boom for the driving spanker.

Then came the riggers with cable and turnbuckle, the blacksmiths with their fittings, sailmakers to design her suit, topmen and taffmen to fit it. They came in teams, the outfitters and craftsmen. Painters and tacklemen swarmed over her, scrubs and trimmers, and carpenters placed the facings in her cabin and deep holds. Pumps were fitted, and a great capstan winch secure on its buttressed stanchion. Coopers and ropemen delivered their wares to outfit a proper ship's lockers. Anchors and chain, casks and pins, slings and boat davits were placed, and a fine jolly boat hung astern.

Even as she grew the economy that fathered her deteriorated, and with it the stability of the realm.

In the spring of the year 1775 she stood at anchor, a schooner ready for sea, and they came down to see her and feel the pride of their creation.

At the top of the ways the shipyard owners and their senior shipwrights tugged at their lips in concern. "The accounts are in arrears," the chandler said. "She stands now, but who will pay the bill?"

"War breeds fortunes," the master shipwright told them. "Yon stands a proud topsail schooner, the best we've done. There'll be one who needs her. Have faith."

"Let's hope you're right, then," the master of yards nodded. "And so we should name her."

Her name was *Faith*.

I

Dawn's line was a promise in the east as Patrick Dalton finished his breakfast, buckled on sword and coat, and went on deck to take *Herrett's* morning watch. Below the quarter rail he paused. The whisper of sea past the ship's sturdy hull had risen in pitch in the night, and her roll was more pronounced. He nodded approval.

High summer was past in this second year of insurgence in the Crown's American colonies, and the winds had gone fickle of late. But now a steady southeaster filled *Herrett's* sails and drove her steadily northward, bound from the Indies to join Howe's fleet at New York Bay.

By the glow of riding lights Dalton cast a practiced eye over the working decks. Pigtailed hands stood aside as he looked at the placement of pins in the fife rails where lines from the maintops were dogged. Their placement told him the set of high sails in the darkness aloft. The set told him the bearing of the wind. He cocked his head at a flutter of sound from

9

above. The main topsail was luffing a bit. To a waiting bosun Dalton said, "Your maintop port sheet has slack, Mister Reed."

The man listened. "So it has, Mister Dalton, Hands a'deck, snug the sheetline on port pin two."

As the tall young officer turned away, Mister Reed pursed his lips and tipped his head, listening aloft as the flutter died in whisper of fine-trimmed sail. It was a matter of wonder among the veteran tars that Patrick Dalton, at twenty-seven years, with his eye for rigging and ear for trim, and with an uncommon service record aboard King's vessels, had not yet been given command of a ship of his own. Most such first-rate officers were captains long since.

But then, Mister Dalton lacked associates among the peerage. And, most important, he was Irish.

Dalton climbed to the lamplit quarterdeck. His watch helmsman, Christie Miles, and his young clerk, Billy Caster, were there ahead of him. With a nod to them he saluted the officer of the deck. "First Officer Dalton reporting for watch."

The man returned his salute. "At the bell, Sir." They stood at ease while final sands ran out, then the officer turned the glass. He called below, "Eight bells, Mister Reed." As the bell sounded below the quarter rail, he saluted Dalton again crisply. "The watch is yours, Commander."

"Relieved, Mister Oates. Take the helm, please, Mister Miles. Course and reports, Mister Caster?"

"Course north. Heading north." Billy's adolescent voice broke and he coughed to regain his unreliable new baritone. "Deadwatch reports no sightings.

10

Navigator charts us past Chesapeake, five knots steady by the line, courses and topsails."

"Wind, Mister Caster?"

"Eighteen and freshening, Sir. Southeast coming south-southeast."

"Very good, Mister Caster. What will it do?"

In the lantern light Billy paused, considering. "Faring" the wind was no part of a clerk's job, but Mister Dalton was forever instructing him in the seamen's arts. "I expect it'll come due south by midwatch, Sir, and freshen to twenty or better."

"And why do you say so?"

"The sky, Sir. There's high overcast with scud below. Besides, if it just keeps doing what it's doing now it'll come to south and twenty, won't it?"

"Very good, Mister Caster." In port, Dalton sometimes addressed crewmen by their first names, but never aboard. It was well understood that Mister Dalton made a deal of correctness aboard and frowned on laxity. It was also understood that no man had a harder time following strict protocols than he himself.

Hands on the stern rail, Dalton looked out over *Herrett's* dark wake. "Has Captain Furney come up yet this morning?"

"No, Sir, though deadwatch says the captain was on deck for a time about three bells, then went below."

"Very well. Bosun of the watch!"

"Aye, Sir?"

"Fresh lookouts aloft to spy the morning."

"Aye, Sir."

"Bring up the duty roster, Mister Caster, then you can go below and have your breakfast."

"Aye, Sir." The boy scurried away on his errand. A waif, barely of age when he ran to sea on a merchantman, Billy Caster had seen his share of navy life in the past two years. Colonial by birth, the boy had been taught to read, write, and cipher, and had instruction in gunsmithing before his young world ashore had been devastated by plague. Orphaned at twelve with nowhere to turn, Billy had gone before the mast on a merchantman. When it was shelled and its survivors taken, he was among them. The boy had come near to being knocked in the head before Dalton took him under his wing as clerk. Dalton was pleased with that decision. Billy was as able a clerk as a ship's officer ever had.

"Ease a'starboard a bit, Mister Miles. Hold full and by."

"Aye, Sir."

A trace of light was in the sky now, and *Herrett's* wake rode ghostly on the swells. She was a fighting brig of twenty-seven guns and boarded a crew of eighty and a company of marines. She carried patches on her sails and fothering on her hull from the action she had seen, blooded twice in encounters with privateers, but she was sound in the knees and taut in the rigging, and she sang her contentment as she coursed northward on the rolling sea.

"On deck!"

Dalton peered aloft. High on the maintop he could see the lookout perched in the trestletrees, silhouetted against lightening sky. He cupped his hands. "Lookout report!"

12

"Sail sighted, Sir! Quarter a'port an' hard down on the horizon!"

"Very well, lookout! Stand your watch!"

Captain Furney's head appeared at the quarter-deck ladder. Compact, grayed, and trim in his seacoat, *Herrett's* master came on deck. "What's the sighting, Mister Dalton?"

"Sail, Sir. Ahead and quarter aport. Sighted from the trestletrees, hard down. That will put her twenty miles away if she's of size."

"Aye." Furney gazed about at the morning. "Visibility's good, then. Fine weather, Mister Dalton."

"Aye, Sir. Any course change?"

"Keep her steady as she goes, Mister Dalton. We are making good time."

By four bells of the morning watch, with the sky a high, bright haze, *Herrett* had closed to where lookout could distinguish two sets of sails, one a tall ship and the other smaller, now some ten miles ahead and on course with the brig.

"They're movin' slow, Sir," deckwatch relayed the report. "The little ship's a fore-and-aft of some kind. Two masts. It's tackin' for the wind, The big one's just layin' back, followin'. It looks like a frigate."

Dalton nodded. Likely a Crown ship with a prize, heading home to New York Bay, he thought, and for a moment let his mind drift. Prize-taking was a heady dream. *Herrett* had taken one . . . the one the merchantman Billy had come from .. and even that battered old hulk had brought enough bounty that Dalton's share as first officer had helped pay some of his debts back in Belfast. He hoped delivery had been made. One day he might return to Ireland, if

13

he could pay the rest of it and a few assorted bribes. On that day he could stand before the Fitzgerald and . . . he shook his head fiercely, clearing away the daydreams. It wasn't likely he would see Molly again, no matter how his purse might bulge. And he wasn't sure he wanted to, when it came to that. He was a fool to long for such a fickle creature.

Near noon the sun broke through, and the distant ships were visible from the deck, specks of sail on the fore horizon. Dalton had finished his watch, and he strode to the forecastle, glass in hand, to take a look.

The near ship was a frigate, and a big one—a first-rate cruiser by the look of her. She lumbered along on reefed sails, staying back from the smaller craft, bearing ever northward. The schooner flew colors of a prize vessel taken in combat. White cross on a red field—that would be the frigateer's prize flag.

The men aboard her would be from the frigate's crew, taking her home for registry and auction.

The frigate itself was a tall, dark-hulled ship, with two tiers of gunports. Dalton glassed her and drew breath in a whistle. He had seen frigates before, but never one so large. Counting the ports in her hull, and the big chaser cannons fore and aft, he reckoned forty-four guns in all—armament enough for a ship of the line, yet a frigate fast and deadly—a great predator of a ship, built to seek out, close, and kill.

"Can you make her colors yet, Mister Dalton?"

Busy with his glass, Dalton had not noticed Captain Furney coming up beside him. "No, Sir, not yet." He offered the glass and the captain shook his head.

"I don't need it. I know that vessel." His brows were lowered in a frown of distaste. "Have you heard of the frigate *Courtesan*, Mister?"

At the name, memory came. "I have that, Captain. A warrant ship, assigned to the fleet but private-owned, as I recall. Her captain is . . ."

"Hart." Furney nodded, the distaste stronger in his features. "Captain Jonathan Hart. They call him the Prizemaster, and for good reason. The man's no better than a pirate. But I'll say this for him, he is a master mariner. It's just a shame his skills and his ship aren't put to more use for the fleet and less to line his own purse."

"We'll close in on him in an hour or so. Shall we hail him?"

"I think not. We'll put over a bit and give him a wide berth. We're due at Long Island, and I don't fancy wasting time in civilities with a pirate, even if he does fly the King's flag."

Herrett heeled two points to starboard, sails were trimmed, and she cruised on, setting a wide course around the frigate and its captive American schooner. In early afternoon they were seaward and abreast, and the schooner veered near on a starboard reach, near enough to make out details of her.

Dalton stood amidships, glass to his eye, and studied the little ship as it angled near. It was a sweet vessel, trim and neat, with smooth-rounded bow that took the water like a lady taking to the dance. A swift and crafty ship, he thought, though those fools at her tiller and sheets had no notion how to make her fly. They were square-rigger sailors, and they handled the sleek schooner clumsily.

15

"She's a trim little lady," Dalton commented to no one in particular. "With the proper master she could outrun the lot of us, on her cross-wind sails. A man could woo a lady like that and take her where the sea's fair and there'd be nowhere he couldn't go."

"Talking to yourself, Mister Dalton?" A grinning second officer stepped up next to him.

"Thinking aloud, Mister Clark. See the schooner there, see how she takes the spray on her bow, though that crew has no idea what it's doing."

Clark leaned on the rail. "She's a sweet one, all right. But a ship's a ship, not a lady."

"That one," Dalton said firmly, "is a lady."

The schooner hove to near enough for its crew to wave at the brig, then swung its big spanker and spencer sails and laid over on a port reach, showing its heels as it danced away. Dalton sighed and put away his glass.

"On deck!"

In the foretop a lookout waved and pointed. Two more ships were in sight, making out from the distant coastline, closing on them under full sail. They came on abreast, stacked sails riding high, gallants and royals billowing above their topsails. They had the look of warships, but they flew no King's colors.

"Privateers," Dalton breathed. He turned and raced for the quarterdeck.

Captain Furney was there ahead of him, at the helm. Bosun's whistles shrilled along the length of *Herrett's* deck, calling hands to battle stations.

"A pair of snows, Mister Dalton. Privateers, most likely, though they could be one of the colonial navies. We'll see their colors in a bit."

16

An officer with a glass turned from the rail. "The frigate's signaling us, Sir. I read his bunting. He's seen the hostiles and wants us to join him. He says close in, Sir."

Furney spat. "Wants us to help protect his prize, it is. Wants me to jeopardize my ship so he can take his bounty home intact. Tell me, Mister Dalton, were this your command, what would you do?"

Dalton kept his peace. It was a rhetorical question, and the captain would make his own answer.

"Aye," Furney growled. "I'll help him, but I'll not enjoy the doing of it. And do you know why I'll help him, Mister Dalton? Because his bunting is a call upon *Herrett's* honor. He could make sail and show his heels to those snows, but he chooses to stay with his little prize. I could show my heels to the lot of them, but he's called on my ship's honor and I can't refuse that. Hard aport, it is, then." A helmsman spun the wheel as deck hands and topmen answered the bosun's calls to trim sails on the new heading.

"Man all guns!" the captain roared. "Maybe we can take home a prize of our own, then."

Billy Caster was at Dalton's elbow. "Are we going to fight, Sir?"

"Aye, Mister Caster. We are going to fight."

Herrett closed course with the frigate and buntings flew. They stood apart three hundred yards, plowing northerly on short sails while the nimble schooner danced ahead of them—short reach to port, long to starboard, short to port again. Behind, coming up, the snows ran full-sailed and hull-up, cresting their bow wakes in long rolls of spray. Guns bristled.

17

When they were a quarter mile away, the frigate *Courtesan* put on sail and leaned, picking up way, making a long sweep to port. The snow on the left, a dark-hulled ship with tattered jibsail, veered to close on the larger vessel. The one on the right, red-hulled and flying a red banner from its topmast, made straight for *Herrett*.

Although smaller than the frigate *Courtesan*, the twin snows had the advantage. They were upwind, coming down on their prey, and neither brig nor frigate was rigged for speed on a crosswind tack, or for coming into the wind.

Furney took *Herrett's* helm and watched the red snow bearing down. At a furlong they could make out the men at its foredeck guns, the swells cleaving under its bow. "They are confident," Furney said. "The red snow has thirty guns I make it. Can you read her colors, Mister Dalton?"

"No navy ensign, Sir. She's a privateer."

"Ah. She's closing to fire." Furney's hands whitened on the spokes of the helm. "Now!" Full out on the courses, bosun! Hands to the topsails. Sheet home! Sheet home!" With a heave he spun the helm hard to starboard. *Herrett* responded, heeled, and veered as a blossom of white appeared at the snout of the pursuing snow. It grew to a sudden white cloud, obscuring the ship, and a great ball shrilled past *Herrett's* beam to churn into the sea beyond, scudding across swells before it sank far ahead. Furney's cheeks went gray. "There is why he's confident, Mister Dalton. That was a long twelve. he has ranging guns."

Even as the smoke cloud drifted toward them, dispersing, another appeared at the bow of the snow, now heeling to follow. The report of the first shot was drowned in a melee of splintering wood and snapping stays as the second ball hummed through *Herrett's* rigging. Far in the foretop a man screamed and fell, debris from a shattered yardarm following him into the closing wake.

Pipes wailed. "Fore topgallant's gone! Hands aloft! Grapples and stays!" Even as the sail collapsed, fouling the course below it, men were swarming aloft on both sets of foremast shrouds to cut away the damage and repair.

"Mister Dalton, command the guns, Sir!" Furney fought the helm, trying for trim.

Dalton braced about. Below him, white faces peered upward from *Herrett's* stern chasers, three at each gun. The twin nine-pounders were loaded and locked. Gunners held slow fuse smoking on linstocks.

"Elevate!" he shouted, glancing back at the snow. "Handspikes!" The gunners pried their cannons upward, set their quoins. "Gunners to notches, bear on his topyards, fire as she bears!"

Herrett rode up on along swell and heeled downward, and both guns roared. Nine pounds of powder hurled two iron balls at the predator in their wake. Smoke rolled over the brig's decks. Dalton steadied his glass. Spume rose ahead of the red snow and a gaping hole appeared in its bow below the jibstays. "Too much range, Captain. Can we close?"

"Aye, we'll have to. Mizzens aloft! Trim for starboard tack!"

Herrett came hard about, losing way as she faced

19

a quarter into the wind. Yardarms swung to lateral. Pipes shrilled to organize the bedlam on deck as frantic hands hauled and dogged sheetlines. Riding tackle clattered. Sails boomed. Tall masts heeled far out over the rising sea.

And now they had the snow off their starboard bow and closing. Dalton raced for the midships catwalk, dodging and leaping through the crowded decks. Here were *Herrett's* big guns, the carronades. Ports open, gunsnouts out, the gunners awaited him. Fire blossomed from the snow's rail. Smoke and thunder rolled across. With the wail of a thousand banshees, chain swept the brig's decks. Directly below Dalton a gunner and two crewmen disappeared in a welter of red spray. Staylines sang and parted. Men screamed and fell. The gunners waited. In the instant's pause following, Dalton's eyes swept from his guns to the snow, now two hundred yards abeam. Far beyond, in the sunlight, dirty clouds grew where *Courtesan* engaged the other snow.

"Ready!" He called to them and linstocks went up with their burning fuse. "Hull at the waterline, lads!" Fire as she bears!"

Gunners knelt to sight, the linstocks went down. *Herrett's* deck shuddered as seven great carronades volleyed in time. Winches rattled. The guns were drawn inboard for reloading. "Marines aloft!" Redcoats swarmed the shrouds, and musketfire rattled from the ratlines, too soon. "Hold until she closes!" Dalton roared. "Then sweep her decks!"

The snow was faltering. Some of the carronades had made their marks. There were holes at her waterline. "Now, by damn, he is not confident," he swore. "He wanted to chase, not close and fight."

The snow was veering, trying to gain distance, but *Herrett* held her arc, still closing. Captain Furney was a fury at the helm. He could wring a ship out and make it do what its designers would not have dreamed. A cacophonous medley of fighting sounds deafened him.

The midships battery had taken its cue. Cannon above and carronade below, *Herrett* spat her venom across the smoking water. Even at this distance Dalton heard the crash as the snow's foremast splintered at its stump. In the haze he saw its tall yards falling lazily back against the fouled main. But its cannons were still talking. A ball cut vacuum past his ear and threw splinters from the main mast beyond him. Screams of agony erupted from the men there.

Like a hound to the kill, Dalton concentrated on his prey, panting through clenched teeth. In a wind-cleared moment he saw the red snow clearly. She was dead in the water, her rigging hopelessly fouled. *Herrett* sat almost still, sails a-sag as Furney put her nose dead into the wind. Dalton looked around. What was he doing? The ship could not move so. But then her high sails crackled, wrapping themselves back against their masts. Confused bosuns laid off their pipes, staring astern. There was no such condition as this in their training. Through the jumble, the tangle and the smoke, Dalton could see Furney at his helm, calling orders. They were relayed along the deck, and hands rushed to loosen sheets. Dalton let his mouth sag open. They were sheeting

21

forward. The lines cleated, sails spanked against their masts, and *Herrett* began to move . . . backward.

"If I lives to tell o' this . . ." a man near Dalton rasped.

"The masts can't take it!" Dalton shouted, his voice lost in the brig's whine. Distressed tackle clattered and sang. Spars shivered. The masts groaned in their pinnings and there were ominous cracklings below.

But they held. Backing water, *Herrett* came about, her bow lining up on the crippled snow. Dalton ran for the forecastle, slipping, nearly falling on the blood-slick deck. "Bow chasers ready!"

Twin long guns snouted out, flanking the brig's heavy jib. "Gunners to your notches! Take her amidships! Fire as she bears!" They thundered. The red snow's hull collapsed amidships. She sagged, with a broken back. *Herrett's* nose continued to swing as the helm fought for wind. Sixty degrees past windward the whistles shrilled and lines were run back to proper cleating. Yards swung and high sails filled. *Herrett* began to move forward, hull-up and climbing. Dalton glanced back at the distant helm, shaking his head in admiration. He wouldn't have believed it could be done. The drifting snow, a shambles on the water, was coming aport, and he hurried to the gunnery catwalk there, but there was no need of another broadside.

Even as he arrived, the red snow's ensign crawled down its halyard. She had striken colors. *Herrett* plowed past, gaining way on her port tack.

Ahead, in the distance, the dark snow had passed the frigate and was driving for the fleeing schooner. *Courtesan* lumbered behind, swinging wide to come about and follow. Neither ship showed much damage from this distance. If both had ranging guns, they had stood off, shooting from a distance. It was obvious they had not closed for combat.

Dalton felt the surge of *Herrett's* deck as the brig heeled and angled to intercept the dark snow. He looked about him. Blood ran red in the lintels. Amidships were crawling heaps of injured and dead. Broken staylines swung loose, their stumps trailing overboard. For the first time he noticed that Billy Caster was beside him. The boy gazed about at the carnage, his young face ashen. He looked about to be sick. He had followed his officer around the brig's gunnery decks through the battle. Dalton had not told him not to.

Dalton put an arm across the boy's shoulders. "Come along, Mister Caster. "We'll be wanted on the quarterdeck."

Captain Furney rode his helm with a devil in his eye. "Look what he has done to my ship!" Dalton knew he meant the frigate. "We're a shambles, Mister Dalton. Him and his bedamned prize! Aye, but we are afloat and away, and we can still fight."

"We could leave him to dispose of the other, Captain."

There was fury in the look Furney shot him. "Damned if we will, Sir! Look off there. While we've bloodied *Herrett* for him, he has stood off and had a shooting match. Not a mark on him! Well, I've

23

fought for him. Now I'm a mind to see him get his own skirts dirtied. We've our wind now, Mister Dalton. We'll turn his prey for him, then we'll watch him do the bloody work."

With a good quartering wind the brig had good legs. She strode out toward the snow, angling to pass ahead. In the distance the erratic schooner still tacked in short sweeps left and right. Dalton pointed toward it. "Why don't they just come about and take a run to seaward? Cross-wind, that schooner could lose the snow in an hour."

"They don't because they're idiots," Furney rasped. "Hart would never put fine sailors aboard such a prize. They might take it into their heads to go off and leave him."

"Doesn't he trust his own crew?"

"Jonathan Hart wouldn't trust his mother with the milk money, Mister Dalton. And *Courtesan's* a warrant ship, remember—not a commission. His crew has signed articles with him, but they're not bound by the articles of war."

"He flies Crown colors."

"He can fly any colors he pleases, he's still a damned pirate."

Running full, *Herrett* came abreast the dark snow in an hour's time and Furney put on more sail, shot ahead, then steered left to cut the privateer's course. In waning daylight the great frigate stood tall, coming up from the rear.

The snow's captain obviously saw the trap he was in. He made a'port, heading for land, but too late. *Herrett* had the wind in her sails and the spray in

24

her teeth. She raced to cut him off. Port batteries unlimbered, Dalton held fire until the brig was close abeam of the fleeing snow. *Herrett* took a volley amidships, but the damage was slight.

Working as a team they closed, captain at the helm and first officer at the guns, and when the range was right Dalton loosed his fore batteries in a sweeping broadside, even as *Herrett* crowded in. The snow heeled to go about. *Herrett* swept on, flanking, turning the hostile back upon the charging frigate. When the two were closing, and guns aboard the frigate bloomed in fiery rosettes, Furney swung *Herrett's* nose through the wind and circled seaward, watching the fight. The snow was hurt but not crippled, and it veered to bring its port guns to play. The great frigate closed relentlessly, firing as it came. Far north, dim in the fading light, the little schooner fled.

"Ah," Furney breathed. "The devil may yet lose his prize."

Thunder rolled across the water and Furney brought *Herrett* in closer to the cauldron of fire and smoke where the ships breasted and engaged. Bright-eyed, entranced, the gray man watched.

"*Courtesan's* bunting flies, Sir!" a bosun shouted.

"Read it, please, Mister Dalton."

"He asks assistance, Sir. He says he's lame."

"Phaw. That frigate is twice the ship that snow is. How can he be hurt?"

Nonetheless, incredibly, *Courtesan* seemed to be drifting, limping apart from the smoke-wreathed snow. With an oath Furney spun his helm and gave orders. *Herrett* made way, driving toward the gap

25

between the two ships. "Starboard guns, Mister Dalton. We'll put an end to this now."

Passing the drifting frigate, the brig dove into the breach, thundering as she came abreast the dark snow. Bright flares answered from its rails. When they were too close to turn, they saw the gaping ports low on her hull, spouting fire. "She has bombards, Sir!" Dalton's shout was lost in the thunders. He loosed his main batteries as the hell of great balls struck the brig broadside. *Herrett* staggered, lost her wind. She drifted. A rumble sounded in the fore, and screams. A mast crumpled, dragging lines and sail down with it.

"Fore battery all fire!" Nothing happened. Dalton turned and peered into the smoke-filled gloom, then caught his breath. There was no fore battery. *Herrett's* entire starboard bow was shot away. Someone was tugging at his sleeve.

"Mister Dalton, Sir, please!" It was Billy Caster, sobbing. "Quarterdeck, Sir. Come now! The helm's been shot away, Sir, and Captain Furney with it."

"Where in God's name is *Courtesan?*"

Billy's voice trailed behind him as he ran. "The frigate's gone, Sir. It turned and ran."

The quarterdeck was a shambles. The helm was gone, and ship's carpenters worked feverishly to rig a tiller. It had grown dark somehow, and they called for lanterns. Dalton took charge. Long minutes passed before he had a chance to look around. The snow, wounded, was listing away, making again for land. And far distant, wind in its high sails, the great frigate *Courtesan* sailed north, following where the schooner had gone. Dalton tried to speak, tried to curse, but the words would not come.

He stood on the slippery deck of a wrecked ship, staring northward, and tears of blind fury washed rivulets in the grime of his face.

II

Little remained of the proud brig *Herrett*. The battered hulk of her struggled northward, shipping water through gaping wounds, torn canvas rough-bound on main and mizzen posts with jury-rigged cables. Her nose was gone, her midships battered and her stern a jumble of wreckage. Massed bombards had beat her to death in a single devastating volley.

Forty-three hands remained aboard her, and only four marines. Some of these would not survive the surgeons' knives. On the blasted quarterdeck, gaunt from shock and loss of sleep, Patrick Dalton struggled to bring her home. The only sail he saw was a distant small boat, fleeing northward near the shore. It passed and was gone.

Her bilges were awash and her bow plowed water as *Herrett* rounded off Sandy Hook, and tow ships came out from Long Island Yards to bring her into port.

Billy Caster watched as the injured were carried off, then delivered up *Herrett's* logs to the port captain. The officer barely glanced at him, accepting the books. He stared at the remains of *Herrett*. "Remarkable," he muttered. "Quite remarkable." Billy went along to the hospital shed to be fed and look for Mister Dalton.

Dalton slept around the clock, then ate and slept again. When finally he was fit, he wandered down to the yards. The bay hummed with activity. Admiral Howe's flagship and escorts were away, but much of the fleet was in evidence. Campaigns were afoot.

Ships of the line stood huge in the anchorage. Frigates, brigantines, and brigs rested stately about them. Ketches, sloops, and low-slung bombardiers were visible across the bay toward Staten Island. Gunboats patrolled restlessly.

A squad of redcoats marched past, eyed him suspiciously, and went on its way. Hessian patrols wended the footpaths. At the docks, he looked again over the bay, seeking the tall frigate *Courtesan*. But the prizemaster's vessel was not in harbor. Off beyond the fish docks, though, a schooner rested at anchor, and he wandered toward it. It was that same schooner, the one *Herrett* had died to save. Trim and proud, it rested at anchor two hundred yards offshore, twin masts with sheer spars catching the morning light on varnished surfaces. There seemed no one aboard, though the prize flag still fluttered at its masthead. It was odd . . . a prize vessel out here beyond the fish docks instead of up at the yards for inventory, registry, and auction.

He got out his glass. Again the beauty of the ship struck him. She was . . . jaunty. She was proud and graceful. She was a lady.

He focused on her bow escutcheon. Her name was *Faith* . . . a good name for a lovely lady.

But was she worth the price *Herrett* had paid? The somber face of Captain Furney rose before him, graying and fierce, yet a fair man and a decent one. No, she was hardly worth such a price. He dropped his glass into his tail pocket and turned away, anger hot within him. He headed back toward the yards, toward the port captain's office. Billy Caster, coming up from the sheds, found him and fell in behind.

In the busy anteroom Dalton caught the captain's eye and saluted. "Commander Patrick Dalton, Sir. Late first officer of *Herrett.*"

The harried man returned his salute, then held out a hand. "Mercer here. Port captain. So you're the one who brought in the hulk. Bit of seamanship, that was."

"May I report, Captain?"

"Ah, Mister Dalton, can it wait? We've got our hands full here right now, things stacked up abominably. We have your logs, of course. Your clerk presented them."

"But there is more than the log entries, Captain. I believe I have charges to bring."

The man's smile faded. He cocked his head and stared suspiciously at Dalton. "Charges? We have a complete report, Sir. The other vessel involved . . ."

"*Courtesan.*"

"Aye, Captain Hart. Everything seems in order, Commander. But of course there will be a board of inquiry in due time. You'll have opportunity to say whatever you want then . . ."

"Have my logs been read?"

31

"All in due time, Commander. I suggest you go along and take a room, rest up a bit, we'll speak later when there's more time." With a half-salute the man was gone, into an inner room beyond, and Dalton turned away. He was frustrated, but it would wait. Such was always the Navy way.

He went across the way to the paymaster and signed a draft. The sergeant looked it over and handed it back. "We got no voucher yet on *Herrett*, Commander. Things have got pretty gummed up since the fleet started massing. Maybe if you'd go to the port captain's office, they could give you a voucher for pay—or at least an advance."

Dalton shook his head and turned to go. "Tell 'em you want an advance," the sergeant said helpfully. "Even if the logs isn't registered yet, no reason not to advance you a bit."

Back at the port captain's office Dalton braced an orderly. The man mumbled, scratched his head, and disappeared into the back room. He returned looking sheepish. "Captain says we can advance you five pounds, Commander. He says come back later when the logs have been read an' registered, then you can draw your pay."

Voucher in hand, Billy still tagging behind, Dalton went to the paymaster's. The sergeant dutifully paid him his advance in coin. "It's got right busy here of late, Commander. How 'bout the boy, there. Will he have pay due?"

"Well, of course he will. Billy?"

"Aye, Sir. Cruise pay, Sir."

The sergeant's brow lowered. "Be you English, boy? You talk like a colonial."

32

Dalton said, "He's my clerk, sergeant. Duly signed and sponsored. But he can share my advance for now. There's enough."

The sergeant continued to scowl. "Patrols been tough on colonials these days, Sir. Signed or not, there's things afoot. I'd keep the boy close by, was I you. He could wind up on a prison hulk awful easy."

They found sleeping space outside the Yards, in the village of New Utrecht, deposited their duffle, and went in search of a meal. At a little inn on a side road Dalton ordered meat, bread, and grog for the both of them. In the gloom of the place he watched the innkeeper stumping about on his pegleg, glancing back at him now and then. The man looked familiar.

When he brought the meal, he leaned over the table and stuck out a weathered hand. "Don't ye recognize me, Mister Dalton? It's me, Clarence . . . Clarence Kilreagh, as was aboard th' ol' *Athene* out of Thames Dock. 'Twas ye that saved my bacon for me, Sir. Don't ye recall?"

Dalton stared at him. Clarence Kilreagh. He had forgotten. The grizzled old seaman grinned and pumped his hand, then sat down with them. "I heard about yer bringin' the *Herrett* in, Sir. Fine bit of work, if ye don't mind me sayin' it, but there'll be some time passes afore ye gets the credit that's due ye. Word is Cap'n Hart's lodged protest on *Herrett*, ye know."

"Protest? For what?"

"Interferin' in th' takin' of a prize, it is, Sir. Oh, it'll all get sorted out. Ol' Hart's done such afore, an' I think they don' care for him much down to th'

33

headquarters these days. Shame it was about Cap'n Furney, Sir. He was a fine man. Real shame. Who's th' lad?"

"This is my clerk. Billy Caster."

"How do, then, Mister Caster. Ye have got yerself a fine officer here, lad. Ye won't know it, for Mister Dalton's not one to gossip, but he saved this ol' tar's bacon, he did. 'Twas after *Athene* had her scrape wi' th' Dutchman off Gibraltar, oh, five-six years ago. That was where I lost me leg, but not an officer aboard *Athene* ever come forward to sponsor me a pension—me bein' Irish, it wasn't seemly, like. But Mister Dalton here, he stepped up an' signed for me right enough. He was barely more than a lad then hisself, but a first-rate young officer he were . . . an' a better seaman no tar never sailed under."

Dalton nodded, embarrassed. "That's all past, Mister Kilreagh. It looks like you're doing well now."

"This?" The old sailor gestured at the inn about them. "Oh, it keeps liver an' lights together. An' I've a bit put away as well."

"How did you come to America?"

"Why, when I got me peg I looked about an' seen how things was goin' in England . . . not good days for a man what's Irish, Sir. So I bought passage on a merchantman an' here I be. Have some more of th' soft tack, Sir. There's honey in th' bucket yonder. Ah, it's good to see yer face again, Mister Dalton. Many's th' time I've wondered how ye be."

Customers came to the door and Kilreagh stumped off to shoo them away. "I'm closed, Sirs. Come back tomorrow." He bolted the door. He stumped back to the table. "Now, we can have a talk. I suppose ye've heard about th' Fitzgerald?"

"No. What about him?"

"Why, Sir, they've taken him for treason. Him an' all those as knew him. I tell ye, Sir, we're well off away from England in these tryin' times."

The Fitzgerald. Taken for treason. It was a blow to Dalton. He had at times detested the fierce old man, but he had always liked him. Him and his daughter . . . firmly he put Molly out of his mind. "How long ago, Clarence?"

"In th' spring, Sir. Word came by packet not a week ago. Things're so gummed up in th' port command of late that th' news sat unopened for four days. Word is they still haven't sorted out the post, it's that bad. Big thing in th' wind, Sir. Th' colonials over acrost the river . . . 'patriots' they calls themselves . . . saboteurs right here in the harbor, aye. Tryin' times."

For the next two hours, Dalton needed do little more than nod occasionally to be brought up to date on the news of the world as collected by Clarence Kilreagh. Kilreagh, it seemed, kept his finger on many pulses. An avid curiosity and plenty of loose-tongued customers made him a wellspring of information.

They talked late, then Dalton woke Billy and they went off to find their beds.

Dalton found it difficult to sleep. Exhausted and drained from the ordeal of bringing home a dead hulk—floating wreckage that had once been a proud fighting brig—still his mind spun from one thought to another. Guns blazed as a graying captain, a man who had been his friend after the fashion of fighting officers, threw himself and his ship into a fray that should never have been his. Again and again he saw the gore on the littered decks, heard the screams of wounded and dying, saw across a darkening sea the tall suit of an unscathed frigate making off after its prize . . . leaving behind the desolation it should never have caused.

And Hart had no sooner entered port than he had lodged protest. *Protest!* Against the very vessel that had intervened at his request, to save his own ship from a shelling at the cost of its own life.

Dalton tossed in his blankets and rubbed hard knuckles into aching eyes. Things were gummed up, they said. So gummed up, with the mustering of Britain's rusty trident—to curb a pack of rebellious colonials—that Dalton had not been able to present his own report on the affair . . . had not even been able to persuade anyone to read his logs . . . could not so much as muster a pay voucher to attend to his needs for the interim, but instead had to settle for the loan of five pounds from a surly port officer.

Gummed up, they said. Yet Jonathan Hart had been ashore an hour and his protest against Herrett was not only on record, it was public knowledge in the taverns of New Utrecht.

In a more distant part of his mind he saw again the fierce, arrogant face of the Fitzgerald. Sean Quinlin O'Day, Lord Fitzgerald, chieftain of clan Fitzgerald of Dunreagh—arrogant old gael, but yet father of Molly. Now the Fitzgerald stood accused of treason against the king. Had old Sean committed an act of treason? Would he know it if he had? Such high crimes, as defined by the ministers of George III, could be as tenuous as saying the wrong thing at the wrong time . . . or, for an Irishman, simply having something that an influential member of the British peerage coveted.

It had happened in the spring. That was all that Clarence Kilreagh knew. By now the Fitzgerald might be rotting in one of Gay Georgie's gaols. Or he might be dead. Justice could be swift for those not adept at court diplomacy and palm-crossing. And for any Irishman.

But again his thought turned to *Herrett*. A taut ship . . . a brave lady. She had performed with valor against the snows, dancing to the hand of a true master, executing a stately and precise minuet of sails and sheets and straining spars to bring her guns to bear. Could he have known about the bombards? He wondered. Should he somehow have divined that below that smoking deck there was another, its ports obscured, its toerails braced with squat monsters designed for bringing down fortresses?

He hadn't known. None aboard *Herrett* had until it was too late. Still, had Captain Hart honored his own request for intervention, and stood his deck and fought, *Herrett* might never have died.

Captain Hart—Jonathan Hart, master of *Courtesan*. The prizemaster, they called him. The hard irony of it made him suck in his breath. Hart had lodged protest against *Herrett*, and *Herrett* was a masterless hulk now, settling on the mud shoals where her wrecked carcass would rot away.

He slept finally, but it was a troubled sleep, with only intermittent reprieve from the harsh dreams of frustration. Reprieve was a dream of Molly's bright eyes, seen distantly now as through a mist. Or the saucy pace of a trim schooner with the wind in her sails and the waves in her teeth—a schooner that would indeed do minuets for a man who knew the manner of her.

Sleep dissolved with a hand on his shoulder and he fought his way out of murky oblivion and sat up, rubbing his eyes. Billy Caster stood a step away, holding a pitcher of water and a battered bowl. "First cock's crow, Sir. I've fetched you a clean shirt and blacked your boots."

Dalton nodded and yawned. It had not been a restful night, and the dregs of it enshrouded him. "Thank you, Mister Caster. I'll attend myself. Why don't you see if you can find us a bit of tea, if you please."

"Aye, Sir." The boy set down his burdens and hurried out, leaving the strap-hinged door open behind him. Morning sounds came from beyond. The place they had found to sleep was a low stall in a decrepit structure that had once been a mercer's warehouse but had been refitted as a barracks with the coming of the fleet. It provided beds only, with no provisions for boarding, but beyond the door he heard his clerk's voice raised in strident argument with someone—proprietor or servant, he didn't know. By the time he had washed the sleep from his eyes and dressed himself Billy was back with a steaming pot and cups. He fumed and muttered as he poured, and Dalton squinted at him.

"That blackguard stood there having his tea and

told me they don't serve tea in this establishment,"
the boy explained.

"But you obviously changed his mind."

"Yes, Sir. I told him that Captain Dalton . . ."

"*Captain*, Mister Caster?"

"Aye, Sir. Landers usually don't know the difference. I told him that you are accustomed to having your tea, and that you would send marines to flog him if he failed in providing the civilities. Your tea, Sir. Bit of lime, perhaps?"

"Thank you, Mister Caster. Please join me, if you will. Oh, and Billy . . ."

"Sir?"

"Permission to stand down. We're ashore now."

"Stand down?"

"Relax, Billy. One may forego a modicum of formality when one is not at sea."

"Oh. Aye, Sir." The boy visibly relaxed, though his expression remained grim. Dalton understood. They had been through much in recent days, and the discovery that a protest was lodged against their wrecked vessel and their dead captain cast gloom over both of them.

"I shall try to see Hart," Dalton decided. "There are words that need to be said.'

"Will you want dress uniform, Sir?" Billy glanced at his officer's dark boots. It was common for gentlemen in the service of His Majesty's Navy to wear buckle shoes with high stockings, in the manner of the Court of St. James. Dalton's preference for field boots had drawn comment upon occasion, but the Irishman ignored it. The flat, foppish shoes were expensive. Besides, he said, they made his feet ache.

To the young colonial, though, his officer's boots were a dashing addition to the tall lieutenant's formal attired—blue tailcoat with white facings and cuffs, trim waistcoat, white breeches, and cocked tricorn hat. With his sword buckled on, Billy would have matched Dalton against any king's officer, stitch for stitch in any court of the realm.

"Aye," Dalton nodded. Billy opened his sea chest and began laying out clothing.

Shaved and refreshed, dark hair brushed back and tied in a trim queue at his collar, coat and breeches fresh-brushed, Dalton strode from the stall to have a look at the morning. Dawn clouds lay wispy on the eastern horizon, and a steady breeze held from the southwest. Flat seas and brisk breeze, he thought. Fine sailing weather for a square-rigger on a north easterly course—or for a fore-and-aft on any course.

The young clerk followed him to the footpath winding away toward the docks, but Dalton stopped him there. "Billy, go and find Mister Oates and Mister Clark, if you will. Ask them to meet me at the old church yonder in an hour. In dress, if it pleases them."

"Aye, Sir."

"And, Billy, look alive and stay away from the shore patrols. Remember what that redcoat sergeant said."

"Aye, Sir."

From a rise he scanned the harbor. There was more activity out there than there had been before, two or three additional ships at anchor—he made out a troop transport and a pair of brigantines that he might not have seen before—and at least one additional ship of the line out in the faring passage. He wished he had brought along his glass, to read her buntings. He did not expect ever to be posted aboard one of the great ships. King and Admiralty in recent years had allowed the fleets to decline until there were not enough berths at hand aboard the line-of-battle dreadnoughts—for that matter, not even among all the first-rate frigates—to accommodate the experienced command officers twiddling their thumbs on numerous beaches throughout the empire. Without court influence or powerful friends among the Anglo-Saxon peerage, even the best of young officers these days stood small chance of posting aboard a *Serapis* or a *General Monk*.

Dalton's highest career ambition, therefore, was captaincy of a frigate—or possibly a gundeck brig or brigantine. But so far, though he had amassed a creditable record as a ship's officer, he had been passed over for command, even of a sloop. The tenor of the times played against him. While the captains of warships pleaded for fighting officers, the Admiralty did not at present tolerate Irishmen commanding their vessels.

At the paymaster's quarter a harried clerk—Navy this time—leafed through letters and shrugged. "Sorry, Sir. We haven't received that voucher."

Dalton set out for the post captain's headquarters, then stopped, squinting into the sun. Off there, standing out from the supply quay, was *Courtesan*. Bright new canvas was being run up to her spars, topmen scurrying on their footropes as slack lines were played and clews rigged. He walked a half-mile along the rutted wagonroad for a better look at the frigate, then swore aloud. *Courtesan* didn't have a mark on her, so far as his trained eye could see. Tall and arrogant, she rode at anchor not seven cable-lengths from the broken hulk of *Herrett*, oblivious to the devastation there. Possibly the frigate had taken a ball or two through her sails but nothing more. Jonathan Hart had not deigned to dirty his skirts.

Protest *Herrett*, would he? Vividly Dalton remembered the distress signal from the frigate, asking assistance of the brig. Lame, he said he was. There was nothing lame about that forty-four-gunner out there. It did not have so much as a scratch on it.

He decided to pick up Oates and Clark first, before pressing his demands with the post captain. They had seen the signals, too. They could confirm Hart's treachery.

Boats scudded around the wreck of *Herrett*, salvaging her guns, fittings, and stores. The hull was not worth repair. It would rot where it sat . . . or be burned or used as a fireship in some blockade.

The arrogance of Hart's report stung him. All for the sake of a pretty prize, the frigate captain had casually willed the brig to its death.

He stopped in at the base hospital, clenching his teeth at the stench there—rotting flesh, sweat and crusted blood on the arms and aprons of the surgeons, the reek of rum and the moans of men in agony.

Only three of the injured he had delivered yet lived. Grizzled Tam Hobb, a veteran anchorman who had served a lifetime on King's vessels, had lost his right arm. The stump of it still seeped blood through soiled bandages. Little Peter Ellis, a topman agile as a monkey, would spend his remaining years in a cart. Both his legs had been amputated. Master's mate Charles Beedle was blind and deaf.

All for the sake of the prizemaster's prize. Outside, Dalton leaned for a moment against a post and gazed with moist eyes to the west, where a trim little topgallant schooner sat at anchor near the fish docks. Distantly, across the bay, he heard the clang of alarm bells and looked that way. Gunboats were making out from Staten Island, slanting against the steady winds. Colors showed over there, and were relayed from ship to ship across the harbor. Saboteurs within the patrolled waters, man lookouts.

According to Clarence Kilreagh, it was a regular occurrence.

He waited by the old church, deep in thought, so immersed in gloomy anger that it startled him when Billy Caster tugged at his sleeve.

"Sir? Pardon, Sir, but I couldn't find either Mister Oates or Mister Clark, so I went and asked the dispatch clerk. They've been reassigned, Sir. Packed off bag and baggage, last night. I couldn't find out where they went."

III

At the foot of the chandler's quay Dalton approached a marine guard, a burly redcoat holding a musket at port arms. "Lieutenant Patrick Dalton to see Captain Hart," he said. "Is the captain ashore?"

The question was a formality. *Courtesan's* bunting said her captain was not on board.

The marine looked him up and down, his gaze fixing momentarily on the officer's boots. He nodded. "He'll be yonder at the chandler's stores, Sir." A trace of a wry grin appeared on the square face, and was gone instantly. "Th' captain prefers to provision his own pantry, Sir."

Dalton started toward the sheds and the marine called to him and pointed. "The officer yonder, Sir. That's Mister Liles, Cap'n Hart's second. He can present your respects for you, Sir."

"What *respects* I have will be presented in person," Dalton muttered. But he went to his left to accost the indicated lieutenant.

Jack Liles was a furtive and sullen man, it seemed

to Dalton—the sort of officer who may have spent too much time on a small deck with a tyrant. He had seen the like before. Still, Liles saluted him correctly and led him up the quay to the chandler's. "Captain Hart is within, Lieutenant Dalton," he said. "Will you follow me?"

Dalton started to follow, then changed his mind. "Ask him to step out, Lieutenant Liles, if you please."

Liles turned and stared at him. "To . . . step out?"

"Ask him to step out here," Dalton repeated. "I should like to see your captain with the sunlight on his face."

Liles disappeared within, looking back at him, and voices came from the interior.

Jonathan Hart was a tall man, as tall as Dalton himself and heavier of build. His blue-faced uniform coat displayed captaincy and seniority—twin epaulettes on his shoulders, the dozen lapel buttons in rows of three. His cocked hat carried gold piping, and his white waistcoat, breeches, and stockings were spotless. He carried a long sword with a jeweled guard. Emerging from the chandlery, he gazed at Dalton for a moment—a long glance that sized, measured, catalogued, and dismissed the junior officer. Dalton was doing some cataloguing of his own. Peerage, he decided. Probably a second son, forty to fifty years old, ambitious and ruthless—a cold man, and a hard one.

Hart tired of the scrutiny. "Well?"

"Patrick Dalton, Sir. Late first officer of *Herrett*."

Hart ignored the civility. "Well?" he repeated.

Dalton held the haughty gaze with eyes of iron. "I

46

have just one question, Sir. Why did you ask assistance of a smaller vessel then turn tail and run away?"

All around he heard the gasps and caught breaths of the men listening. Hart's cheeks paled and he stiffened. "Do you know who you're talking to?"

"Yes, Sir. I am addressing a cowardly betrayer in the uniform of His Majesty's fleet. Answer my question, if you please, Captain Hart. Or reserve your answer for a court of inquiry. But now or then, I intend to hear your response."

Hart's eyes blazed. Abruptly he stepped forward and struck Dalton a resounding slap across the face. "There's all the response you'll have from me!" he hissed. "How dare you confront me with accusations!"

Dalton put a hand to his cheek, felt the sting there, and smiled coldly. "Is it an affair of honor, then, Captain? You have dishonored flag and ship . . . will you honor me?" His hand went to his sword.

Hart backed away. "I'll not soil my hands on the likes of you . . . *Irishman!* Mr. Liles . . ."

The lieutenant pushed forward, his hand at the hilt of his saber. "Sir!"

Abruptly they were surrounded by redcoats, and a captain of marines stepped between them. "That will be enough of that," he told Liles, pushing him back. To Dalton and Hart he said, "Post commander's order, Sirs. If you have private disputes, you may settle them privately. But not in this compound."

Dalton nodded. He pushed his half-drawn blade down into its scabbard and lifted his hand away from it. "Any time and place you like, Captain Hart. But you shall do me the honor in person. I've seen you turn tail and run. I should like to see if you can stand and fight."

Hart went for his sword, but the marines hustled him back. He shrugged them off, circled around Dalton, then turned his back on him. "See to my launch, Mister Liles," he said. "I am due aboard." He paused, then half turned to glare at Dalton. "I shall not forget this! I promise you I shall not."

Courtesan sailed on the tide. New suit of sails, the dock foreman said. Captain Hart had gone out to shake her down. Through the hours of daylight Dalton wandered about, out of action and out of sorts, wondering how long it would take to schedule a court of inquiry regarding *Herrett*.

The trim schooner *Faith* still rested at anchor, out from the fish docks.

It was dark when Dalton returned to Kilreagh's inn. The place was half filled and he went to a dim back corner to find a table and a bench. Billy Caster, exhausted from keeping up with his officer's ramblings, lay down by the hearth and went to sleep.

For a time Dalton sat unnoticed, but eventually Kilreagh came with a mug of ale and a worried frown. "Sir, I did hope ye'd come soon," he breathed. "Pray keep yerself back here in th' corner until we can talk a bit." He looked around, glancing at others in the room. "There be mischief afoot, Sir."

He was gone then, and Dalton sipped his ale, puzzled. After a time Kilreagh returned, looking more worried than ever. "Sir, do ye see the stairs yonder? I wonder if ye'd go up there to my loft an' wait. The place'll clear after a bit, then we can talk. It's best,

Sir. Leave the lad, he's in no danger. But Sir, you are."

He had no reason to doubt the old man. Quietly he got up, crossed to the loft ladder, and went up. In the dimness above, he found a mattress and sat down to wait.

It was an hour or more. Finally all was quiet below and he looked down. The common room was clear. Kilreagh was mopping near the door as the last belated customer shrugged into his coat and paid his pennies. Kilreagh bolted the door behind him and put down his mop. "All clear now, Sir! Come down an' I'll serve ye hot rum. There's a thing I must tell ye."

"Sir," the old man said softly in the empty room. "They have a warrant out on ye, for high treason."

He was quiet then. Dalton sat stunned, letting it soak in.

"It came aboard the post packet, Sir. It's been lyin' there in th' post office for near a week an' none had sorted it. But I've a friend there, Jamie Sloane— I've lent him a deal of money now an' again—so when I got to thinkin' about th' Fitzgerald an' all, I got onto Jamie an' he looked through. It's warrants for all those as ever was known to know the Fitzgerald, Sir, by name. An' sure your name is there, right on th' list."

Dalton folded his arms on the table and put his head on them. What more? What else could occur? Treason. In wartime. His chances of ever being returned to England for trial were nil. No, he would simply go to the stockade, and after a hearing go to a prison hulk, and that would be the end of Patrick Dalton. Ironically, he thought how simple it was to end a man's career and life. Just put his name on a piece of paper. So simple.

The thought angered him. He raised his head to gaze across at Kilreagh. "When will the post be delivered?"

"It has been, Sir. Today. And Jamie couldn't hold it off. That's why I wanted ye to wait in the loft. No tellin' who's read the warrants by now, Sir. They could be searchin' for ye this minute."

"I've left my duffle at my room. I don't suppose I'd better even return there."

"I've got a thing or two ye might use. What do ye think ye might do, Mister Dalton? I'll help if I can."

"I don't know, Clarence. I need time to think things out."

The old seaman's weathered face was pale with dread. "I have room here, Sir . . ."

"No, I can't hide here. They'll look."

"Then I know where there's a few abandoned shacks. What about the lad there?" Billy Caster lay sleeping beside the hearth.

"Aye, I'll need to attend him, too. He's a colonial, and he'd go to the stockade without a sponsor."

Kilreagh's face wrinkled in thought. "Up past the yards, less than a mile, there's a wee cut where I keep a skiff. You an' the lad might make across to Manhattan in darkness. New York City's been burned an' it's bad there, but there might be some colonials could help ye."

"No, I'll not go to the colonials. But the boy . . . aye. Maybe that's best."

In morning darkness he cupped a candle in his

hand and shook the boy awake. "Mister Caster, come with me and make no sound."

Through the dim ways of Long Island Yards they crept, Billy shivering in his threadbare coat. At a turning Dalton pulled him back into darkness as a Hessian patrol passed. Leaving the yards behind them they walked in darkness past the civil docks and along the bay. Dalton led down through a littered cut, and a skiff was pulled up there under the bank. He herded the boy aboard and thrust a small purse into his hand.

"Do you see over there, Mister Caster, the head of land across the way? New York is there. You lay to those oars and make for that point with a will."

In the same hushed voice Billy asked, "Mister Dalton, will you tell me what's wrong?"

He hesitated, then nodded. "There's a warrant on me, lad. There has been treason in Ireland and they believe I am involved. I can't protect you now. But over there somewhere are colonials. Be very careful, and maybe you can find help over there."

"Can't you come with me, Sir?"

"I have to go my own way. And I have no love for the rebels." He stooped to push the skiff off the mud bank. "Now, row, Billy. For all you're worth. And good luck ride with you."

The boy pulled, the oars bit water, and the skiff slid away on the dark channel. Dalton turned away, then crouched. Men were coming. He leapt to the washed bank above the cut, ducked, and pulled himself deep under the sheltering roots. First false light of dawn was in the sky. Voices came, and hurried footsteps. A voice called in German and another, heavily-accented, "Sir, look. There goes a boat."

They came to the very edge of the cut. Debris rained on him as they halted directly above. An English voice, heavy with impatience, commanded, "Open fire." Muskets roared.

"Blast you," the man spat. "You've missed him." A pistol sounded, then another musket. "It was the Irishman," the accented voice said. "I am sure of it."

Dalton held his breath and hugged the cold, wet soil. Finally they went away. When he was sure, he crawled out and peered across the murk of the channel. Barely, dim with distance and dark, he could see the boat. And in a sudden ebb of morning breeze he heard the chunk of oars.

Helping the boy escape, he realized, had sealed his own fate. They had seen the skiff. They thought it was him. Now the word would be out. Patrick Dalton had deserted, crossed the river to the enemy beyond. Now he was not only a traitor but a turncoat as well. A sour grin pulled at the corners of his mouth.

It was amazing how quickly a man could go to hell without ever meaning to.

IV

The prison stockade on Long Island was no stockade at all, but a crudely fenced compound just up from the admiralty yards—railed sapling poles set a foot apart encircling a sturdy block building that had recently been a fisherman's smokery, and a pair of sheds where, in less troubled times, boat tackle had been stored. With the coming of the White Fleet, these had been appropriated and fenced for the keeping of culprits. It was, in fact, three compounds in one. Guards routinely patrolled the block building, where those accused of capital crimes were kept. The sheds and the little yards fronting them were less closely guarded. Their occupants, despite being technically incarcerated, were unlikely to attempt escape. They were all king's men—a ragtag lot of sailors, marines, and pressedmen stockaded for every petty crime conceivable—and all subject to eventual assignment back to active duty. Even should they wander away from the stockade, there was nowhere to go.

For these, stockade life consisted of a hammock under a shed roof and a daily meal provided by various merchants, with tallies kept for payment and each man charged against his next wages. Clarence Kilreagh was one of those who supplied the stockade, and it was his custom to linger there each morning and visit with some of the prisoners while they ate. Several among them, before being jailed, had been customers at the inn. Some would be again, when their sentences were served and shore leave came around.

But on this day, although Kilreagh sat with them while they emptied the baskets and pails he had brought, he was distracted. The charge of treason against Patrick Dalton troubled him, and he turned it over in his mind, searching for a means to assist the young officer.

Though Dalton knew nothing of it, Clarence Kilreagh had made it his business for several years to keep track of him. Kilreagh had followed his career, through the proven means of forecastle scuttlebutt, virtually from the time Dalton had stood for the old sailor's pension. Kilreagh felt a fierce loyalty to the young officer and prided himself that there would come a day when he might do him a service.

But now Patrick Dalton was in need—desperate need. And Kilreagh could think of no way to assist him. Oh, he could arrange to hide him for a time— maybe indefinitely. Kilreagh had friends among the farmers up the island, and not all of them were involved in the insurgency. Things had come to a pretty pass, he told himself, when a man must rank his friends in rows of three—like separating melons—in order to determine who to ask for help for an innocent man. Yet so it was. With the calls for a Continental Congress of the colonies' delegates had come division among neighbors. Some who before had only grumbled and gone on their way now were whiggish radicals who might gleefully pitch in to do a disservice to the King, but who could not be trusted to provide shelter for a king's officer. Others were glowering Tories who would as soon turn a fugitive over to the king's justice as they would steal land rights from those who did not share their views.

Some, though, were neutral—people simply going about their business and trusting that the chaos around them might end soon, one way or another.

As the inmates around him chewed their biscuit and chatted among themselves, Clarence Kilreagh sat and scowled, barely aware of their presence. They were a baker's dozen, these clients of his within the pole fence—sailors from a scattering of king's vessels thrown together now in the camaraderie of captivity. Most wore the pigtails of the British tar. Several had the striped shirts and buckle shoes of able seamen, others were more motley garbed—ordinary seamen, deckhands and sheet-cleaters. Few among them had any notion of why they were in the Americas, and some had no idea why they were in the stockade. The brothers Grimm, for example—Brevis and Solamon—had told him candidly about their offense. They had enjoyed the favors of a lady. But why that lady had objected strenuously enough to land them both in the stockade was beyond their comprehension. And Robert Arthur, a huge, strong ship's cook with half a beard, puzzled at length over why the cracking of a pair of landlubber skulls should have brought punishment upon him.

Samuel Coleman, Victory Locke, and Ishmael Bean had come to the stockade together, drunk as lords and bloodied from brawling. Charley Duncan and Purdy Fisk were victims of mayhem—their own mayhem, committed on various other people.

John Abernathy had been apprehended in the thieves' market trying to sell some officer's braided saber. It was unclear what crimes Martin Smith, Cadman Wise, and Claude Mallory might have committed, but they were here as well, as was Donald Oates, whose final stockade meal this was. By noon he would be aboard the brig *Quester*, with cat stripes on his back and a cruise to the Indies ahead of him. To a man, the rest envied him. The prospect of feeling the lash was unpleasant, and the day-to-day duties of shipboard life on a king's brig seeking American privateers was little better. Still, the dull discomfort of long days in the stockade made one wish for something a bit more exciting.

Charley Duncan took the last smoked fish from one of the pails and handed the container to Kilreagh. "It's rare that I've seen you so distracted, Clarence," he said.

Kilreagh glanced at him. "Aye, I've much on my mind this day, Charley. And no answer to it all. I've seen a good man becalmed on a lee shore, and naught can I fathom to keep him from runnin' aground."

"A friend, is it?"

"Aye, a friend. Nor ever was there a better one to me. A God's own shame it is that such a one should be made to suffer for the doin's of another."

"Is it an injustice, then?" Duncan removed his cap to rub a hand over his sandy-red hair. "I've no liking for injustices, myself."

"Injustice as ever was," Kilreagh agreed. "The man is the very soul of innocence, but he'll be lucky if he escapes the confines of that prison hulk yonder in the mud flats."

Martin Smith, squatting nearby, shuddered. Most of them had seen the island's prison hulk. The sheered hull of a line ship it was, towed into the shallow cove known as Wallabout Bay to serve as a final prison for those felons who would not see either action or freedom again. The hulk out there was home to hundreds of pallid scarecrows rotting in filth and hunger. Some were prisoners of war, some convicted felons. Their fate was all the same. Few would ever leave the holds and spattered decks of the hulk that had once been a proud ship, the *Jersey*. Ports from which sixty-four great guns had once fired were now nailed shut, and the only air and light below those decks came from two tiers of square holes ten feet apart. Hessian grenadiers patrolled the quarterdeck behind a ten-foot barricade notched for muskets, and each morning escorted pitiful parties of prisoners to the mud shoreline to bury the dead laid out on deck the night before.

It was the nightmare of every man jack of the fleet that he might one day be consigned to the hulk that had once been *Jersey* and was now nicknamed *Hell Afloat*. Few who went there ever saw freedom again.

Men who had faced the howling death of a riven deck in pitched battle—and who might face such again—quailed at the thought of rotting aboard the hulk.

Victory Locke chewed on a bit of biscuit and gazed at Kilreagh thoughtfully. "This friend, Clarence. Would it be one we might know?"

"You all know *of* him, right enough—I've talked about him since he came ashore."

Duncan stopped eating and stared at him. "The brave lieutenant, Clarence? The one as brought *Herrett* home?"

Others gathered closer to listen. "The very one," Clarence nodded. "Yesterday a hero, today a fugitive in hiding, falsely accused by those as should know better."

"So what's he done, then?"

"It isn't what he's done, lads, but who he's known. Patrick was acquainted once with the Fitzgerald—a chieftain of Belfast. Now the Fitzgerald stands marked for treason, and not an Irishman that ever was seen with him is likely to escape the king's wrath."

"Long live the king," someone muttered.

"Aye." Clarence shook his head and sighed. "Long live the king. Did I tell you lads what he did at the chandler's quay?"

Victory Locke blinked. "The king?"

"No. The lieutenant. When that low pirate Jonathan Hart was ashore—no disrespect to a fine captain, but that's what he is—why, Patrick went and found him and braced him face-to-face for bein' a coward and leavin' *Herrett* to fight his battles for him. The prizemaster went into such a rage that he slapped the lieutenant and offered the blade of his sword. Oh, I've heard many a word on that, I have. For a day, those havin' custom at the inn could speak of little else."

"Did they fight?" John Abernathy's eyes glittered with excitement. A tale such as this was fine meat in the dullness of the stockade.

"The lieutenant offered to, they said. But Hart would not honor his challenge. The man turned his back."

Cadman Wise snorted. "Disgraceful. No way for a gentleman to behave."

Abernathy turned aside to glance at him. "And what would you know of gentlemen, then? Your place is the forecastle, same as the rest of us."

Distantly there was the sound of cannon fire on the bay—not the familiar boom of a salute being sounded, but a pair of hollow coughs as of long chasers being fired in pursuit. Two or three of the men walked to the fence to look out across the yards.

"Gunboats," someone said. "They're chasin' a boat of some kind, yonder off Staten Island."

"There's been talk of saboteurs in the harbor," Duncan commented. "Even in here we've heard of it."

Those at the fence came back. There was nothing more to see.

"What will he do now?" Duncan pressed.

"The lieutenant? I don't rightly know. I'm thinkin' I might find a haven for him somewhere, at least for a time."

"He could make for Manhattan, I suppose."

"And join the rebels?" Kilreagh shook his head. "No, Patrick is a proud man an' loyal to king and country. No matter what they say of him, he's no traitor."

Duncan nodded. "I could follow a man like that."

"And I," Smith agreed. Others nodded.

"As fine a seaman as ever was," Clarence sighed. "I sailed with him on *Athene*. And if I could help him now I would, but I just don't see a clear way to do that. A God's own shame, that's what it is."

Grenadiers were at the gate, and a ship's clerk to take Donald Oates into custody. As he was escorted out, the others looked after him wistfully. He would feel the lash, but at least he would plant his shoes on a deck again.

A few miles away across Kill van Kull, where the Jersey swamps began, six men in the dress of colonials hawled a stub-mast launch into screening reeds and turned to look back at the open water where they had been.

"We were lucky that time," Guy Neely muttered. "Much too close for my comfort."

"Had we wanted to," Virgil Cowan said, "we could have holed a pair of them while they were shootin' at us."

"Holed 'em with what, Virgil? A musket? What we need is a cannon. We should have brought one."

"There's rifles aboard the schooner. If we'd had a few of those, the Georgies on those gunboats would have had a mite to think about."

The launch carried no cannon, nor was there a place to mount any. It had made the run up from Delaware Bay loaded to the gunwales with people

60

and cargo. The cargo consisted of a water keg, a few days' supply of food, and several squat kegs painted with tar. With all the people aboard, there was no room for anything else.

Cowan turned away from the screen of reeds and pointed toward the end of the tiny swamp cove where others were snugging the launch. "For a while, then, I guess this is home. What will we do now, Mister Neely?"

"I expect we'll try again tonight. It's what we're here for."

"She isn't one to give up, is she?" He tipped his head toward the seventh member of the company, a smaller figure in dark bonnet and long skirts.

"Not likely," Neely shrugged. "She's like her father that way, Virgil. Once she sets out to do a thing, she'll jolly well get it done one way or another."

"Aye," Virgil agreed. "Even if it means takin' on the whole of the King's Navy."

"The thing I wonder about, though, is whether her father knows about any of this. Somehow it just don't seem like he'd have let her go off on this errand in the first place. Maybe he doesn't know she's here."

Triumph was a privateer. Though not much longer in the keel than a large launch, she was cutter-rigged and armed to the teeth, and her tall mast with its spars and rising laterals could carry as much sail as a medium sloop. Commissioned in Connecticut after the occupation of Newport by the British, *Triumph* was both a warship and a profitable enterprise for her master, and Isaac Purdue had supply bases ranging from the Connecticut coast to the Chesapeake, all paid for from the spoils of *Triumph's* adventures. In the year since the arrival of the White Fleet of Admiral Lord Richard Howe, with the troops of his brother General Sir William Howe, *Triumph* had roved the waterways above Long Island. Five king's vessels had felt her sting, and two of those were no longer king's vessels. Colonial investors had paid well for the sloop *Gratitude* and the bomb ketch *Jove*. Both were now on the Hudson, wearing new colors and harassing British shipping.

On this day *Triumph* put out from her lair below Bridgeport and turned her jutting sprit southwestward toward the throat of the Sound.

"We've good wind today," Isaac Purdue told his second. "A few hours and we'll lay by in a cove and go ashore. Let's see if we can't find a dispatch runner to tell us what the Georgies are up to at the moment."

"Are we going to make for Delaware?" the second asked. "It's been a time since I've slept under my own roof."

"A few days," Purdue said. "I've a mind to do one more sweep up here, just to see what comes our way. Then we'll head out and put her south. If that woman of yours has been faithful to you this long, Mister Jones, then I warrant she can contain her passions for a few days longer."

V

Like a fox that has broken the scent, Patrick Dalton went to ground. It was well that he knew the lay of Long Island. One of the bright young officers of the King's Navy, twice cited for valor and now lauded as the seaman who'd brought the battered brig *Herrett* safely home, Dalton huddled now in an abandoned shed a half mile above the yards, bracing for flight each time he glimpsed the red coats of patrols or the blue of Hessian guards. His Irish mind toyed with the awful irony of it.

Less than a year hence he had been posted as first aboard the fighting brig of Captain Furney. Just four days ago he had almost single-handedly brought the wreck of *Herrett* into anchorage. Now he hid in a verminous shed, venturing out only in darkness to steal to the inn where Clarence Kilreagh still welcomed him.

Clarence Kilreagh, he thought, may God bless your scabrous old heart. If ever a man had needed a friend . . . Dalton remembered well the brigantine

Athene out of Thames. It had been his first posting as a ship's officer. And he remembered the running battle off Gibraltar with that Dutch pirate. But he barely recalled signing warrant for old Kilreagh's pension. He supposed it had seemed a stalwart thing to do at the time . . . or some such thing. He had hardly known the old man.

But Clarence had never forgotten. And now that Dalton so desperately needed a friend, here he was. The fierce loyalty of the Irishman . . .

His thoughts turned to the Fitzgerald, and he felt regret. There had been few times in the years he'd known him when he'd have cared if they'd carried the old warlord's head off on a platter. Him and his "emancipators," his cronies spying in the night, his never-ending lambasts at King and Parliament for the "plight of poor Erin," as he termed it. Dalton had found the old man distasteful. But of course, not so his bright-eyed daughter Molly. Dalton had courted Molly ceaselessly and shamelessly, without requite. He had loved her as those old heroes of Greek mythology had loved their goddesses. And he half suspected, thinking on it, that it was from there he got his pattern. But Molly had never been for him.

While she was aloof, it had been relatively painless. But the day she had toyed with him, led him on, encouraged him . . . and then betrayed him, he could never forget that.

He had deserved it, of course. He was not of the peerage, not even of the Irish clans. He was nothing more than an ambitious waif who had shouldered his way into academy at an early age—had borrowed, finagled, fought for the privileges he thought he deserved. Oh, he had come far. But he remained what he had been . . . a landless Irishman without good family or strong friends in an empire that demanded both.

To this day, though, true to the classics that had so thrilled him as a reading child, his honor and loyalty burned fiercely within him. He was a subject of the Crown. He did wonder at the moment if he were quite British enough to remain loyal to a Crown that had so used him.

His finances were pressing. Only a few coins remained between him and starvation, and he had no mind to beg from Clarence. With the warrant on him, there was no way he could ever draw his accumulated pay, and his accounts were, of course, sealed by now.

Through the long day he slept, waited for nightfall, and kept his attention on the yards and the harbor beyond, where masts stood tall and tenders edged about. Far in the distance he could see the twin masts of the pretty little schooner that had cost him his ship and his commission, the prizemaster's latest prize. She had been a wealthy colonial's pride and joy, surely, before Hart had taken her. Well, Hart and all his crew would be in line for a fancy bounty on that one. He hoped they all choked on it.

If a man had a vessel like that, he mused . . . and shook his head at the direction his idle thoughts were taking him. You didn't just row out and go aboard a ship and sail quietly away with her. Preposterous. But to while away the waning day he played with the notion as a game.

Twenty men could crew a craft like that in comfort—ten in a pinch. A captain, a first officer—or two lieutenants, to avoid the grueling schedule of standing watch-and-watch. Then she'd need a good boatswain and a sailmaker, a carpenter and a cook. These and a dozen capable hands would be a'plenty, both to man the ship and to man her guns if they had to. She had four guns, he thought—six if there were deck swivels, but he had noticed none.

If they had to? Of course they would have to use her guns. They would be essential to a fugitive ship. As a matter of fact, a pair of long twelves would be a nice addition to her double brace of four-pounders. He grinned at the idea of a little schooner with twin thirty-two-hundred-pound long twelves mounted fore and aft as chasers. By the Lord, fire them together and the poor little ship would pleat like a music box.

It was an irony—Lord, would this day never end? His stomach growled—an irony that the only two ships big enough to mount long twelves were those too big to really need them. That red snow had had long twelves. And its sister had boarded bombards. His eyes misted and he pulled his mind back to the game. He ticked off the provisions a fugitive expedition on a stolen ship bound to nowhere might require, then grinned and shrugged at his foolishness. Impossible.

Yet after nightfall he made his way down to the cut above the harbor and watched lantern lights play distantly on the silent schooner where she bobbed sleepily in the choppy bay. And later, slipping to the inn after its last customers had gone, he asked Clarence about her.

"The little fore-an'-aft, Sir? Aye, I know her. Pretty thing, she is. Belonged to a colonial gentleman, is the word, till Cap'n Hart took his *Courtesan* into Delaware Bay and plucked her out like a plum from a pudding."

"Her name is *Faith*. I could read her escutcheons when I went to look at her."

"Well, Hart'll surely change the name if he decides to keep her."

"Keep her? But isn't she Crown registry now? As a prize?"

"Oh, no, Sir. Hart's not declared her as a prize. That's why she's anchored off by the fish docks. Word is, he means to keep her as a toy, to take home with him to England. No sir, neither sponsors nor crew are likely to get bounty money on that one."

The sound of boots in the street hushed them. Kilreagh stumped to the shuttered front and listened. "They're swarmin' like ants out there tonight. Rumors a'flyin' . . . some says General Washington has thirty thousand rebel troops across the two rivers and will attack. Others say the colonials have abandoned the bay. Some say they're amassed in Jersey, others that they're on the Hudson. Ah, for the time when a good spy could be trusted."

Dalton made to leave. "If they catch me here, Clarence, you'll be in the soup with me."

Kilreagh's hand went up in gruff denial. "Sir, was it not for you I'd be beggin' now on the Liverpool docks. There's naught they can do to hurt me."

"They could put a ball through you."

"Aye," the seamed face grinned. "An' hasn't that been tried afore!"

He hobbled to the pantry and came back with hot rum. "What's got 'em riled now is, there's saboteurs about the harbor. A small boat's been seen the past night, makin' from across the bay. When they chased it off, they foun' a keg o' Greek fire tied to the stern of *Constant*, just a'waitin' for somebody to strike a light."

"Audacious," Dalton nodded, deep in his hot rum and his thoughts.

"Aye, it was," Kilreagh pressed on. "But *Constant* is a fleet tender, wi' near twelve hundredweight o' powder in her holds. Now wouldn't *that* ha' made a wondrous sight had they touched her off!"

"Clarence, are we at war with Spain right now?"

Kilreagh squinted at him, lost in the sudden shift of subjects.

"Spain, Sir? I don't know. We might be. Then again, maybe not." He peered at his guest in the lamplight. "Ye do seem most interested in Spain, Sir. I wonder why."

"I'm thinking about my problem, Clarence. I can't go back to England now, even if I could get there. I can't stay here much longer, and I'll not join the colonials. But if a man could make his way to New Spain, now . . ."

Fists thundered at the inn door. Dalton jumped, his hand going to his sword. Kilreagh snatched up one of the mugs from the table, dashed its contents into a slops jar, and pointed. "There, Sir, up the stair. On the loft landin' is a ladder to the roof. Hurry."

Dalton flew up the stairway into darkness. As he found the ladder he heard Kilreagh's peg leg stumping across the floor below. He reached the ladder top and pushed upward. It was lighter here, and he swung up through the trap and onto the roof, then let the trap down silently. He heard the inn door unbolted and opened, and an angry voice shouting, "King's men! Make way, make way!"

Easing down to the edge of the roof, he looked over in time to see red-coated guards entering the inn. In the darkness he thought there were others posted outside, but could not be sure of it. Back at the roof's peak he eased the trap up slightly to listen. Clarence was protesting, ". . . bustin' in on honest folk! Ye got no call . . ."

"The King's warrant is call," another voice said. "Produce the traitor Dalton or face the King's mercy, Innkeeper!"

"I don't know no Dalton."

The voice was cold and precise. "He came here the night he came ashore. He left here another night and escaped across the river. He has returned and was seen coming here again tonight. Produce him."

Kilreagh's voice went sullen. "I don' know what ye're talkin' about, Sir."

"Take two men upstairs, Sergeant. You men, through there. Search the place, turn out anyone you find, and bring 'em to me."

Boots on the stairs. Dalton closed the trap and looked around in the darkness, trying to remember the lay of Kilreagh's roof. Carefully he crawled along the peak until his fingers found an edge. He lay at full length and swept his arm below the lintel, hoping to find a brace—anything he could cling to. He found nothing. He looked back over his shoulder as the trap began to rise, torchlight shafting through it. Pray God this place is built as it should be, he thought. He twisted around, slipped off the peak, hung by his fingers on the damp wood shingles, and swung his body forward, his knees up.

The angle beam he prayed for was there. Clawing at the shingles he got a knee on it, slid it upward, and got a boot across as his fingers lost their grip. He doubled, nicking his head on the lintel, and grabbed. His fingers closed on stout wood.

He clung there under the eave peak, holding his breath as boots whispered on the shingles above him. The torch lit the ground below him and he pulled back as tightly as he could against the wall. The light lifted away and he heard the booted steps receding toward the other peak. He heard footsteps on the ground, coming around the building. They stopped just beneath him and he held his breath again. Then they went away.

The faint glow above the roof faded and he heard the trap slam shut. Dimly through the flimsy wall he heard commotion inside. There seemed to be another commotion off in the distance, far away, but he couldn't make it out.

Carefully, trying to make no sound, he edged out and up on the angle brace, hanging from it, reaching out to find the edge of the roof. At first he could not reach it, but with extreme effort he got one hand over it, then the other. Taking care not to swing, his fingers clamped at the shingles, his nails dug into the wood, he released his hold on the brace—first one leg and then, carefully, the other. The pain in his fingertips was agony. Slowly, gritting his teeth against it, he pulled upward.

He lay for several minutes on the shingled roof, sprawled and soaked with sweat, rubbing his fingers gingerly to bring back the circulation. He could hear the other commotion more clearly now, distant voices shouting somewhere down toward the harbor. He looked, and the low clouds to the south had a faint glow. There was a fire down there.

He crept to the far end of the roof peak, hoping to see what was happening, but his view was blocked. The cloud reflection seemed brighter.

He heard the front door of the inn slam open, and voices in the courtyard. Clarence Kilreagh shouted, "You can't do this, Sir! I'm just a poor business-man . . ."

"If he opens his mouth again, Sergeant, rap him on the head to quiet him. Now take him away."

There were running footsteps coming up the path. The voice of authority below called, "Ho there, you! What's amiss?"

The footsteps faltered and stopped. "The sabo-teurs, Sir. They've come back, and the *Rapelle* is afire. They're tryin' to extinguish it, Sir, but water just seems to make it spread."

"Greek fire! Sergeant, put this man back in his inn under house arrest, with two men to guard him. Then you and the rest, come with me, quickly!"

Dalton eased down the roof slope in time to see a man in dark clothing hurrying away toward the har-bor, a squad of redcoats trotting behind him, mus-kets at the ready. When they were gone he squatted atop Clarence Kilreagh's house, gathering his thoughts.

Clarence was in it with him now, and he cursed himself for bringing his troubles to the old seaman. "Well," he muttered, "First things first." The low clouds over the harbor had a definite glow now.

Easing the trap open, he peered into the darkness of Kilreagh's loft. Faint lamplight came up the stairwell. He let himself through, let the hatch close silently above him, and crept to the head of the stairs. In the common room below, Clarence stood glaring at a pair of red-coated guards. Clarence, Dalton asked himself, are you as clever as you once were? From his waistcoat he extracted a coin, bounced it twice in his hand, then flattened himself against the wall cornering the stairwell. He flipped the coin over his shoulder. It rang as it bounced on the stairs, then hit the floor below. Then there was a moment's silence. He waited.

He heard muffled, careful steps below, then on the stairs. The soldier climbed slowly, trying to make no sound, and Dalton counted the steps. The man's shadow preceded him. Dalton held his breath. The muzzle of a musket slid beside him, came further, and he whirled and grasped it, wrenching it toward him. With his other fist he swung hard into the soldier's midriff and the man doubled over. Dalton loosed the musket barrel and brought a hard fist up under the guard's jaw, cartwheeling him down the steps. Below there was an instant's pandemonium.

When Dalton came down the stairs, one soldier lay sprawled at their foot. The other was face down in the center of the room and Clarence Kilreagh stood over him, a bung starter in his hand.

Dalton said, "I am sorry, Clarence."

Kilreagh grinned at him with pure glee in his eyes. "Make nothin' whatever of it, Sir. Where are we goin' from here?" He dropped his bung starter on the table, went to the fireplace, and lifted a heavy hearthstone. He pulled a pouch from beneath it. "All I've got is here, Mister Dalton. A man's a fool who'd not be ready to travel fast in wartime."

"We'd best make for the river, then."

Carrying the soldiers' muskets and pouches, they left the inn and turned warily down the alley, then pulled up short. The light in the sky was bright now. Somewhere a ship was blazing. Clarence licked his lips. "She's not the *Constant*, Sir . . . too far down. Be one o' the line ships, maybe." Taken by a sudden impulse, he grabbed Dalton's arm. "Sir, there's a way, there sure enough is!"

"What are you . . ."

"No, there's no time, Sir. Just trust me. Can ye make your way to the fishin' dock?"

"I can."

"Then go there straightaway, Sir, an' find two or three stout boats with oars in 'em. There'll be some about. I'll be along direc'ly, Sir."

"But . . ."

"Trust me, Sir." Clarence was gone into the darkness.

Keeping to the dark ways, Dalton reached the upper dock. Several small boats lay there, and he found oars in a cradle on the short dock. The boats were seining vessels used by the men of New Utrecht village. He waited, hidden in the darkness by the dock, allowing his eyes to wander out to the little schooner where she rode at anchor. Far down the harbor a ship blazed in the night. Its light was strong enough to strike reflections from *Faith's* varnished booms.

Somewhere up in the yards or beyond he heard a musket shot, then another. Within minutes there came the sound of running feet and Clarence Kilreagh's voice, low and urgent, *"Where be ye, Sir?"*

"Here, Clarence."

"Ah, good. Come along then, lads, an' look lively now. Be as quiet as ever ye can, though." A dark mass of men dropped from the grassed bank and down onto the flats, hurrying toward the fish dock.

"Ah, there's boats. Hurry along there, boys. There's good lads. Grab some oars as ye come by. Now, let's aboard."

As they scurried past him, Dalton counted a dozen men. Most wore the short britches, jackets, hats, and pigtails of Royal Navy tars.

There was no time for questions. He followed and boarded the third boat. Two of the men locked oars and pulled hard after the others, skimming out toward the anchored *Faith*. In moments they closed on her and swarmed aboard. As Dalton clambered over the rail he heard a thump across from him, and a moment later a muffled splash.

"Thought there might be a guard," someone said.

Kilreagh came up beside him in the near-darkness. "These lads mayn't look like much, Sir . . ."

"I'm sure I can't tell, Clarence. I can hardly see a thing."

"But they're all seamen. There's a fair breeze

makin', Sir, an' we're all aboard. So if ye'll just give the orders now, Cap'n, we'll be about our business."

And little enough choice I have about it, Dalton thought. He squared his shoulders. "Very well, Mister Kilreagh, we seem committed. All hands to make sail, and look alive. But quietly, if you please."

Dim glow from the distant fires confirmed what he recalled. Bare topsail spars glinted on both tall topmasts. Blocks and stays were all in place. The schooner's great spanker boom lay heavy with triced canvas alongside the tiller and across the stern rail. Bow and sprit sails and the midships spencer were triced and ready for hoisting.

"Topmen aloft," he ordered. "Release gaff tackle and stand by the rising blocks."

In red-mottled darkness they sorted themselves to stations. Four vanished aloft, one up each shroud of each mast. Kilreagh relayed orders in a hoarse half whisper that Dalton knew should carry a half mile on still water. He went aft to find the tiller and mainsheet dogged down, and loosed them. Downharbor the firelight flared to daytime brilliance, and a rolling boom echoed across the bay. Some ship's magazine had exploded.

At mast tops men secured rising tackle, and those on deck hauled lines to raise sail. "Up anchors," Dalton ordered. Then, when the capstan winches began squealing, he barked, "Belay that. Cut the lines." Drawing his sword he hacked at the light aftanchor line while Kilreagh went forward to cut the bowline.

Someone amidships said, "I coulda swore I saw a boat just then, when the fires went up. A little boat."

Another voice hushed him. "No time for watchin' boats, Brevis. Put your back into that sheet an' haul."

Southeasterly breeze caught rising sails and the schooner drifted, turning on its still-held forward anchor. Kilreagh was up there in the darkness, hacking at the great line, swearing at it.

There were shouts from the fish dock and Dalton saw men there with torches, a hundred yards away. A musket blazed. Simultaneously he felt the ship's quiver as the anchor line parted. "Mister Kilreagh!" he roared. "To the jib. Trim foresails for port reach! We need wind in our nose!" Grasping the tiller he hauled the spanker sail's sheet line from its cleats and paid it out as the ship's swing ceased. "You forward! Up staysail!" In the dancing light he saw men in the bow, gathering sail, hauling on the sheets. Grommets rattled. *Faith* shrugged, righted herself, and raised her bow, edging forward as wind took her sails. She was deep-keeled, he noted as more musket fire rattled from the dock. She held the water well, though with an odd inertia amidships, as though her weight pivoted there.

Someone aloft called down, "Cap'n! We're bein' boarded aport!" Even as he said it dark forms swarmed aboard at the port rail. Dalton stared at them, then looked back at the fish dock, seventy-five yards away now and just starting to slip astern. "Holy Mother of Christ!" he muttered.

Of his dozen men—Kilreagh's dozen men—four were in the tops, two were lofting sail in the bow, and four were occupied with sheet lines. Clarence Kilreagh, bent to the strain of cleating sail to escape the fish dock, looked around at the dark forms across the hold hatch from him and roared, "Repel boarders!"

The newcomers hesitated, stared about in confusion. Dalton shouted, "Belay that! Secure your rigging!" Two men less occupied than the rest had started around the companion hatch armed with belaying pins. At his shout they halted in confusion.

A musket ball chipped the spanker boom. Another whined through the foreshrouds, clipping a stay line and causing a man at the masthead to cling there, kicking wildly for a new foothold.

As one, the figures at the port rail scurried across to starboard, around the hatchway, under the straining foresail, and split into two groups. Ignoring the harried crewmen, they went to the starboard guns, a pair of four-pounders, hauled them back, rammed to check for load, and snugged them to the rails, a man on each line. A small figure in dark struck spark to tinder, got a fuse alight, and touched it to the fore cannon, and the gun roared. Water erupted at the foot of the fish dock, now sliding smartly astern. From there the gunner raced the aft gun, aligned it swiftly, and touched it off. One of the piers under the fish dock collapsed and red-coated figures there teetered, waved, and plunged into the water.

"Right smart gunnery," Clarence Kilreagh announced.

Faith had the wind in her wings on a broad reach, and dark water hissed past as her bow sought the dark horizon across the bay. Frozen at the tiller, fighting for trim, Dalton looked back. The fish dock was far behind. Off beyond it the sullen, dancing light continued to flare as a hulk steamed in the water and a ship alongside it blazed.

To the south across the bay, on Staten Island, were the British General Headquarters was situated, sparks of light had appeared and there were distant bells ringing. *Faith* stepped up on her bow wave and raced into darkness toward the Jersey shore.

Dalton watched the red-tinged dark sails. When the light was gone from them he eased the tiller over and brought her about, dead in the water, her bow to the breeze. The sails slacked and hung. His crew—Kilreagh's men, whoever they were—had gathered around him in the stern, various weapons in their hands, and were staring forward at the dark clusters of strangers there.

Kilreagh stepped out, a cutlass glinting in his hand. "Shall we put them over the side, Sir?"

"You there!" Dalton ordered, "Declare yourselves or be put overboard."

One of them, the smallest, stepped forward and pulled off a dark hood. Long auburn hair fell loose about the face of a confused and angry pixie. She looked straight at Dalton and demanded, "Just who in God's name are you, Sir?"

Dalton took a moment to close his mouth. Then he squared his shoulders and frowned back. "My name is Patrick Dalton, Miss. And who then, in the same God's name, are you?"

"My name is Constance Ramsey," the girl announced. "My father owns this ship."

VI

From the darkness above an urgent voice called, "On deck!" They peered upward. Dalton asked, "Who is that up there?"

One of the men said hesitantly, "That's Charley Duncan, Sir. He's got tangled in the foretop lines an' can't get down."

Dalton shook his head. "What is it, Mister Duncan?"

"Sir," the disembodied voice came back, "There's ships makin' sail in the harbor back there. I make it three of 'em."

"I understand you can't come down, Mister Duncan. Is that right?"

"Aye, Sir. I've got fair tangled in the bloody ratlines."

"Then be so kind as to remain there and keep watch."

"Aye, Sir."

Kilreagh was aft, at the rail. "They'll be after us, those ships."

"*Faith* can outrun them," Constance Ramsey declared.

"Outrun them where, Miss? This bay's no more than five miles in any direction."

"To sea, of course!" she snapped. "Run right past them in the dark."

Dalton turned from his study of the blazing pyres downchannel. It appeared another ship had caught fire. "Mister Kilreagh, put those people below for now."

Several eager hands stepped toward Constance. Kilreagh roared, "Vast there! This is a job for a gentleman."

"I will not go below! This is my ship!" She held a pistol in her two hands. Dalton pointed at the dark figures around her.

"You men there! Will you take my orders or swim ashore?"

They hesitated, muttering among themselves. Then one spoke up. "Only one of us can swim, Sir."

Constance whirled on them. "You're supposed to be on my side!"

"Put just the woman below, then, Mister Kilreagh, and those men amidships on the lines. Have one of your men find the sail locker and see what sort of suit we have."

"Aye, Sir."

"And take that pistol from her as well."

From the rigging Charley Duncan called, "It is three ships, Sir! They've made sail! Two have turned this way!"

"The third'll block the harbor," Kilreagh said. "They intend to rout us out."

One of the men suggested, "Maybe we ought to go to New Jersey."

"We could abandon there and make through the swamps," another agreed.

"I'll not have my ship abandoned!" Constance rapped.

"New York is right over there . . . or what's left of it. Canvastown."

From the huddle amidships came, "Sir, we were mistaken. None of us can swim."

Dalton set his jaw. "Mister Kilreagh, how are you coming along with getting that woman below?"

"Not very well, Sir. You men, give me a hand here. But mind where you put 'em!"

The clap of the companionway hatch did not entirely drown out the fury of Constance. In the darkness to the east Dalton could discern two riding lights making for them. "Mister Kilreagh, hands to the sheets. Trim for starboard beam reach. Secure those people's boat in tow. Stations!"

"On deck!" Duncan's distant voice was plaintive. "When you have time, could somebody come up here an' help me get loose?"

"Send a man up to help him, Mister Kilreagh."

As the spanker boom swung aport, *Faith* took the breeze and started to slide backward. "Foresheet aport!" Dalton called. "Look alive, there!" He heard lines crackling and *Faith* stopped her backslide, heeled lightly to port, and began to fill her sails. The motion reversed itself. Slowly, gingerly, she came about and gathered way, directly toward the oncoming bowlights of the two warships.

A man amidships, securing the foresail, asked,

"Who is that back there?" Another rasped, "That's the captain, ye idiot!"

"Fore lookout," Dalton called, "How do those warships lay?"

"Moment, Sir," the answer was muffled. "I got a rope aroun' my head . . . there, that's better. They're close abreast, Sir, an' comin' on apace."

"Mister Kilreagh, can the starboard guns be loaded?"

"No, Sir, 'less we can find powder an' shot below-decks. There's none up here."

"No time for a search. Get hands on the aft port and fore starboard guns and trade them around."

"Aye, Sir."

"You men there in the hoods . . . you have fuse with you?"

"Aye, Sir. We brought it along for settin' off the Greek fire."

"Then get two pieces alight and stand by those guns."

"Sir, that's a pair of warships out there, an' we got only two loaded four-pounders."

"Do as ye're told!" Kilreagh thundered.

"Mister Kilreagh, how deep do you reckon that East River channel to be?"

There was a pause. "Can't say, Sir. Should make two fathom . . . then again, maybe not."

"Then see about rigging a sounding line, Sir, and pray douse that light as soon as you can."

The lamp was put out and *Faith* ran in darkness, Dalton manning the tiller with his eyes on the twin lamps ahead to estimate his direction. The overcast had thickened, and it was utterly dark on the bay.

Against the glow of dying flames to the east he made out the dim silhouette of one of the warships, a huge, sailed shape framing the speck of light that was her bow lantern. The other lantern was just off his port quarter. Can it be, he asked himself, that they have not seen us yet? As if in answer there was a flare of yellow-orange and a ball threw water behind him. The ship directly ahead had fired one of her bow chasers. He pushed the tiller to ease *Faith* aport. "Ease those sheets," he told the men beside him.

The ship's second bow chaser put a ball where *Faith* had been as she heeled. A moment, and Dalton's hands on the tiller told him the feel of her, the feel of the water beneath her, the sliding pressure on her keel. She rode easily, agile except for a slight heaviness amidships. He counted to fifteen, then hauled back on the bar. "Haul sheets," he barked. "Two points!" *Faith* righted herself, heeled a bit to starboard, and plunged for the gap between the warships. They were less than a hundred yards apart.

"Stand by the guns!" he called. In the faint glow now he could see the warships standing over him on both sides. *Faith* slowed and settled momentarily as she entered the lee of the one on his starboard.

"Train amidships!" he called to the gunners, and then they were directly between the warships. "Fire as they bear!"

The range was so close that he could hear splintering wood to port as the four-pounder there roared. Then the starboard gun spoke and he heard a thump to that side. *Faith* came out of the lee of the frigate and her sails filled again. On both sides of her, overhead, batteries of heavy guns fired full broadsides.

83

"Rig for running wing and wing!" Dalton shouted while the thunder still rolled and chaos echoed on both sides behind them. "Ease the sheets main and fore! Full out aport! Fore full starboard!" The rudder bit water and the tiller tugged at him as *Faith* got the wind on her tail and the big sails swung wide to catch it. Her hull came up and she rode a crest, heading north into darkness.

"Lord a'mercy!" Clarence Kilreagh announced. "They shot hell out of each other!"

Twenty minutes later the schooner crept close-hauled into the nect of the East River. The fleet yards were less than a mile to her right, and the New York bank the same distance to her left. Patrick Dalton watched the sky and wished for three things: that they could get well into the channel and out of sight of the yards before dawn exposed them; that there was a channel deep enough to clear the schooner's keel; and that he were somewhere else entirely. His first wish was granted. By the time there was light enough to see the silhouetted banks, *Faith* was two miles up and hidden from the fleet yards. She was also aground on a mudbar.

There were six oars in the Wilmington party's launch and four with the schooner's little jolly boat. Two lines were secured to the ship and ten pairs of shoulders pulled at stubborn water.

"We should have tide a bit after dawn," Kilreagh assured his captain. "She'll move then."

"We'll be seen then, too," Dalton said bleakly. "And there'll be redcoats lined up on that bank to use us for musket practice." He squared his aching shoulders. "We'll probably have to leave the ship and go ashore on that bank. What is that land there?"

"Manhattan Island, Sir."

"She's a sweet craft, Mister Kilreagh. I will hate to leave her. Who are these men you brought? Where did you get them?"

"Oh, them. I turned them out o' the stockades, Sir. They're mainly a good bunch o' seamen, decent souls caught ashore an' thrown in for drunkenness or rapine or the like. Nothin' serious, except maybe that one there by the capstan . . . the one wi' half a beard, ye see? His name's Arthur an' he cracks heads on occasion. Yon two with the beaks on 'em, they're the brothers Grimm. They're good lads, except around ladies. And they do get mean when they're not fed."

The deck lurched slightly, settled, and stirred into lazy motion. "She's aweigh, Sir. Those dear lads ha' tugged her free."

"Very well, Mister Kilreagh, holler them aboard, ship the jolly boat, and put a fresh crew in the launch. Line to the bow. From here it'll be tow and sound. Did that man ever get loose from the foretop lines?"

"Aye, Sir. This is him right here. Charley Duncan."

"Thank you for standing lookout, Mister Duncan."

Duncan blushed with pleasure. "It wasn't anything, Sir. I was stuck up there anyway."

Kilreagh frowned. "What are you doin' back here, Charley?"

"Oh. Well, Sir, I wanted to tell you, we're bein' overtaken by somebody back there in a skiff."

They peered astern. Coming up the dark channel was a small boat, its oars plowing water. There seemed to be only one aboard.

"What do you make of that, Mister Kilreagh?"

"Hard to tell, Sir. But he does seen to be coming our way."

"Very well. If he gets here before we are gone, bring him aboard. How are you coming with our rig for tow?"

"I haven't started on that, Sir. We've been discussing that skiff since you gave your orders."

"Well, hop to it."

"Aye, Sir."

"Oh, and you can let that woman come up for air now, providing she will be quiet and not interfere. And when she's safely on deck, Mister Duncan, you can send one of our decent souls below to see if this ship carries any cargo and whether there are provisions aboard."

"Aye, Sir."

With a towline secured to the bow and fresh rowers in the launch, *Faith* crept upchannel, gradually picking up enough speed to create a slight wake. Dalton looked back. The skiff was closer now and coming on, its occupant leaning to his oars. "Mister Duncan, when that skiff overtakes us bring that man aboard and secure his boat in tow."

"Aye."

"Aye, *Sir*, Mister Duncan. I'll have no laxity aboard."

"Aye, Sir."

The girl seemed subdued when she came up out of the ship's tiny stern cabin. She blinked and looked around in the dim light. "What have you done with the ships?"

"What ships?" Dalton asked.

"Those warships that were coming to get us. I heard the firing."

"They seem to have broadsided each other, Miss. Now if you will please just stay out of the way . . ."

Constance squinted up at the gray light. "You have us going the wrong way!"

"Skiff's coming alongside, Sir!"

"Very well, bring him aboard. Mister Duncan, have the men looked below for provisions?"

"Aye, Sir. Th' larder's got some stock. Hardtack and colonial coffee. Maybe a tub of salt meat. We haven't looked at the holds yet."

"Mister Kilreagh, do you have someone among the crew who knows how to cook?"

"Aye, Sir. That Arthur's a cook."

"When he isn't cracking heads," Dalton muttered, then called, "You, Mister Arthur! You are assigned ship's cook. Please go below and see what you can find to make breakfast."

"Aye, Sir."

"Mister Dalton, I said you have us going the wrong way."

"We are in the East River, Miss Constance. It goes only two directions. I have chosen this direction because there are large parts of the King's Navy looking for us in the other direction, probably because we have stolen a prize vessel belonging to a gentleman known as the prizemaster, and because at least three ships of the King's fleet have been burned and two others broadsided as a result of our activities. For these reasons we are in the East River, heading approximately six degrees east of north."

"I only meant that Delaware is south of us, Mister Dalton. You seem to be taking a long way around."

"Please stand aside, Miss. Mister . . . ah, you! What is your name?"

"Me, Sir? Abernathy, Sir."

"Mister Abernathy, where is the person from the skiff?"

"Just comin' up now, Sir. He seems fair wore out, he does." With Abernathy's help a slight figure clambered over the rail. "Come along, lad. Cap'n wants ye."

They made their way aft, the boy leaning on Abernathy. At sight of Dalton, his eyes grew to the size of shillings. "Mister Dalton, Sir. Is it you?"

Dalton stared. "Mister Caster, I thought I sent you home to the colonials."

The boy looked completely done in. "I tried, Sir. But the town has been burned. Everyone there is hungry and they tried to take my purse, an' there's redcoats all around. So I got away and went back and sat in the little boat. Then I saw the fires and heard the guns, and when this ship passed I guessed it was a patriot ship, so I came after it . . . you. I don't suppose this *is* an American ship, is it, Sir?"

"It is not. *Faith* is a British prize."

"She is not!" Constance declared. "*Faith* is American, and she belongs to my father."

"Miss Constance, stand aside or go below."

"Beg pardon, Sir." It was Kilreagh. "I wouldn'

send th' young lady below right now. Th' brothers Grimm are down there, doin' inventory. It wouldn' be safe, Sir."

"Sir? What should I do with this lad? He's saggin' quite a lot."

"Mister Caster, when did you eat?"

"Ah, maybe it was when we were at the inn, Sir."

"Take him below, Mister Abernathy. Have Mister Arthur feed him, then rig a hammock somewhere and let him sleep. Ah, Mister Kilreagh, your brothers Grimm . . . I suppose a lad is safe around them?"

"Oh, aye, Sir." Kilreagh sounded shocked. "The brothers Grimm are harmless, Sir. Except for the ladies, is all."

Out on the brightening river, the singsong of the man sounding depth aboard the launch continued, then stopped. There was a shout, relayed by a sailor in the bow. "Sounder says she's shoaling, Sir. Readin' is 'an' a quarter, two.' "

"Mister Kilreagh, how sounded the shoal where we bottomed?"

"It was 'an' a half, one,' Sir."

"Then go forward if you please, Mister Kilreagh. Read us through, but should it come to 'by the mark, two,' then belay the tow and report."

Faith crept over the shoal with inches to spare. Beyond it the channel widened, and in the distance seemed to split into two narrow cuts. "I believe it's like an island, Sir," Kilreagh said. "Runs about two miles, then it's one channel again. After that I don't know. Th' charts o' this river I've seen only showed the mouth of it."

Constance Ramsey's eyes widened. "We're in a river? You have us going up a river?"

Dalton looked around. "I could have sworn I ordered you aside, Miss. I intended you stay there."

"It seems to me, Mister Dalton, that the nature of rivers is such that if you go up one, the only way out of it is to turn around and go back down it again to the place where you began. I really do not see what that will accomplish."

"This isn't exactly a river, Miss," Clarence explained helpfully. "It's more a tidal cut between two bays. Was it not for the East River having two ends, the Long Island over there couldn't rightly be an island, don't ye see."

"Well, of course in that case . . ."

"Please stand aside, Miss Constance."

"Best do as th' cap'n says, Miss."

"Mister Kilreagh, aid my memory. What navigating has been done of this channel?"

"Small craft all th' time, Sir. An' after th' fightin' on Long Island, ol' Black Dick . . . ah, his Lordship . . . Admiral Howe, I mean . . . he took his transports up here to gain the Sound. Wide-beamed they was, Sir, but not deep-keeled. This vessel's deep-keeled, Sir. I don't know about her."

"Then we must make shift as we go. Let's have a fresh crew in the launch to row ahead and sound those channels. And let's get an anchor down here, please."

"We got no anchors rigged, Sir. We left bower an' stream grapple back there in the bay. But there's sheet anchors stowed below."

"Very well. You amidships! Aye, you four. There

90

are anchors in the forehold. Get a line from one to the capstan and hoist it out, please. Then rig chain and line and anchor a'starboard."

"Mister Dalton . . ."

"Please, Miss!"

"I just wanted to tell you, there are four casks of Greek fire in the launch, under the tarp."

"Mister Duncan, take two men and hand those casks aboard. Put them in the chain locker, where no spark can reach them."

"I don't think we should anchor here, Mister Dalton."

"Miss Constance, I've told you . . ."

"But won't they be coming after us?"

Dalton took a deep breath. He was tired. "Miss Constance, this schooner has already bottomed once in this channel. While you and your saboteurs were raising havoc with the King's fleet back there, did you see anything that might seek us out up here?"

"Gunboats, Mister Dalton. There are gunboats."

A half-bearded head popped out of the galley hatch and bellowed, "If anybody can stomach this slop, it's ready!"

Dalton secured tiller and sheets. Come gunboats or the devil himself, he intended to have breakfast and a nap.

Captain Jonathan Hart held his deteriorating temper in check as he held the eyes of the bemused, indifferent man seated before him. "I am certain, Sir, that if I wait patiently enough you will eventu-

91

ally explain to me why I cannot have gunboats to go after my schooner."

Post Captain Roger Mercer gazed back at the man standing across the table. He had little interest in Jonathan Hart's problems and less in his company. "You might have noticed, Captain Hart, that there have been some changes here since yesterday. I shall itemize them for you." He counted gravely on his fingers. "Items one, two, and three are those charred hulks out there in the anchorage. As recently as yesterday, those were capable ships of the fleet. Now one is burned to the waterline, one is blown to kingdom come, and one is rather badly scorched.

"Item four is the brig *Voluble,* presently under tow with her starboard beam collapsed from cannon fire. Item five is the frigate second class *Menage,* which you can see from here with a glass. She will make port on her own, but she is heavily damaged. You see, Captain, we have had a bit of sabotage here in your absence."

Hart kept his fury barely in check. "Then doesn't it occur to you, Sir, that it might be a splendid idea if someone were to go and apprehend the saboteurs?"

"It would indeed," Mercer nodded. "If we knew where they were at the moment. But assuming someone does turn them up, I expect I will need my gunboats for just that purpose, Captain—not off trying to reclaim your private property."

"The *Faith* is a prize of war!" Hart bellowed.

"Of course, Captain, of course. But you chose not to consign her to registry, as I recall. Therefore she remains yours, not the King's."

"Balderdash! The sabotage was a feint. Those very same people in all likelihood stole my schooner."

Mercer cocked an eyebrow at him. He didn't care at all for this man they called the prizemaster. Mercer was Royal Navy from heels to cockade, and had little use for adventurers who used war—or even the business of squelching obstreperous colonials—as an excuse to indulge in piracy for personal gain. "I understood you to say, Sir, that it was the traitor Dalton who took your little ship."

"That is exactly what I said. The evidence is clear. Mister Croney's harbor guards had located Patrick Dalton—even had an accomplice in custody—when your damned harbor lit up like a bonfire. As a result Dalton got away. He went directly to my schooner and stole her. He is in league with your saboteurs, Sir. They are all the same."

Mercer spread his hands on the table. "My dear Captain, that does seem rather far-fetched, don't you think? The Irishman has been ashore only a few days—after bringing in the unfortunate *Herrett*. He could hardly have organized so precise an undertaking in that time."

"He has accomplices, Sir!" Hart was losing control. "Who knows the extent of the turncoat ring operating here?"

Mercer gazed at him sadly. "Captain Hart, while you and your *Courtesan* have been out, ah, taking prizes, I have remained here keeping my finger on the business of this harbor. I venture, Sir, if anyone knows the extent of anything here, it must be me."

Hart's face went livid. He strode to the table and

pounded the top of it. "By damn, Sir, I demand gunboats!"

Mercer came to his feet. "And by damn, Sir, you shall not have them!"

"By whose authority?"

"By my authority, Sir, over port and tender vessels assigned to this command in the absence of Admiral Lord Richard Howe!"

In the icy silence that followed, Hart's purple face drained white. "And by damn, Sir, that does not include the *Courtesan*."

"No, unfortunately that does not include the *Courtesan*."

"Then good day to you, Sir, and I will attend to the matter myself!" The door he slammed behind him rattled the building.

Before the sun was high, crew officers from the big frigate *Courtesan* had swept the bars, bins, and brothels of New Ultrecht and Long Island Yards and herded the ship's full complement staggering aboard her. "Mister Mace," the prizemaster ordered, "All hands to make sail. Courses and tops'ls past breakwater, then I'll want gallants and royals."

"Aye, Sir."

As he strode to the quarterdeck, casting an eye over the forty-four shining great guns at his command, Hart's mind was racing. "Take to the East River, will he?" he muttered. "Well by God, he's got himself in a funnel now, and I know where the funnel comes out."

Courses and topsails sheeted home as he took the helm. The tall frigate nudged water, creeping into the choppy lower bay. By the time she cleared the breakwaters she rode hull-up and keening. Captain Jonathan Hart, the prizemaster, brought her a quarter to port and set his course upcoast for the distant head of Long Island Sound.

Post Captain Roger Mercer watched from the door of his command quarters. Then he turned back to the three men awaiting him inside. "Well, gentlemen?"

Croney, head of the guard unit, nodded firmly. "It was the traitor Dalton, Sir. We missed him at the inn, but my men saw him and his accomplice the innkeeper row out to the *Faith* with the gaol fugitives."

Mercer's eyes went to Captain Damian Snook, master of the brig *Voluble*. He had a bloody bandage around his head, and one arm in a sling. "It was the *Faith*," he assured Mercer. "The devil ran between us and provoked fire, then got away."

Mercer turned to the third of them. "Commander Blessing, is it possible a ship with the keel of that schooner could navigate the East River?"

The harbor patrol master scratched his chin. "Aye, Sir. I suppose it is possible. But only with a real master seaman at her helm, Sir."

"Your gunboaters have run the channel, I believe?"

"Oh, aye, Sir. For gunboats it's easy. We had boats up there to harass when Sir William pushed the rebels back to Manhattan."

"Suppose a schooner like *Faith* had entered the East River, Commander Blessing. Would your gunboats have any difficulty catching it?"

"No, Sir. None at all."

"Very well, Commander Blessing, you are authorized to send a squadron up the East River to take the *Faith*. Take her and return her . . . no, belay that. Sink her, Commander. Sink her where she lays."

VII

Billy Caster awoke in a hot, dim place and suffered a moment of disorientation before he remembered where he was. The forehold of the *Faith* was ranked with shrouded heaps barely discernable in the reflected light from the open grating. He heard distant chanting voices, and his hammock moved to the tempo of them as it swung a few inches one way, a few the other, an interrupted rhythm foreign to the roll of a vessel in water.

He rubbed his eyes, squinted around, and swung to the cargo decking, careful not to raise his head in the low space. Working around the shrouded heaps, he found the short ladder and went up on deck. They were in a narrow channel, with heavy forest on both sides coming right down to the banks above tideline. The ship surged, then rested; surged, then rested; and the chanting was plain now. Long lines had been secured to her bow quarters, spread out ahead to the two banks of the channel. Crews of sweating men, six to a line, alternately hauled and rested, chanting as a peg-legged man in the bow called time. Judging by the way the forest crept past, *Faith* was making steady time.

Astern, a sandy-haired man was at the tiller, holding it steady against the thrusts and eases from alternate sides. Beyond him Patrick Dalton leaned on the after rail, looking back the way they had come.

There was a man at each masthead above, and two at each midships rail holding long poles for fending. Directly before him, a young woman sat on a little stool by the capstan.

"Mister Caster!" It was Dalton's voice, from the stern. He grinned at the red-haired lady when she turned, then hurried along to the stern deck.

"Well," Dalton nodded. "You look much improved. I trust you've had a good rest."

"Aye, Sir. What ship is this, Sir?"

"Do you recall the schooner that ran away when *Herrett* fought the snows, Mister Caster? The prize vessel? Well, this is the same schooner. We have appropriated her in order to escape. Her name is *Faith.*"

Billy looked about in wonder. He had never been on a schooner. "She has no courses, does she, Captain?"

"No, she's fore and aft rigged. She carries square sails only on the topmasts. This big sail here at the stern, this is the spanker. It is the mainsail. That one foreward, on the foremast, is the spencer. But I'll tell you about her as we go. Right now I'd like you to look for records, papers, and ink. The past few hours I have left a great deal undone that I need a good clerk to attend to."

Billy turned to obey, then turned back. "Then am I still your clerk, Mister Dalton?"

"You are. And the proper address is 'Captain' Dalton. I'll have no laxity aboard this vessel, Mister Caster."

"Aye, Sir."

In the tiny stern cabin below the afterdeck Billy crouched in the tight space searching cabinets and lockers. He found sheaves of stiff paper and an inkwell with quills. He also found two maple-stocked flintlock rifles of the kind his uncle had once designed, and he stared admiringly at them.

Then with his hands full he hurried back up on deck. "Captain's clerk reporting, Sir. We have rifles in our stern."

Dalton looked at him amused. "Yes, Mister Caster, I know. And there are approximately fifty more in the hold, along with some, ah, other instruments. You recall how the musters were kept aboard *Herrett?* And the hold manifests you copied? You can start on those things. Two of the men, the brothers Grimm, have counted the cargo but lack the skills to produce a manifest. Also, I need a roster of people aboard. Name, qualifications, and status."

"Aye, Captain."

Dalton turned back to the after rail. Out there, at the end of a long cable, a launch was in tow and there was a man aboard her. Billy moved to look curiously past the captain. The man in the launch sat with his back to the schooner, cranking at something. There was a keg on either side of him.

"Captain?"

"Yes, Mister Caster?"

99

"What is that man doing, Sir?"

"He is grinding gunpowder, Mister Caster. We have no fine powder for those rifles, so he is using a coffee grinder to make cannon powder into rifle powder."

"Oh. Captain, why is he out there in the launch?"

Dalton turned to him. "You are the expert on small arms here. Perhaps you can tell me."

Billy thought about it. His eyes widened. "Does the coffee grinder have iron gears, Sir?"

Dalton nodded. "Exactly."

"Then possibly I should list his name first, Sir? While he is still with us?"

Dalton fought back a grin. "Go about your business, clerk, if you please."

With the channel's end in sight, Billy completed his inventory, as recited by the two hook-nosed men who listed themselves as Brevis and Solamon Grimm, able seamen, late of His Majesty's Sloop *Louise*, recently of Long Island stockade, four years' service apiece.

The cargo included fifty colonial rifles, fifteen casks of oil, two-and-a-half hundredweight of beeswax, forty ingots of lead less five assigned to Mister Arthur in the galley for making rifle balls, twenty hewn rooftrees, ninety bales of wooden shingles and thirty kegs of drawn nails. There were also twenty of what the brothers Grimm described vaguely as "different kinds of fiddles." Billy went to see for himself.

"This last is five violins, ten dulcimers, three cellos, and two violas," he explained to Dalton when he handed him the manifest. "I counted them."

Dalton read through the list, then raised his head. "Miss Constance! Quarterdeck, please!"

When the red-haired young lady arrived aft Billy stepped aside.

"Mister Dalton," she placed her hands on her hips, "you know very well *Faith* has no quarterdeck."

"I was curious whether you'd know the difference, Miss. Can you read? You can? Marvelous. Be so good as to read this, then. This seems an odd lot of cargo, does it not?"

As she took the paper her hand trembled. She looked frightened. But when she read it, her composure returned. "No, not odd at all. There is a settlement in the hills where my father trades. The people are Germans there, and very clever with their hands. My father bought their produce for resale at Boston. That, of course, was before your English pirates came and stole his ship."

"They make fiddles?"

"Of course they do. They make all kinds of things." She frowned. "This says your men have taken some of the lead. Please replace it."

Dalton took the list from her. "Thank you, Miss. You may go forward again, now."

"I believe I'd rather remain here for a while."

Billy excused himself and wandered off, uncomfortable in the presence of laxity.

As the channel widened, towlines and shoremen were brought aboard. Billy met them as they came, making out his roster. Some of the credentials seemed odd, but he listed them as given. Clarence Kilreagh was complaining to the captain, "That boom took a fair bit of our suplus cable, Sir, and all our spare grapples and hooks. I hope it wasn't wasted."

"Actually, Mister Kilreagh, I hope it is wasted. I hope there's no one after us at all. But just in case, that cable boom should slow them down."

"That's a river tactic, Captain. Where did you learn such a thing?"

"The same place I learned sailing, Mister Kilreagh. The north of Ireland can be a hard school at times."

"Aye, my ol' Pa told me, though I've been mostly English all me life, except for bein' mainly Irish."

Billy handed over the roster. "Some of the credentials are a bit odd, Sir."

Dalton read through it. Of the Delaware men, Constance Ramsey's men, two were able seamen and three had some sailing experience. Only one was a landsman, a carpenter. "Miss Constance, where did you find your crew?"

"Mister Neely works for my father, in his shops. I think one or two of the others do, too. Mister Neely found them." Neely was the carpenter.

"It seems odd to me that a band of men would set out on such a harebrained venture, under the leadership of a young woman."

"Not odd at all. I promised them we would sink some English ships. I trust we have done so."

Dalton shrugged. Life was full of mysteries. He read on down the list. "Mister Kilreagh, this is a strange mix you have brought me. All but two are competent seamen, as you promised, though they have a strange way with their credentials. One qualifies himself as a lover, three as grog testers, and two as sandpipers."

"The lads are just high-spirited, Sir. I'll arrange floggings if you like."

"Not just yet, thank you, Mister Kilreagh. It wouldn't be proper to flog men who haven't been read the articles of war, would it? But where did you get these two . . . Peter Tarkington and William Moses . . . a Southampton beekeeper and a Virginia tinsmith?"

"I didn't rightly know we had them, Sir. When the lads slipped the stockade, those two just got caught up in it, so to speak. They've been pressed men on a tender, I believe, before bein' stockaded."

"Miss Constance, which of your men is Mister Neely?"

"That one with the wide hat. You see?"

"Please fetch him for me, Mister Caster." Billy went forward and brought back the carpenter.

"Mister Neely," Dalton said, "have you done ship's carpentry?"

"No, Sir. But I've built many a storebin and crate, as well as a house and two barns."

Dalton was disappointed, but shrugged it off. "Very well, Mister Neely. Please go below and find the carpenter's locker. Acquaint yourself with the tools. You'll be ship's carpenter."

"All right."

"Mister Neely, say, 'Aye, Sir.' "

"Aye, Sir, all right."

"Mister Kilreagh, I'll leave it to you to select a bosun, bosun's mate, navigator, master gunner . . .

and if there's a man aboard who's handy with knife and saw, we'll make him ship's surgeon."

"Aye, Sir." Kilreagh looked crestfallen. "Captain?"

"Yes?"

"Sir, I was kind of thinkin' I was your bosun, Sir. Forgive the presumption, Sir, but I was."

"You cannot be *Faith's* bosun, Mister Kilreagh."

"Oh. Aye, Sir."

"You are my first officer, Mister Kilreagh."

The old man's shoulders squared and his stump thudded the deck as he saluted. "Aye, Sir!"

Phillip Blessing, commander of boats, His Majesty's harbor fleet, stood ankle-deep in rancid mud on the bank of a wilderness island, wet from head to toe, and stared at the wreckage before him. "Damn his soul to hell!" he repeated. "Damn his soul to everlasting torment!"

Out in the channel, men aboard three gunboats worked frantically to salvage what they could from the wreckage of a fourth which lay stem-down in the water, its entire bow submerged. A crewman waded ashore dragging a length of torn-ended rope with pikes, hooks, and grapples knotted into it at intervals of about three feet. "It were a cable boom, Sir, stretched just below the surface. This here's a piece of it."

"I know what it was," Blessing growled, then turned away. The diabolical device had taken the bottom out of his best boat, the only boat in his fleet with an eight-pounder aboard. His best gun now was sunk deep in the silt bottom of the channel, the ruined boat resting stem-down and anchored to it. Only the stern of the ten-sweep craft jutted above the water, standing at an impossible angle. The grapples had gutted her.

After cursing Patrick Dalton, Blessing cursed himself as well. He should have suspected . . . he should have been more wary. But with sails swollen by a fair, following breeze and an easy quarry close at hand, who would have expected a cable boom? What kind of madman would rig such a thing, anyway?

He watched the scurrying of men in the water, the slow dance of the three remaining gunboats on their six sweeps apiece, and closed his eyes tightly. He had four men injured. "Mister Rand!" he called, "that will be enough! Bring the boats into the shallows!"

He looked at the heap of soggy salvage on the bank. "Mister Mason, put this tack aboard number four, with the wounded, and you and the rest of the crew of number one get aboard her. When you have loaded, return to port and ask the yardmaster to send a barge with a windlass up here to retrieve that cannon."

"Aye, Sir."

The three boats nudged the shallows, their four-pound cannons jutting from their bows. Blessing said, "Mister Rand, take stroke, if you please." He waded out, clambered aboard the bow of number two boat, and waited for Rand to get settled in the stern. Men were loading salvage aboard number four. "Number three, follow my lead, please! Back us off, stroke, and we shall continue upriver. Jibs and sweeps, please, and a sharp eye to the fore. We don't know what other surprises he may have left to amuse us."

All the gunboats were high-rigged, but mainsails remained furled, only the slim jibsails catching at the long-channel breeze to assist the sweating rowers. Slowly now, carefully, a pair of gunboats crept after the fugitive *Faith*. In the bow of number two, Commander Philip Blessing squinted at the water ahead and muttered, "Sink her, shall we? Sir, it will be my pleasure."

With but a mile of channel ahead, one small island to round, and opening water beyond, Patrick Dalton mustered his ship's complement amidships, counted heads, and quoted to them the articles of service and the articles of war, both from memory. Under the articles of service, each officer and hand aboard must bind himself by pledge and mark to the service of the ship and obedience to command. The articles of war seemed a bit extraneous, with their ominous recitation of dire penalties for misbehavior, but they were the most impressive document he could call from memory and he recited them for effect.

"I have now a complete roster of ship's company," he concluded. "Mister Caster, my clerk, will take your marks. Any man unwilling to sign aboard as ship's company for the remainder of this cruise may so state now, and will be put ashore."

One by one they came forward and made their marks, and he was pleased to note that Constance Ramsey's six men were among them.

When all had signed, he addressed them again.

106

"Mister Kilreagh shall be your first officer, Mister Duncan is your bosun, Mister Wise is bosun's mate, Mister Arthur is cook and surgeon, Mister Solamon Grimm is chief of navigation. We still lack a gunner. You colonials," he looked beyond his Englishmen at the Delaware contingent, "I saw you operate the starboard guns last night in the bay. Which among you is the gunner?" They looked blankly back at him. "Well? Speak up, lads. Who was it fired the guns at the fish dock, and later when we ran the broadsides?"

Virgil Cowan raised a hand, hesitantly, and cleared his throat. "Beggin' your pardon, Cap'n, but it wasn't none of us. We just dogged 'em in. It was Miss Constance done the shootin'."

"On deck!"

Dalton looked up at the man squatting atop the main crosstrees. "Report, Mister Smith!"

"Mast tops, Sir! Two, I make it, sheer and separate!"

"Whereaway, Mister Smith?"

"Beyond that last bend, Sir. I see 'em over the trees. They're comin' this way!"

He looked back at the fidgeting group before him. "Dismissed, then, and to stations! Mister Wise, please bring those forward guns aft and set them as stern chasers. Mister Neely, we will need two sets of ring bolts in the after rail and deck. Mister Wise will show you where they belong. Mister Kilreagh, please stand by as gunner, and three of those colonials can crew for you. Up anchor, Mister Duncan, please, and stand by to make sail. I'll want jib and jigger only until we've cleared that island."

"On deck!"

"Yes, Mister Smith?"

"I make 'em gunboats, Sir, a pair of 'em. They'll round the bend any time now."

He stepped aside as the fore cannons were trundled past on their oak carriages, their crews waiting as Neely installed ringbolts to snug them. Men manned capstan and cathead and the anchor came aboard. *Faith* drifted lightly in the breeze and Dalton loosed the tiller. "Up jibs'l, Mister Duncan!"

The sail rose, the sheet paid, and Duncan hauled it taut and took a turn around a cleat. "Sheet home, Sir."

Dalton tested the breeze. "Quarter aport."

"Aye, Sir," The jib crept to port, reefed foresail raised and filled as Duncan secured the sheetline and topmen secured the gaff. With the light sails nudging her, *Faith's* slight heel was almost imperceptible. Inertia held her motionless for long seconds before she began to move. The cut ahead along a small island was narrow. The better channel opposite was blocked. Dalton would have preferred to haul through with lines, but that option was gone. He held his breath, waiting for the inert tiller to come alive under his hands as *Faith* gained enough way for the rudder to take hold.

"They're in sight, Sir." Kilreagh said quietly from behind him. He looked back. The second of them was just rounding the bend a half mile back. Their sweeps were out and their bows up as they came on, and in a hush he could hear the faint call of their strokes. What was precarious quarters for the schooner was running room for them, and they were taking advantage of it to close the gap.

Faith faltered and lost what little way she had as the breeze slackened, and then the foresail filled again and she quivered. All along her rails men looked down at the water, waiting for rills alongside that would show movement. Lazily she responded to another nudge of breeze. Dalton felt life in the tiller and heard mutters of relief about him. With terrible slowness the schooner edged itself into motion, and he pointed her stem at the cut.

"They're coming up fast, Sir." Kilreagh said.

"Are your chasers in place, Mister Kilreagh?" Dalton's fingers were iron feathers on the tiller bar, his eyes dancing to take in trim of sail, the rippling of the uncertain air on its cloth, any surface sign on the water that might lead him to the best course to find his wind, and always coming back to the narrow channel ahead, where he must spirit her through on the breath of air available.

"Secured, Sir. Shall we send a ball their way?"

"What range are they, Mister Kilreagh, and what do they carry?"

"Closing a cable length, Sir, and they have four-pounders, by the looks of 'em."

"Then wait, Mister Kilreagh. Wait for half a cable."

"They'll hole us before then, Sir." As if to punctuate his remark, a ball sang under the starboard rail and threw a plume of water sheeting onto the foredeck. The gun's roar reached them simultaneously. Dalton glanced back. Even as the drifting smoke thinned, he could see trained hands ramming another shot home in the gun. *Faith* plodded, barely making a wake, and the agile gunboats leapt forward for better range. Their guns sounded almost together. He felt the crunch of a stern hit beneath his feet. The second host sprayed water over the port after rail. Three shots, all low. "They're out to hole us below waterline, Mister Kilreagh. They aim to sink us. Have you range yet?"

"Barely, Sir."

"Then see if you can greet the lead craft, if you please."

One of the guns roared and reared back into its securing lines. Kilreagh shouted, "Reload!" and the three who crewed him hurried to comply. Dalton glanced around in time to see water erupt a dozen yards short of the lead gunboat. "Elevate, Mister Kilreagh."

The Americans were good crew. Their reloading was quick and efficient. But before they were done, two more balls came their way. One splintered the afterdeck pinion. Dalton saw pieces of his ship spraying off to speckle the water to starboard. "Fire at will, Mister Kilreagh. Mister Neely, go below and repair damage astern."

Before Neely reached the companionway cover, it erupted upward and Constance Ramsey scurried topside. "What the devil are you doing to my ship—" Her words wer cut short by the roar of Kilreagh's second gun. She watched the ball go wide of its mark, saw the billow of smoke from the lead gunboat, and heard the crash as *Faith's* port hull was grazed. "Are those people trying to sink us?"

110

"That is exactly what they are doing, Miss Constance." Dalton's face was pale, his jaws tight, his eyes in constant motion as he edged the creeping schooner toward a channel he could only guess was there.

Constance whirled on Kilreagh, grabbing the smoldering slow fuse from his hand. "Get out of the way! Which gun is ready?"

In his surprise, Kilreagh gestured and Constance stepped to the starboard gun, giving quick instructions to the men securing its riding lines. "Taut aport. More. Ease the off line, blast you! Now, hold!" Kneeling behind the gun she sighed along its notches, then stepped aside and touched fuse to its priming hole. It bucked and roared, and there was a splintering noise behind them, the howls of men. As the smoke drifted they saw the second gunboat, which had been moving into position to fire, dead in the water with its mast down and its mid-locker a shambles. Its crew was scattered, some in the water, some at the wales, clinging wide-eyed.

"Good gunning, Miss!" Kilreagh roared in delight.

The other gunboat had drawn off to reload, and now it held back, its officer and gunner standing in the bow. Kilreagh squinted. "I know that man, Sir! It's Commander Blessing! He's a regular of mine."

Dalton didn't look around. "We don't have time to stop and visit, Mister Kilreagh."

Several men came out of the forward hold carrying rifles. Billy Caster prodded them along. The boy grouped them on the foredeck, produced powder, ball, and patching, and instructed them in the load-

111

ing of the long, slim firearms. They were clumsy. Few of the seamen had ever used a musket, much less a rifle.

Dalton watched the neck of the cut edge closer. Kilreagh said, "They're comin' again, Sir. This time they've got their gun on loose point. They'll bear in an' sweep our beam, most likely."

It was what he had dreaded. There was no time to remount the pair of cannons. If the gunboat swept alongside it could hole them at will. *Faith* was already taking some water. He could feel it in her sluggish rudder. He glanced around. The gunboat was two hundred yards out, racing toward them on a wide course that would keep it out of range of the stern chasers.

Billy Caster had his motley rifle crew lined at the port rail. "Use those sights," he told them. "Look along them till the front blade is in the back slot and it's on your target. Then touch the trigger."

One rifle discharged up through the rigging. "No! Mister Locke, don't touch the trigger until you're ready to fire!"

"Shan't we wait till they're in gun range?" a man asked.

"These are rifles, Mister Fisk. They are well in range of rifles right now."

To demonstrate, Billy took a rifle and leveled it, steadying on the rail where he knelt. He hesitated, then the rifle barked and one of the men on the distant boat howled and spun over the side.

"Phew!" Fisk looked at his own rifle in admiration. "Let's see can I do that." Imitating the boy, he knelt, rested, and touched trigger. The flintlock spat and a splinter burst from the boat's mast. "How 'bout that? Look what I did!"

"Please reload, Mister Fisk," Billy said around a mouthful of patchcloth. Two others fired from the rail. One missed, one put a hole in the boat's gunwale. "See the gunner in the bow," Billy said. "When he stoops to fire, see if you can hit him."

Eagerly, those with ready rifles knelt and sighted. A hundred yards out, the gunner stooped to sight. The rifles crackled along the rail. "I got him! Look!"

"Hell you did, I got him!"

"That was my shot!"

"It was mine!"

"Gentlemen, please reload," Billy urged.

Out on the gunboat there was panic and confusion. They didn't know what to make of the range of the rifles. Blessing scurried forward to take up the fuse, but as he applied it, a line severed by a rifle ball parted and the cannon nosed down. Its shot plowed water alongside the boat, skipped and glanced over the surface, then sank short of the schooner.

Faith nosed painfully into the cut, her bow slipping past screening vegetation, then midships, and finally her stern. Dalton didn't look around. Again he noticed the ship's odd heaviness amidships. Quick to turn, she was a bit lethargic in responding. Kilreagh blurted, "Cap'n, that commander back there, Sir, damned if he didn' stand an' salute us just then."

113

VIII

Through the evening Patrick Dalton manned the tiller, eyes red-rimmed from the effort of deducing channels among the many little islands and low-tide reefs off the opening of Hell Gate. Neely and some of the crew were below, rigging patches and plates on the damaged stern structure, while seamen with ropes on them dangled in the water astern, fitting copper plates over the holes in *Faith*'s hull. Crews of four worked shift and shift at the midships bilge pump.

By shifts, he had Charley Duncan send them below to fill their bellies with the salt pork, bread, and coffee that was Mister Arthur's particular menu. Cadman Wise had his crew up in the rigging for a time, checking for damage, but found none that hadn't already been repaired. The gunboats had not gone for the rigging.

With sundown the breeze swung around to the northwest and soon became cool. "We'll lose our wind in an hour," Dalton told Kilreagh. "Do you see that largish island off port bow? Send a man up to look at it with a glass, please. If it is not inhabited, we will lay over there for the night."

In last light he eased the schooner close to the open shore of a jutting wooded island and dropped anchor. Its flukes held. Dogging the tiller, Dalton stretched himself and rolled his head to relieve the tension in his neck and shoulders. Calm was settling, and a mist began rising from the still water, shrouding all about.

With the creak of the anchor line Constance Ramsey came aft. Now she said, "I really think we should keep moving, Mister Dalton."

He kneaded the back o his neck. "Miss Constance, we have been aboard this vessel approximately eighteen hours. During that time we have mustered a crew, committed sabotage and high treason, fought two naval encounters, sunk or crippled at least seven times our own weight in shipping—all of it, by the way, vessels of my own King—and navigated a course some would consider difficult. For my part, I have managed only about two hours' sleep in the past three days. I believe Mister Arthur has tea brewing, Miss Constance. Or possibly coffee. If you like, I'll have someone bring it around to you. Excuse me."

In the close, smelly confines of the aft galley he sat down with the men there and had his supper. Then he took a mug of colonial coffee and clambered back into the tiny stern cabin, where he lit a lamp and read again through the musters and manifests prepared by Billy Caster. There were two bunks in the cabin, and he was tempted to sleep, but decided

116

the girl would be safer down here than anywhere else. Billy Caster stuck his head in, and Dalton said, "Mister Caster, please find Mister Duncan and ask him to see to the rigging of twenty-three hammocks—in the holds and galley—wherever he can manage them."

"Twenty-three, Sir?"

"At least twenty-one, Mister Caster. We'll need lookouts, but I want us all to get a good night's sleep."

"Aye, Sir."

"Oh, Mister Caster, do you know whether the young lady has eaten yet?"

"Aye, Sir. Mister Arthur fed her first, Sir. Her and the cat."

"What cat?"

"Why, Bernice, Sir. Mister Arthur's cat. She's our ship's cat, Sir."

"I suppose she's listed on the ship's muster, then?"

The boy's solemn eyes widened. "No, Sir. Do you want me to list her, Sir?"

"No, Mister Caster, it won't be necessary."

"Aye, Sir." The boy disappeared and Dalton leaned back against the bulkhead, his mind reeling with facts and figures, strategies and plans. Twenty-four souls aboard the vessel—twenty-five, counting Bernice the cat—and they were all his responsibilities. They, and the *Faith* herself. He had taken her. He must protect her. In his mind he calculated distances, times, provisions, disciplines that must be maintained, the memorized charts of the region springing into focus as he called upon them.

His course now lay northeast up Long Island

Sound, a distance of about a hundred and eighty miles. With a fair wind the schooner should make eight knots or better, but he must consider the possibility of having to dodge, backtrack, beat into the wind, or run and hide. Word could move faster along these close waters than any ship could outdistance. There were settlements here and there along both shores of the Sound, fishing villages and ports, and where there were settlers there would be both Whigs and Tories. From Lord Howe's headquarters on Staten Island, a message could be sent both ways and would spread as fast as horses could travel. For *Faith* there would be no safe harbors.

Patrick Dalton was a condemned man among British and Tories, condemned as a traitor and turncoat. Yet among colonial Whigs he would be an enemy, a subject of the King.

Billy Caster returned. "Sir, Mister Duncan says he can make your twenty-three hammocks, but without shifting cargo twelve below decks is the best that can be done, and anyone sleepin' in the open without a fire will surely catch the vapors, cool as it has got."

"Very well, Mister Caster. I had thought there'd be more space in the holds. Please ask Mister Duncan to arrange his dozen hammocks. Is there bedding aplenty?"

"Oh, aye, Sir. Right here in this large locker, there's quilts and blankets enough for everyone." He lifted the lid. Dalton got tiredly to his feet, pulled out a pair of quilts, and started for the ladder, ducking low to miss the beams. "Bring two mugs of coffee, Mister Caster, and follow me."

On deck it was nearly dark, just a haze of violet

118

light filtered through the mist from the sun's last glow. "Mister Kilreagh?"

"Here, Sir."

"Mister Kilreagh, I want you to take the skiff and ferry yourself and ten of the crew ashore on that island. Take bedding with you and make a camp back among the trees behind that cove where your firelight will be hidden. Sleep there tonight and come back aboard at dawn."

"Aye, Sir. Which ten, Sir?"

"Take Mister Neely and the other five Delaware men. No sense in offering temptation, is there? And take the brothers Grimm, and Misters Smith and Coleman. Get a good night's rest, Mister Kilreagh, and keep a fire burning to ward off the vapors."

"Aye, Sir."

"I have the coffee here, Sir," Billy said from the coaming ladder.

"Very good, Mister Caster. Bring it along, please."

Dalton turned to where Constance Ramsey huddled on the sailmaker's bench by the main fife rail. "Miss Constance, I've brought a quilt you can wrap in, and Mister Caster has coffee for you. You should avoid the vapors."

She wrapped herself in the heavy quilt. Dalton took one of the mugs and handed it to her. "This will warm you."

"Thank you, Mister Dalton." She noticed the second quilt and mug, and eased over for him to join her.

"Are you quite comfortable, Miss Constance?"

119

"Quite. Do you think we will escape, Mister Dalton?"

"I shall try very hard to. After last night, I suspect we are none too popular in this region."

"It's only a short way to the Connecticut ports, I expect. We might find haven."

"I have no wish to go over to the colonials, Miss. I am a faithful subject of the King."

"Oh, phoo. The king's a moron."

"Of course he is, but that's no reason not to be loyal to him."

"Well, then, maybe we could go to Rhode Island. They don't seem to be on anyone's side, particularly."

"That's slaver coast. And pirate ports. Not to mention the Crown fleet at Newport. We'd be fair game for privateers in those waters. No, I'm looking for a direction that will get us away from all aspects of the war."

"Mister Kilreagh says you're a fugitive. That's why you took my ship." When he didn't respond she added defiantly, "I intend to have *Faith* back."

Over the rim of his mug he studied her—a pale, dark-eyed blur in the failing light. Her eyes were huge, dark smudges. Her hair . . . he thought of Molly Fitzgerald and tried to compare the faces. They were alike, somehow, but then he wasn't sure. He found he couldn't quite remember details of Molly's face. "Miss Constance, I assume your father had an insurance arrangement on this vessel."

"Well, yes, of course."

"And her cargo is nothing extraordinary—no great value, certainly . . . hardly enough to even warrant shipment, it seems to me. So I continue to wonder why you, such an unlikely adventurer, should go to such risk . . ."

"That is my business, Mister Dalton."

"Does it in any way concern the safety of this ship? Or the manner of our pursuit?"

"There is nothing you have any business knowing that you don't already know." Resolutely she turned away. Dalton was very tired.

"In that case, Miss, I'll say good night. The stern cabin is yours, and I'll set a reliable watch on it." He stood, folded his quilt, and paced off toward the bow. Billy Caster came to her. "Can I show you below, Miss?"

She stared into the gloom. "He's a cold man, isn't he?"

"Cold, Miss? Oh, no—not in the least. He isn't even stern, though he tries to be. I expect you just haven't heard him laugh, that's all."

"I can't imagine him laughing."

"That's because he's aboard his ship. Captain Dalton doesn't care for laxity aboard ship."

Kilreagh met Dalton at the fore rail. "The first boatload's away to the island, Sir. The rest of us will follow when the skiff returns. When we're ashore I'll send back the skiff."

"Why not just keep it ashore until morning?"

"Well, Sir, it's all those colonials. They seem right lads, but who can tell? They might just run, Sir."

"And take the skiff," Dalton nodded. "Yes, we might need the skiff."

When Kilreagh turned away, Dalton stopped him.

121

"I've wanted to ask you, what do you know of Captain Jonathan Hart?"

"I heard about that." Kilreagh frowned in the darkness. "How ye faced him down an' all that, Sir. He's a cruel man, wi' a killin' temper about him. Fine seaman he is, an' *Courtesan's* as fine a warship as ye'll see. But he uses her like the lowest pirate. He's not a one to be trusted, Captain."

"Yes. I've learned that very well. Good night, Mister Kilreagh."

Amidships Dalton paused by the mainmast. "Where is Mister Duncan?"

"Here, Sir." In the gathering dark a figure dropped from the lee shrouds to the deck.

"Mister Duncan, why were you in the stockade on Long Island?"

"Which time, Sir? First or second?"

"This latest time. What was the charge?"

"Mayhem, Sir."

"Against men or women?"

Duncan sounded deeply hurt. "Men, of course, Sir."

"Very well, Mister Duncan. Miss Constance will sleep below. I'd like you to position yourself across the companionway. Mister Caster can spell you on watch. Should any man attempt to get past you, you may commit as much mayhem as you see fit."

"Aye, Sir."

Dalton paced the deck of the schooner, his mind on the trim vessel. I don't yet know her well enough, he thought. I must learn her moods, her tempers. In his mind he traced Faith's lines, puzzling again about the odd center-heaviness of her. Yet for all that, she was a trim lady—a living creature, a dancing thing, a dynamic balance of tensions that could come alive for a proper master. The man who would master *Faith* must know her as he would a mistress.

The touch of a hand, the utterance of a word could master her if done with infinite, intimate knowledge. He considered hull design and superstructure, set of masts and angles of stay. I must know her better, he thought, his mind tired and turning slowly. But what he found in his mind suddenly was not *Faith*, but a girl's face—like Molly's face yet different, somehow better. He shook his head, clearing away the uninvited thoughts. "I'll have no laxity aboard my ship," he swore.

"Sir?"

"Nothing. Go below and get your rest."

On the island, Clarence led his charges up, past the fronting rocks and into forest, each man carrying his bedding and part of the equipment—a dip-pan or a saw, an ax or a lantern. Clarence carried one of the rifles, charged for firing. From a distance he had seen movement on this shore. And while the place showed no evidence of habitation, he wanted to take no chances.

Beyond the cove he found a little wooded glen sheltered all around. "Make a fire," he told them. "Spread your beds around it."

The old man stumped around a little, wary on his peg leg in such wilderness, but saw nothing amiss. He returned to the fire, wondering idly what the movement had been that he had seen from *Faith's* gunwales. He had taken it for a beast of some sort, but it could have been human.

The beds were spread, but not necessarily around the fire. The colonials were grouped on one side, with Martin Smith and Samuel Coleman on the other, each delegation eyeing the other suspiciously.

"What's this, now?" Clarence demanded.

"We don't know which one of us is to stand watch over these renegades," Coleman said. "You didn't say, Sir."

"Renegades be damned!" Hannibal Cranston growled. "Patriots is the word, you bleeding limey. *Patriots!*"

"It's what General Arnold told us to be, Sir," John Cranston explained to Kilreagh. "He didn't say a word about renegades, not once. He said patriots."

Martin Smith glared again at the glowering colonials, then spread his hands mystified. "You can't be patriots. You are not patriotic."

Neely the carpenter, oldest among the colonials, waved a finger at him. "Mind your words, sonny. There isn't a man here who isn't patriotic and proud of it."

"Beg pardon." Smith lowered his head, rebuffed.

"But not to the *King*," Coleman insisted. "Isn't that right, Mister Kilreagh? Aren't these people at war with the King?"

Martin Smith gained resolution from this idea. "That's right, that's what Mister Biddle said. He said all these colonials are opposed to the King. How can any good Englishman be against the King?"

"The King isn't English," Neely pointed out. "He's a German."

Coleman goggled at him. "The King of England?"

"The very one."

"Besides that," Hannibal added, "he's a lunatic. I heard that for a fact."

Coleman bristled. "I'll not stand by and hear the King of England called a lunatic . . . even if he is a German, which just doesn't seem right, some way."

Neely raised a hand. "Lunatic is a harsh word, Hannibal, and you don't know that for a fact. You just heard somebody say it."

"Well, that may be," Hannibal conceded. "Maybe he isn't a lunatic, and I apologize for spreading such stories. But he *is* an idiot."

"That's better," Coleman conceded. "Apology accepted."

Kilreagh had been trying to say something. He gave up, stood his rifle by a tree, and sat beside the fire. Neely squatted beside him. "Politics is a young man's sport," the carpenter muttered. "Those of us old enough to understand it generally don't care for it."

"I'll second that," Kilreagh nodded.

The exchange had relaxed some of the hostility among the men, and they began settling into their blankets and quilts—except for Samuel Coleman, who eased around to where Clarence sat. "You never did say which one of us was to stand guard, Sir," he pointed out.

"I expect Mister Neely and I can take first watch. Then you and Mister Cranston there, then Mister Smith and Mister John Cranston can take the dogwatch."

125

Coleman chewed on that for a moment. "Colonials on guard duty, Sir? Whose side are they on?"

"At the moment, Mister Coleman, it seems they're on our side."

"Oh. Well, then, Sir, whose side are *we* on?"

"We're on our side, too, Mister Coleman. For the time being, unless Captain Dalton says otherwise, I believe we should all concentrate on being proper fugitives."

"Aye, Sir."

Midnight was long past and there was a riding moon abaft the island when John Cranston nudged Martin Smith. The tar came awake with a start.

"I keep hearing noises," Cranston said. "Out yonder in the dark."

Smith tipped his head, listening. "What kind of noises?"

"Well, sort of like somebody was startin' a fresh ox at a millstone," the colonial clarified. "There. There it is again—did you hear it?"

"I heard something," the tar admitted. "Kind of like weatherline bein' hove on a capstan. What is it?"

"I don't know. Suppose we should go look?"

"We can't leave our watch," Smith scolded.

"You've been sleepin' through it. I don't see what difference it makes. Listen, there it is again. Sounds like it's past the rise yonder. I'm going to take a look. You suit yourself."

Cranston crept past the sleeping Kilreagh, picked up the rifle, and disappeared into the forest. Smith stared after him and shook his head, his pigtail bob-

126

bing in the moonlight. "Bleedin' colonial wouldn't last out a day on a proper deck," he muttered.

He was about to awaken Mister Kilreagh, but then he hesitated. The awakening of an officer to point out that his watchmate was gone—along with the officer's smallarm—was beyond his experience and he wasn't sure just who might get the blame. He glanced around at the sleeping camp, then heard the sounds again—an odd, repeated scraping sound somewhere past the little peak of the island.

"Well, wait up for me," he muttered. On silent shoes he took off after the vanished Cranston.

He almost stumbled over him. Cranston squatted at the top of the rise, at a point where the brush broke away to give a view of the little island's far shore. There was lantern light down there, and men at work.

"How many do you see?" Cranston whispered.

Smith counted them. "Three. What are they doing?"

"Using a winch, it seems to me."

"Maybe they're fishing."

The strangers were less than a hundred yards away. They had a frame of bound poles set on the shore, a tripod whose top was twenty feet above its footings. Behind it was a rude windlass secured to a pair of trees. The three were heaving at the windlass with capstan bars, drawing a heavy cable a foot at a time across the high frame. The line was lost in darkness beyond, diving toward the water of the cut, but moonlight showed ripples of movement beyond, and something large creeping over the surface.

"They're not fishing," Cranston decided.

"I think we had better wake Mister Kilreagh. You go and get him, Mister Cranston. I'll wait here."

Smith heard Cranston's shoes scuff the hard ground and he turned, "You had best leave me that . . ." he began. But Cranston was gone, rifle and all.

Martin Smith watched, fascinated, as the men below worked. Something was being hove ashore, right enough, and dimly on the moon-blessed surface it resembled a dismasted gunboat.

IX

Kilreagh came huffing over the rise within minutes, followed by most of the others, with the Cranston brothers leading the way and Samuel Coleman dogging their steps. They squatted on the rise while John Cranston and Martin Smith pointed out what they had seen. The dark form on the water was nearer to shore now, grinding audibly as it was dragged over rocky shoals. The stub of a shattered mast rocked above it, and a blocky dark finger jutted from its snout.

"It is a gunboat," Kilreagh said.

"Then what are those people doing with it?" Coleman wondered. "They appear to be landsmen, not sailors."

"I guess we could go ask them," Neely suggested.

"They are having a hard time of it with that windlass," Smith noted. "Possibly we should help them."

"They might not welcome help," Kilreagh said. "Whoever that gunboat belongs to, I doubt much it belongs to them."

"Could it be one of them as chased us? It's dismasted, right enough, and the lady did shoot the friggin' mast right off one of those."

"If it is, what's it doing up here, then? That was miles back."

"Maybe those people are scavengers. Shouldn't we at least find out, Mister Kilreagh?"

The old man scratched his stubble, wondering whether they should all go back and hale *Faith*. This might be an important thing, and Dalton would know how to deal with it. On the other hand, the captain had moved like a walking corpse when last Kilreagh saw him. He had sorely needed a night's rest. Besides, Kilreagh was in charge of the landing party. Therefore the decisions were rightly his.

"I need a detail of volunteers," he said, "to go down and talk with those people. You, Mister Coleman, and Misters Cranston and Cranston. You'll do nicely. The rest of us will wait here for you." He fondled the long rifle he held. "If ought is amiss, just give us a shout and I'll put a ball into their scuppers."

The three started away and he stopped them. "While you're about it, you might show them how to snug that windlass there. They *are* making a poor job of it."

"Aye, Sir," Coleman nodded. Followed by the colonials, he headed for the beach.

For a time, those on the rise lost sight of their detail. Then the men at the windlass abruptly paused in their work and one pointed into the intervening brush, and a moment later Coleman and the Cranstons walked out and approached them.

130

Kilreagh cradled the rifle, trying to remember the instructions Billy Caster had given the hands in the firing of such things. He was not at all sure whether at this range he could hit anyone at all. And if he should, he was not sure who it might be.

But the moment passed and no alarm was raised. In the lantern light down there they could see the men talking, gesturing, and walking down to the water to look at the gunboat, then back to the windlass. They saw their detail pointing and gesturing, explaining the proper way to snug a windlass. Then all six of them were working at it, and the burden in the water grated and groaned and moved toward shore at a good pace. When it was full aground, all six went to it and wandered about it, looking and talking.

"What are they doing now?" Neely peered, blinking his eyes.

"They are discussing that gunboat," Kilreagh said.

One of the figures below strode away from the rest and disappeared into the brush. Moments later they heard footsteps ahead of them, and Samuel Coleman came into the moonlight. He glanced at them, then hurried on past. "We need a mallet," he said. He disappeared over the rise toward the camp. Long moments passed. Abruptly, then, Coleman was among them again, heading toward the lantern-lit beach. "Found a mallet," he announced over his shoulder as he disappeared into the shadows.

"Whatever it is, they seem to be working it out," Neely offered.

They saw Coleman arrive at the winching site, and one of the strangers disappeared behind a shoulder of bluff and came back along the shoreline, towing a small boat at the end of what seemed to be a fending pole. Others waded out to the boat, searched in its bilges, and returned carrying a small thing that the watchers above could not make out.

The whole crowd moved to the gunboat again, and there was the unmistakable clear ring of a heavy hammer against metal.

"Whatever are they doing down there?" Neely demanded.

"Kilreagh shrugged. "I don't have the slightest notion."

The ringing went on for more than a minute, while people waded back and forth between gunboat and dinghy, carrying things. When finally the sound stopped, the watchers saw those below again assembling, gestures and posturings in the lantern's light, and then a general shaking of hands all around. Three of the figures disappeared into the shrubbery, and the other three pulled down their winch frame, released windlass and cable, loaded it aboard the dinghy, then took their lantern, got aboard, and dipped oars.

The little boat was gone from sight when the delegation returned to the rise.

"Landsmen, sure enough," Samuel Coleman explained to Kilreagh while the rest gathered around. "Decent folk, but they didn't know what they was about."

"They found that gunboat seven miles down," Hannibal Cranston picked it up. "They've been most of the night trying to tow it home, but it finally sank. That's why they were winching it ashore."

"Probably the same one the lady hulled," Coleman said. "The men there said it was roped in and marked with a salvage flag. But it was Navy salvage, and they don't hold with the Navy, so they took it."

"That's well an' good," Kilreagh urged. "But what was all the hammering about?"

"Oh, that. Well, Sir, we thought since they couldn't get it home, the least they ought to do was spike the cannon. They didn't know how to do that, Sir, so I showed 'em."

Kilreagh chewed his lip. It occurred to him that Captain Dalton might have welcomed an additional gun aboard *Faith*. But Coleman seemed so pleased with what he had done, and the Cranstons were so taken with their newfound knowledge of cannon spiking . . . and anyway, what was done was done.

"It might be for the best," he told them all, "if what we've seen and done this night just remain amongst us, so to speak. I believe the captain has enough to worry about, without recounting every detail of every landing party we might have need of."

The sun of morning brought a neat wind sweeping smartly from south-southwest, and Patrick Dalton stood alert, fresh and crisp at the port rail as the boat brought the last of the shore party alongside. They didn't all look as rested as he had hoped, but apparently they had encountered no problems.

"Good morning, Mister Kilreagh. Did you sleep well?"

"Quite well, Sir. Yon is a cozy little island.

133

"Come aboard, then, and have your breakfast. Is there anything to report?"

"Nothin' of consequence, Sir."

"Very well, then," Dalton smiled. "Let's be ready to make sail on the next bell, Mister Kilreagh. We have tarried in tight waters long enough. I've a mind to learn our ship today."

Faith came alive. By the time the sun stood clear of the horizon, the mist had cleared and he had the launch lashed in tow. One of the tests he had in mind was of the soundness of *Faith's* knees and timbers. With hands at stations Dalton strode to the tiller and loosed it. "Hands to make sail!"

John Abernathy and Brevis Grimm swarmed up the main shrouds, Martin Smith and Samuel Coleman up the foreshrouds. Virgil Cowan and Victory Locke followed to take station at the mastheads. The rest stood by sheets, fife rails, and capstan, ready to put the ship to work. "Hoist the spanker!" The big mainsail lofted, rising with its gaff. "Foresail and staysail!" It came out "Fors'l and stays'l." The spencer amidships rose and canvas lifted from *Faith's* nose on rattling grommets to meet it. "Jib and jib tops'l!" Two more triangular canvases stood to take the wind.

"Hands to the sheets!" he called. "Starboard tack, broad reach on a quartering wind!" Lines were hauled to trim. She took the wind in her nose, came about, and heeled nicely as spencer and spanker strained at their leashes. She moved. She quickened. She raised her nose and danced. She exulted. Within moments she was hull-up and running.

Constance Ramsey had come from the galley. She

paused in the hatch to watch the performance. Dalton stood above her and a few steps away, and she saw his gray eyes dance, the pull at the corners of his mouth as *Faith* pleased him, the roll of hard shoulders as he brought her over into broad reach. Sensitive hands caressed the living tiller.

"Mister Duncan," he called, "put a man out on the bowsprit to guide by dark water! Mister Grimm, stand by the capstan and relay signals."

"Aye, Sir."

He caught sight of Constance as she came up to stand by him. Her head barely reached his shoulder. For an instant he lost his fine touch on the tiller. "Mister Kilreagh, have the lashing tightened on that skiff. It rattles on the deck."

Constance gazed up at him sternly. "You seem to be having a very good time with my ship, Mister Dalton."

"Aye, Miss, she's a lively vessel, soft and sweet as a girl's, er . . ." *Faith* shuddered again, "That is, as a gull in flight."

Eighty feet ahead of them Michael Romart scrambled nimbly along the bowsprit to the butt of the jib boom and sat astraddle it, with his knees over the spreader yard. Solamon Grimm, by the capstan, spread his arms and began signaling in response to Romart's calls. Dalton added the arm signals to his running inventory of forces and stresses, and his hand on the tiller became more sure. With dark water under the jib and a watcher there, he could bring her up to speed. Today he would get to know her better. A man could grow to love her.

"Mister Kilreagh," he said as the one-legged man

135

came stumping astern, "Take a look at those top riggings. Are those blocks for gaffsails?"

"Aye, Sir. There are gaffs in the sail locker so new they still smell of bindin' oil."

"Then break them out, Sir, and let us try them. What are you grinning at, Mister Kilreagh?"

Kilreagh's face went stern, with some difficulty. "Beg pardon, Sir, but I was enjoyin' the music."

"Then keep enjoying it, Mister Kilreagh. There's little enough in a man's life."

The grin returned. "Aye, Sir." He hurried away, calling orders as he went. By the capstan Solamon Grimm's right arm went up and Dalton eased the tiller a degree to starboard. Off the port bow an islet jutted from the water. The bottom would rise toward it.

"What did he mean?" Constance frowned. "What music?"

He looked down at her, eyes alive with the mating of man and vessel. "Just listen, lass. Listen with your ears and your eyes and the soles of your feet. Hear how the shrouds sing? The beat of wind in the sails? There—she flutes as her keel cuts a wave. It's the ship's song, lass, and she'll dance to it."

She stared back at him, puzzled and strangely annoyed. The man talked as though *Faith* were a living creature—as though she were a woman. "It's just a ship," she declared. "Just a silly ship."

Billy Caster was at the rail. She joined him.

"She didn't sail like this when Mister Dalton and I first saw her," the boy said. "She sailed like a barge, then. Mister Dalton said it was because she had idiots aboard."

"You saw *Faith* before?"

"Oh, aye, Miss. When that Captain Hart was takin' her. We fought for her, we did, and . . . and *Herrett* died. So did Captain Furney, and a lot of others." His eyes when she caught them were misted. "That was when *Courtesan* ran and left us. He left us and came after the schooner. . . ." His voice trailed off. There was more here than she knew about.

"Where is your home, Billy?"

"I don't rightly have one, Miss. I was born up from New Haven, but after my folks died and then my uncle too—he was going to apprentice me at gunsmithing, but he died—well, I went to sea. And I was pressed . . . look, Miss, see how she cuts the swells. Ah! Anyway, Captain Dalton made me clerk so I wouldn't go into irons. I guess this is my home now, Miss. I guess a ship can be home. *Faith* does seem right for it."

He turned away, and now her eyes were moist too. There was more than she understood. Some of the men had brought new sails up and were rigging them to hoist. Dalton plied the tiller.

"Tops look alive there! Hoist gaffs'l fore and main!"

Kilreagh had the two pressed men in tow. He had taken it on himself to teach them a bit about ships. At present both looked green and unhappy. "The gaffsails," he said, "goes up on top of the spanker and spencer—on their gaffs. It makes 'em bigger to take more wind."

Snaprings were placed and the triangular sails rose high atop the gaffs, fluttering like great batwings.

137

They opened and sheet lines drew taut. As though pushed by a great, gentle hand, *Faith* heeled further from the wind and the keen of her bow wake rose in pitch. Bright water sang along her sides. The launch in tow slapped fast water behind them. "Mister Wise, bring three men! Haul in the launch and raise it on the jolly-boat davits!"

Cadman Wise brought men aft and looked dubiously at the big boat bucking in the wake. "Shouldn't we come about first, Sir?"

"You're a seaman, Mister Wise. Haul her short, secure davit hawsers, and hoist. Bow and stern, Mister Wise. Bow and stern."

"Aye, Sir."

Constance watched fascinated. Dalton seemed to be taking unnecessary chances. The heavy launch, full under way, might pitch and tear a fragile davit from its mounting. It might even lunge and crash into *Faith's* stern. But as they pulled it in close, it becalmed there, it seemed, riding the ship's stern-slick. The davits groaned as they took its weight on block and tackle. Throughout the hoisting Dalton never once turned to watch. Was it confidence, Constance wondered, or arrogance?

"Mister Wise," he called over his shoulder, "find Mister Neely and have him break out one of those rooftrees in the hold and cut it into five-foot sections. Look lively, please."

She could no longer contain herself. She asked, "Mister Dalton, what are you doing?"

A gust caught *Faith* and strained hoists shrilled. "I'm shaping up a ship, Miss, and shaping up a crew." Solamon Grimm's left arm went up abruptly.

Dalton hauled hard on the tiller. *Faith* heeled smartly and the sails boomed as shifting wind recurved their fill. The straining boat davits groaned piteously as the launch heaved below them. Deep in the ship's hull something cracked, and the keen of waters a'port took on a gurgling note. "We'll have to repair our patching, I'm afraid," Dalton said.

Clarence Kilreagh came hopping back along the deck. His charges were forward, being sick over the bow rails. "Sir, the channels here be a bit erratic. Not what ye might call open water, as they say."

"Quite right, Mister Kilreagh. Have you any notion what might make the ship feel center-heavy? It's a bit strange."

"Don't rightly know, Sir." *Faith* heeled again, into another channel of dark water. Five-foot sections of rooftree were sprouting from the forward hold, being hauled astern. Neely came with his tools and crew.

"Mister Neely, I want a pair of stayframes, one on each side of the deck here, just at the rails."

"Stayframes, Sir?"

"Wooden triangles, Mister Neely. Plate them to the deck and lap the joint to take the weight off those booms there."

"Aye, Sir." To the ship's song was added a cacophony of hammering, studding and swearing. *Faith* sailed on. Finally Neely stood back. "I think the're done, Sir."

Dalton glance around. "Excellent. Mister Wise, rig stays from those peaks to the booms."

They had rounded another islet before the stays were in place, driving off on a new course that shook every joint in the little schooner's knees. Amidships

Charley Duncan caught Kilreagh's arm. "Do you suppose the captain has had a bit? He certainly is shaking this ship out."

"Putting her through paces, Mister Duncan. He'll know this ship's whims ere we're through."

With the stays taking the weight, the davits settled back into shape and the launch rested easy. The added weight astern had raised the schooner's nose an inch or so and she sang at a new pitch. Her wake curved back among a jumble of islets and shoals.

From the capstan Solamon Grimm called, "Clear water ahead, Sir!"

"Ah," Dalton breathed. "Mister Duncan, trim her for a broad reach! Let's shake the sleep out of her." To Constance he added, "We know now she'll run. Let's see if she will fly."

X

Vice Admiral Sir Walter Jennings, epaulettes glistening on tailored shoulders above an ample belly, paced around the chart table in the little office of Post Captain Roger Mercer, his fingers drumming the table as he went. "I fail to understand how you could have lost him in the East River," he said. "I simply don't see it."

"It wasn't so much I lost him," Blessing explained for the second time. "I just couldn't reach him, with those American rifles nipping at us. The range of those weapons is incredible, Sir."

"But four gunboats, Captain! A full squadron, and you couldn't take one small, poorly armed, channel-bound civilian vessel? That is most difficult to accept."

"Aye, Sir. It is." Blessing looked at the floor. "Of course I had only two boats when I overtook him. His cable boom took one, and necessitated another be read off for salvage."

"And then he crippled another."

"Aye, Sir. With a shot from a stern gun. And those rifles . . ."

Sir Walter stopped his pacing. He eased his ample bottom into one of the post captain's chairs. "You were close enough to get a look at the man. Describe him, please."

"A tall young man, Sir. Ruddy, dark hair. He wore a dark blue coat and white breeches, with field boots . . ."

Guard officer Croney wagged a finger. "That's Dalton, Sir. The description fits."

"I have a list of the men with him," Post Captain Roger Mercer said. "Rummies, rascals, and not a one that hasn't felt the lash, though most are able sailors. But none of them are colonials, Sir. They are all British. Mostly good service records, except when they're ashore."

Blessing shook his head. "Those rifles were colonials, Sir. They had to be."

"If I understand it," Sir Walter said, "the harbor sabotage had already been done when those men escaped from the stockade. And Mister Croney's men had this Dalton cornered in an inn at the time. Dalton and the fugitives were seen to board the schooner after the escape. And no one else was seen to board. Is that right?"

They nodded.

"Yet now it appears that the schooner *Faith* is manned by colonial rebels, according to Commander Blessing."

"Aye, Sir." Blessing was emphatic.

"This is a bloody mess, gentlemen. Especially with the admiral due to return any time now. I fear we will be doing some explaining before a court of inquiry."

"Our case would be stronger, Sir, if we could put an end to his mischief."

"If *we* could, yes. However, it will be a bit humiliating should Jonathan Hart attend to the rascal alone. Wouldn't our prizemaster crow then, though."

They remained in gloomy thought for a few minutes, then Sir Walter hitched himself up out of the chair. "Captain Mercer, please draft an order to all ships of the command, and get your packets and signals working. Provide them with a description of the schooner. They are to sink her on sight. Do not attempt to capture or board. Do not attempt to reclaim. Make it clear, Captain. They are to find the *Faith* and, very simply, sink her."

Blessing frowned. "With all hands, Sir?"

"Do you want to try the patience of a court of inquiry with a story that might take weeks to unravel, Sir? Do you want to chance that after what we have already suffered? No, I think not. This is war, Sir. We must do what we must do. The order stands. To all ships: find and sink the *Faith*."

Aboard the little sloop of war *Wolf*, standing in at the mouth of Flushing Bay to cut wood, Commander Lewis Farrington and his bosun, William Moweth, puzzled over the strange orders delivered by a post dispatch rider. "Th' gold braid mus' want that'n somethin' fierce, Lewey, to put out a sink order on 'er. What ye make of it?"

Farrington shook his head. With the *Wolf* technically a ship of the fleet, although commonly banished to the most remote and mundane of assignments to avoid embarrassing the Admiralty, he did occasionally receive general orders from post. It was understood, however, that an order delivered to *Wolf* was only for protocol's sake. No one expected the sloop and its young master to actually participate in the war. *Wolf* rarely ventured beyond sight of land since the time a year before when she had remained lost at sea for a day and a night in Long Island Sound.

"I expect we had better watch for her," Farrington said. "When the rest of the men wake up, Will, you tell them about it."

"Tell us about what, Cap'n?" James Mudd sat cross-legged atop the hatch, splicing a much-repaired hawser line.

"We're supposed to be on watch for a schooner. Jamey. She's a fugitive."

Mudd scratched his stubbled chin. "What's a schooner, then?"

"A Dutch-looking ship, not very big, two masts with fore-and-aft sails on them, maybe some spars on the topmasts."

"That sounds sort of like the one as went by last evenin', Cap'n. Come beatin' out of Hell Gate under sail, an' you don't see that very often."

Moweth frowned. "How come you didn't report the sightin', Jamey?"

"She did'n fire on us. She just went by."

Farrington scratched his head and cocked a brow. "You suppose it might have been the same ship, Jamey?"

"Sure would'n know, Cap'n. But that's sure enough what she looked like."

Lewis Farrington mulled over the implications of the sighting. Being half-brother to an upland nobleman had enabled him to become an officer. Being unwelcome in his half-brother's home had got him command of a ship of the fleet. But at twenty years of age he had gone as far as he would go on his half-brother's reluctant generosity. He never claimed to be either a sailor or a disciplinarian, but it did strike him that an encounter with the enemy might give him a leg up on a career, especially if he should win.

Unfortunately the schooner already had passed, and Farrington had no illusions about his ship. *Wolf* would be hard-put to outrun a jolly boat, much less a fast schooner.

But with general orders out on her, the schooner might encounter some opposition before she left the sound . . . in which case, she might go to ground. And in a year and a half of avoiding colonial privateers, Lewis Farrington had learned just about every hiding place on the sound.

Could he go schooner hunting without orders? Of course he could. He got out the piece of paper and looked at it again. This *was* an order. He was ordered to find and destroy the schooner *Faith*.

Bill Moweth was asleep by the hatch coaming. His bosun's whistle lay beside him. Commander Lewis Farrington picked it up and blew on it as hard as he could. The resulting wail brought Moweth to his feet and several of the crew running from the woods on shore.

Shaking the sleep from his head Moweth snapped, "What'n hell you doin', Lewey?"

"Get the crew aboard, Will. Load up those guns and let's make sail and see if we can get out of this neck without running aground."

The privateer *Triumph* out of Bridgeport lay screened and waiting in Eastchester Bay, a predator laying for game. Slim-hulled and long-prowed, *Triumph* seemed all guns and masts as she lay low in the water, her shallow keel waiting to rise on the waves and chase down slower prey.

Isaac Purdue, commanding, looked again at the crumpled sheet of paper in his hand and back up at his first officer. "Where did you get this, Mister Jones?"

"Some of our Whigs ashore ambushed a post rider down on the Bronx road. They knocked him in the head and these were what he was carrying. Looks like the Georgies want that schooner pretty bad, doesn't it?"

"Aye, it does. One wonders why."

"Could be her cargo, Captain."

"Aye, it could be her cargo. One can presume she's in the Sound by this time." With a nod of decision, he thrust the paper into his coat. "Mister Jones, let us make sail. Perchance we might take this one before the Georgies catch her."

The packet *Caper* never got the word at all. Slim-hulled, cutter-rigged, and carrying a crew of three, the packet out of Boston was just rounding Cape Cod, leaning westward. It would beat its way down to Newport and from there across the sound to deliver mail to Northport and Brent.

Caper was a coaster, shallow-drafted for the tidal shoals, high-walled and false-keeled for the rolling deeps. And because there were always predators she carried a six-pound cannon in her bow and a swivel gun.

As evening calm descended on Northport Bay, the ring of hammers and the reek of pitch pervaded the still air around *Faith*. She had flown. And in flying she had loosed and lost two of the copper plates covering her wounds. Now shielded from the open Sound by a wooded point of land, she lay to in the bay, making repairs. As darkness descended they broke out lanterns and continued with the work.

Dalton kept men in the high crosstrees of both masts as lookout. Billy Caster and his riflemen were out in the launch, between the ship and the shoreline where residents of the village of Northport had come down to watch. Clarence Kilreagh remained aboard to supervise the manning of bilge pumps. Patrick Dalton, aboard the jolly boat with the brothers Grimm as his rowers, circled nervously about *Faith's* hull as they worked to mend her wounds. The makeshift deck braces rigged to reinforce the stern davits were doing service now to hold a scaffold slung astern where Mister Neely and his mates worked at waterline.

As the jolly boat rounded *Faith's* stern to view the

patching underway there, a ragged volley of rifle fire sounded from beyond her toward the shore. The port hull lifted an inch in the water as those on deck scrambled to the far gunwales to look. The pressed-man holding the lantern in the skiff for those working on the hull raised his light a bit higher and pointed. "Look a'there. They's a seam sprung right under the water."

Dalton drew the jolly boat in and looked. The part was a foot beneath where the ball had grazed *Faith's* side. Concussion from the blow had impacted her wooden skin, parting planks to open a half-inch slit more than two feet long.

"That's why we keep drawin' water, Sir." Charley Duncan looked up from where he knelt in the skiff. "We didn't see that crack when we plated her before."

"Will it plate, Mister Duncan?"

"Aye, Sir, I reckon. But it'll take a while, an' we'll need more freeboard than this to work with."

"Very well, Mister Duncan. Get to it. I'll arrange your freeboard for you. Back us off if you please, Misters Grimm." When the boat was out from under the schooner's fife rails, Dalton cupped his hand to his mouth. "Mister Kilreagh, if you please!"

A moment passed, then in the near-darkness above Clarence Kilreagh appeared. "Aye, Sir?"

"Mister Kilreagh, we need freeboard on the port hull. Please have everyone go and sit on the starboard gunwales, and move the port guns to starboard."

"Aye, Sir. But I'll have to keep these pumps goin', Sir."

"I mean everyone not manning the pumps, Mister Kilreagh."

"Aye, Sir."

As the boat came around the stern again, the launch approached.

"What was the shooting about, Mister Caster?"

"Those people ashore, Sir. They tried to put out in a boat, and we drove 'em back."

"Do you suppose they might have been coming to help?"

"No, Sir. If they'd wanted to help they wouldn't have waited till dark."

"Very well. Please return to your patrol, then."

"Yes, Sir, but I have to send a man aboard first, Sir."

"Why?"

"Because we had an accident, Sir." The boy's voice, floating back from darkness, sounded exasperated. "Mister Mallory was standing up to pee, and when we volleyed those people, he got disoriented and wet our cannister of powder. We had to come back for more so we can reload."

A splash sounded from around the starboard side, and someone thrashed and sputtered in the water. Dalton strained backward in the boat, holing out his dim lantern. He could make out nothing. "Mister Kilreagh, who is overboard?"

"One of the lads, Sir. I think it's Mister Locke. We're getting a line to him."

"Well, what happened?"

"We were all sitting here on the starboard gun'l, Sir, and he might have tried to bother Miss Constance. Anyway, she pushed him over."

Constance Ramsey appeared at the stern rail, her eyes flashing in the glow of the work lanterns. "Mister Dalton, I will not be bothered aboard my own ship! Not by anyone!"

"Miss Constance," Dalton said as patiently as he could manage, "I do wish you would stop arousing my men. We have a great deal to do and they are most frightfully busy."

"Well, they're not busy enough!" She turned and disappeared.

Dalton pursed his lips and shook his head. "We fly like a bird," he muttered. "But we don't nest very well."

"Sir?" Solamon Grimm asked.

"Nothing, Mister Grimm. I was talking to myself. Just let that be a lesson. Do not bother Miss Constance."

The brothers looked at each other, then back at Dalton. "It wasn't us, Sir."

A tentative breeze touched erratically in the bay, fading toward calm. Dalton drew in close to watch the work Neely and his men were doing. "We are about to lose our wind, Mister Neely. How soon can you complete the repairs?"

"Still be a while," Neely grunted without looking around. They had sheeting fothering the holes and were applying tar. "If you move this here vessel tonight it'll be with oars . . . Sir."

From high above a voice called, "On deck!" and Kilreagh answered, "What is it, Mister Coleman?"

"Light off the port quarter, Sir. Looks like a ship coming into the bay."

"Bring us around to starboard," Dalton ordered.

The Grimms hauled on their sweeps. As the boat thumped the ship's hull Dalton stood, grasped the main fife rail and swung himself up to the gunwale. On deck he hurried to the stern and broke out his glass. Kilreagh was beside him. "Can you make her out, Sir?"

Dalton peered through the glass, then shook his head. "It's a ship of some sort. Bow and stern lights, and I can see sailcloth, but it's too dark."

"Shall I douse our lanterns, Sir?"

"No, we need them to work. Besides, she's becalmed over there, just as we are here." He leaned over the rail. "Mister Caster?"

"Aye, Sir?"

"There is a ship out there across the bay. I'd like you and your riflemen to stand off in the launch and keep an eye on her, if you please."

"Aye, Sir. We've got dry powder again."

A glow of light had appeared above the trees off *Faith's* bow, past the slim neck of land that separated the bay from the Sound. Dalton gazed at it ruefully. Those Tories ashore had built a bonfire over on the Sound, a beacon for anyone within miles to see. When there was wind, *Faith* had better be ready to move with it, because others would be coming this way.

Into the night the lanterns burned, hammers rang, and the sharp, hot scent of tar hung over the schooner. Once, in the distance across the bay, there was the sound of small-arms fire—the thump of muskets and the distinctive crack of colonial rifles. Those on and around the schooner paused to listen. In the distant darkness they saw tiny specks of light, and after

151

a pause the crackling of rifles came again. Another pause, and twin blossoms of fire appeared and were gone instantly. Dalton swore. He had instructed the boy to watch the ship, not to attack it. The thunder of cannon rolled across the still night. "Mister Kilreagh, please lay on your whistle and see if you can pipe that launch back to us."

The bosun's whistle howled, echoed from under the port side by Charley Duncan's whistle and from the shrouds by Cadman Wise's. The triple wail was deafening. When silence had returned, Dalton peered across the dark water. If they weren't sunk, that should bring them home.

The companion hatch opened and Constance Ramsey came on deck, pinning up her skirt in the way she had worn it when she and her Delaware men boarded, like breeches.

"Are we fighting again, Mister Dalton?"

"No, Miss. Some of our lads are off there in the launch, amusing themselves with that vessel across the bay."

"Oh." Constance went below again and returned in a moment with a wrap. "I'll sit on deck for a while, Mister Dalton. It is very close in the cabin, and those people are doing me mischief with their infernal hammers. It is like trying to sleep inside a drum."

"Very well." He turned and peered forward. "Who is that? Is that you, Mister Grimm?"

"Aye, Sir."

"What are you doing, Mister Grimm?"

"Looking at the lady, Sir."

"Then go below and bring up some of Mister Arthur's coffee for her, if you please. We don't want her catching the vapors."

"Aye, Sir . . . Sir?"

"Yes, Mister Grimm?"

"Me and my brother've been making a chair for the lady, Sir. Can we bring it up?"

"A chair?"

"Aye, Sir. There's all them shingles below, an' some rail stock, an' we used just a bit of it."

"Would you like a chair, Miss Constance?"

It was, indeed, a chair. The brothers brought it up from the fore hold and coffee from the galley. Then they hovered there, their attentions plainly divided between gentle protectiveness and frank lust. Dalton chewed on his lower lip. "Thank you, gentlemen. That will be all."

At the midship rail he found Kilreagh. The peg-legged man was working a sounding line. "Tide's lowering, Sir."

"What's the mark, Mister Kilreagh?"

"An' a half, two, Sir. Shoals to the fore, seems like."

"Then let's keep sounding off the bow, Mister Kilreagh. Report if it lowers to and a quarter, two."

"Aye, Sir."

Charley Duncan and his crew had completed the port hull patch. As he and Jubal Foster came over the gunwales Duncan said, "Good as new, Sir. Should the rest of the hull rot away, that patch will still sail on."

"Very good, Mister Duncan. When you bring the skiff aboard, lash it down properly, please."

"Aye, Sir." Below the rail the lantern was put out

and the port side was in darkness. There was a frantic creaking of oars and rush of water. Duncan whirled to the rail. "Ahoy, there. What's amiss?" There was no answer, but the sound of oars increased, then drew away. As it diminished, Duncan said, "I'm afraid they've run, Sir."

Dalton was at the rail beside him. "Who was it? Who ran?"

"Both the pressedmen, Sir. Moses and Tarkington."

Dalton sighed. The launch was out in the darkness somewhere and the jolly boat had been hauled up. There was no way to bring them back. The loss of a Virginia tinsmith and an English beekeeper was no great concern, but he hated to lose the skiff. "You should not have left pressedmen alone in a boat, Mister Duncan."

"No, Sir." The bosun sounded shamed. "I wasn't thinking, Sir."

A while later the launch appeared. Billy Caster came aboard. "You piped us, Sir?"

"I did, Mister Caster. Why were you firing at that ship over there?"

"It was the men, Sir. They do enjoy firing their rifles. Some of them fired and the ship returned fire, so we had at it."

"Do you have any casualties?"

"None, Sir. It was too dark to hit anything."

"Very well, Mister Caster. Did you learn anything?"

"Aye, Sir, she's a sloop of war, the *Wolf*. Crew of eight beside the master and the bosun. She carries two eight-pounders and a four-pounder on a swivel.

154

The commander is Captain Farrington, and they'd been cutting wood ashore when they got orders to come and sink us. Did you know there is a general order out to sink the *Faith*, Sir?"

After a long silence Dalton asked, "How did you learn all that, Mister Caster?"

"We got to talking, Sir, while we were reloading and all. I thought you'd like to know. Oh, and *Wolf's* aground on a shoal, Sir. Captain Farrington wonders if we could give him a tow."

"Mister Kilreagh, what is the mark?"

"An' a half, two, Sir, off the bow."

Dalton calculated. "He'll have tide before he has wind, Mister Caster. He'll not need a tow."

"Shall I go and tell him, Sir?"

"Never mind, Mister Caster. He'll know when it happens."

Soon after midnight the stern repairs were finished. They were done right this time. *Faith* was high and sound, as good as new. Neely and his carpenters came aboard, hauled up the scaffold and were sent below for supper. There was a commotion below-decks and shouting voices. Dalton hurried to the hatch, down the ladder, and into the tiny, low galley. One of the men was sprawled half under the table, and two others had a furious, babbling Mister Arthur pinned up against a bulkhead. "What in thunder is going on?"

"Mister Arthur found a keg of rum somewhere, Sir. He seems intoxicated."

With a heave of his great shoulders the half-bearded cook threw his adversaries across the galley and started forward. Neely dived under the table.

With his arms spread wide to grapple, Robert Arthur virtually filled the galley. Dalton crouched, ducked a battering-ram swing, and backed into the companionway. As Arthur charged him there Dalton feinted to pull the big man's guard wide, then put all his power into a straight-arm punch that caught the man squarely on the chin. Arthur swayed, went glassyeyed, and toppled backward. Hauling Neely out from under the table, Dalton ordered, "Get a line on this man and tie him securely."

Dimly, from above, he heard, "On deck!" He went back up the ladder as Kilreagh responded to the call. The lookout in the foretop called, "Ship sighted, Sir. Bow and stern lights. Must be using sweeps."

"Whereaway?"

"Port quarter, Sir. Past the point. She's blocking the mouth of the bay, Sir."

In the dark silence following, Patrick Dalton lowered his head and shook it slowly from side to side. Then he turned and strode resolutely to the companion hatch. At the bottom of the ladder he asked, "Mister Neely, did Mister Arthur leave any of that rum?"

XI

It was indeed a keg of rum. Dalton stood in the tight little galley with Guy Neely, Solamon Grimm, and Billy Caster, examining the evidence by lantern light. It was a full keg, minus what Mister Arthur had managed to absorb, and it was prime Jamaican rum.

"I surely don't know where he kept it hid," Grimm asserted. "Me and my brother Brevis, we went all through the vessel, Sir, like you said, and we tallied everything. The lad here can testify."

Billy nodded. "He's right, Sir. When I scribed the inventory I went through the holds and lockers and looked in every place anything could be. I didn't see the rum, Sir."

Dalton dipped a ladle into the keg and sampled it. It was very good rum. Neely and Grimm licked their lips. Dalton took another sample to be sure. It had been a long day. He gazed across at the inert Mister Arthur—bound, reeking and snoring between the tack lockers. "Drunkenness on watch is a very serious offense," he said, and the heads around him nodded seriously. "I want each of you to witness that Mister Arthur does seem intoxicated."

"Aye, Sir." Solamon Grimm stepped across and peered down at the unconscious cook-surgeon with his half-beard. "He does seem that, Sir." Neely moved around beside him and nodded.

Dalton tried another sip of the rum. "And this keg seems to contain rum, which could have accounted for Mister Arthur's condition."

"It seems to, Sir." Grimm peered into the keg. "At least, it looks like rum."

Dalton handed him the ladle. "Assure yourself, Mister Grimm."

"Aye, Sir." Grimm filled the ladle, tossed it off, choked and sputtered, then wiped his mouth. "There certainly is a resemblance." With a judicious frown he dipped the ladle again and drank. "Sir, I'd be hard put to disagree about that being rum." He handed the ladle to Neely, who repeated the performance.

"Mister Caster?"

"Maybe you should ask some of the others, Sir, if there's doubt."

"Capital idea," Dalton said. "Please go ask Mister Kilreagh to come down here, and bring some of the lads with him."

By the time all hands had examined the evidence, there was substantially less evidence than there had been. Victory Locke was in the foretrees now, barely visible against a moonlit sky. The bay was like dark glass, unrippled by the slightest breeze. Two miles southwest lay the sloop *Wolf*, becalmed and aground, a speck of light. About a mile due west, a pair of lights indicated the strange vessel blocking the channel.

Might they put boats out? Dalton ordered the jolly boat launched. "Provide three men with rifles and a lantern, Mister Wise . . . three who have had some rest. They can stand patrol about us until first light."

"Aye, Sir."

His stomach still aglow, Dalton strolled aft. There seemed to be music coming from the ship's forward hold, and he paused a moment to listen. It wasn't very good music. He went on past. Constance Ramsey was seated in the stern. When he neared she stood and stepped back to the rail, hugging her quilt about her.

"Good evening again, Miss." He smiled his best smile, realizing at the time it was wasted in the darkness.

She stepped back, startled at the spirits on his breath. She seemed . . . dismayed? Frightened? "Good evening," she said.

Propping himself firmly against the rail, Dalton ventured, "I've been wanting to ask you something, Miss Constance. Why are you aboard this ship?"

She stared at him. "I told you."

"Oh, yes, that. But it just doesn't hang together, you know. Why, you must have traveled—what? Two hundred miles?—to reach New York Bay from Delaware." He raised fist to mouth to stifle a satisfying belch. "And just to try—obviously in vain, since you couldn't know you would find help—to recapture an insured vessel? Come now, Miss Constance."

"Mister Dalton, you've been drinking."

159

"Only a little. Cook had a keg of rum we didn't know about. Thought we'd better test it, you know."

"Oh." She sounded inordinately relieved. He noted it, lost it, and returned to his subject.

"I simply can't imagine your father allowing you, a young lady . . . an attractive young lady . . . might I add, a very attractive . . . no, I said that before, didn't I . . . allowing you—your father, I mean—allowing you to set out on such a venture. I can't."

"I think I lost you. You can't what?"

"Can't imagine."

"That's because my father believes I am visiting my aunt. My father is not at all well, Sir. And you are overly inquisitive."

"How did you learn to fire great guns, Miss Constance?"

"Cannons? Oh, I am quite good with cannons. When I was just a little girl my father had a small sloop that he used for hauling stores from the Chesapeake to Wilmington. He often sailed it himself, and sometimes he would take me with him. I would get so frightfully bored with just sailing that he would let me play with the cannons. I became very skilled at it."

"I can't imagine your father allowing you . . . a young girl . . . probably even then a rather attractive . . . aside from that, allowing you to play with cannons."

"Your speech has become circuitous, Mister Dalton. Is it the rum, do you suppose, or the Irish?"

"It is getting late. What I mean is, what kind of man is your father to endorse a girl firing a cannon?"

"What on earth is so special about firing a cannon, Sir? All one does is point the bloody thing and touch fuse to the vent."

Dalton sighed. "We have gotten off the subject, I'm afraid. I simply do not understand why you came to New York Bay and why you are aboard this vessel. And more to the point, I assume it was you placing Greek fire on those ships?"

"I felt we needed a diversion."

"But Greek fire? Where did you . . . no." He raised a hand. "Don't tell me. You learned from your father."

The sounds drifting from the fore hold had grown in volume if not in quality. Constance pulled her quilt more tightly about her. "That rum you, ah, tested, Mister Dalton . . ."

"Patrick."

"What?"

"My name is Patrick."

"I assume the other men tested it, too?"

"Aye. There needs be witnesses. I'm afraid we finished most of it."

"You didn't offer me any."

"My oversight, Miss Constance. Mister Duncan!"

"Aye, Sir."

"Did Mister Kilreagh secure the remainder of the evidence?"

"Aye, Sir."

"Then go unsecure it and bring it up here, please." To Constance, "I could use a tot myself. And afterward I shall see you to your bed."

"The devil you will. I can find my own way."

161

A frightful yowling had begun, accompanying the medley from the hold. Duncan returned with a jug. "Here's a bit that was kept out when it was makin' the rounds, Sir. But I can't find the keg. It doesn't seem to be there."

Dalton put hands to temples to rub away a growing numbness. "There is a disturbing quantity of noise in the fore, Mister Duncan. That might indicate where the remainder of the rum has gone."

"I'll go see."

Dalton hefted the jug. It was near full. He poured two cups.

Duncan returned quickly. "Some of the lads are playing with the fiddles, Sir. Mister Mallory and Mister Bean are fair hands. Some others are down there singing."

"I thought that might be singing. Did you find the rum?"

"Oh, no, Sir, that's gone. The three that went off in the jolly boat, they took it with them—for safekeeping, they said."

"I see. Then I'll wager the boat is growing jollier by the minute. Which men were they?"

"Mister Coleman, John Cranston and Hannibal Cranston, Sir."

"Have another tot of rum, Mister Duncan."

"Aye, Sir."

"And you can pour again for Miss Constance and me."

Clarence Kilreagh came aft at the next bell. "Secured for change of watch, Sir." He held a muted lantern aloft and peered at the jug. He hefted it. "It looks as though we've lost our evidence, Sir."

162

Dalton unwrapped himself from the quilts—his and Constance's had become inextricably overlapped as the air grew colder. When he stood he swayed. "We'll need sea anchors if this keeps up," he muttered. "Have all the lads turn in for rest, Mister Kilreagh, except deck and topwatch. We'll need our faculties in a few hours. There are ships out there, you know."

"I know, Sir."

"Miss Constance, you had best go below and get some rest."

"Sir?" Kilreagh cautioned. "The brothers Grimm have set watch on the companionway. Do you think the lass might be escorted past them? Safety's sake, you know."

"Of course. Miss Constance, would you like me to escort you below?"

"Absolutely not!"

"Very well. Mister Kilreagh can escort you. And Mister Kilreagh, please find someone less, ah, enthusiastic to replace the brothers Grimm in the companionway."

"I suspect that narrows it to Mister Caster, Sir."

"Mister Caster, then. And issue him a pistol."

"On deck!"

"Yes, Mister Locke?"

"Boat putting out from the spit, Sir. Making for us."

"Thank you, Mister Locke. Mister Duncan?"

"Aye, Sir?"

"Please bring up one of Mister Caster's rifles. See that it is properly loaded."

Rifle in hand, Duncan followed his captain to the

bow, where they peered out across the starboard gunwale. A small boat crawled across the water.

When it drew near Dalton called, "Ahoy the boat! Identify!"

A familiar voice came, "It's just us, Cap'n. We came back."

"That's Mister Tarkington, Sir."

"The pressedman?"

"Aye."

The skiff drew under *Faith's* bow. Dalton leaned out. "Where have you been, Mister Tarkington?"

"Ashore, Sir."

"I know that, Mister Tarkington. Why did you go ashore?"

"We thought we might just, ah . . . ,"

William Moses' voice came. "While we was out we went down to the end to see that ship down there, Cap'n. It's just sittin' out there in the water. Did you know there was a ship there, Cap'n?"

"Mister Duncan, bring those men aboard. And haul up the skiff, if you please." He shook his head, trying to clear it.

On deck, the two pressedmen slouched before him, heads down. "You men attempted to run," he said coldly. When there was no response he asked, "Why did you come back?"

Moses, the Virginian, said, "Those people ashore, Sir. They're Tories or somethin' and . . ."

"They are not!" Tarkington corrected. "They're Whigs. Anyhow, we was afraid of 'em, Sir."

"So you went to look at the ship."

"Aye, Sir, but it seems to be a Tory ship . . ."

"It's a Whig ship . . ."

164

"We don't know what kind of ship it is, Sir, and we were afraid to call out."

"Well, tell me about the ship."

"It's pretty long and skinny," Moses said, "and it has a lot of guns."

Tarkington looked at his co-conspirator with contempt. "It's a cutter, Sir. I know that."

Moses erupted, "You don't know any such thing! You're a beekeeper."

"Well, I've seen cutters."

Dalton held up a hand. "Never mind! What was she doing?"

"Who?"

"The ship, Mister Tarkington. The ship."

"Why, nothing Sir. Just floating there in the water, that's all."

His head swimming, Dalton turned away. "See if you can learn anything useful from these two, Mister Duncan."

"Aye, Sir. Would you like them flogged?"

"I'm thinking about it, Mister Duncan."

He stowed the rifle and climbed the shrouds to the mainmast top. The air was sharply cool, and clearer at mast top than on the deck. He made out the big bear and followed its point to the North Star, standing cold in the sky. Fists at arm's length he counted down from it. There should have been five handspans to the horizon. There were no more than three. Below was darkness. He returned unsteadily to the deck. "We'll have a northerly wind, Mister Kilreagh. And there'll be fog before first light."

Leaving Cadman Wise as watch officer, Dalton,

Kilreagh, and Duncan swung hammocks amidships and lay down for an hour's sleep. "Wrap tightly in your quilts, gentlemen. Let's not catch the vapors, shall we?" The quilt Dalton pulled up to his ears smelled disturbingly of the warm scent of Constance Ramsey.

In the tiny cabin Constance stripped to her chemise and crawled into the bunk, pulling heaped covers to her chin. Four feet away, beyond the curtained portal, Billy Caster checked the load in a large pistol, wrapped himself in a quilt, and sat cross-legged on the companion deck. "Are you all right in there, Miss?"

"I'm fine, Billy. You can go to sleep if you want to."

"Oh, no, I'd best not. Some of the crew are a bit spirited."

There was silence for a time. Then, "Billy, tell me, what is it your captain broods about?"

"I expect it was because he had a good ship destroyed around him, Miss, and an act of treachery it was. Captain Dalton respected Captain Furney, I know. And he was fond of *Herrett.*"

"*Herrett?*"

"A fighting brig, Miss. A real lady of a ship, as the captain would say. She was shot to death, and Captain Dalton brought her hulk home."

"Were you there?"

"Yes'm, I was. So I know how he feels about what was done."

166

More silence. Then, "Billy?"

"Yes, Miss?"

"You were right about Mister Dalton . . . about his not unbending aboard ship. It does lead to laxity."

XII

By three bells of the morning watch, Dalton had
what he had waited for. There was fog, and he sent
Charley Duncan and Cadman Wise quietly through
the dark ship to awaken the crew. No standing fog,
this. It was a dense bank of cold vapor that rolled in
low and thick off the Sound, and with it came the
winds of autumn.

Through the night he had made a dozen contin-
gency plans, cataloging them in the sober portion of
his mind.

He would have preferred a good southerly breeze
in the dark hours, a clear, starry sky, and a port
reach midway across the bay followed by a dash
straight out the mouth of the estuary into open water. He didn't know what vessel it was that stood
there in the mouth, but he knew it stood bow-forward
to the bay, ready to come nosing in with morning.
Sailing on broad reach with a mile or more to gain
way, he could be past her in an instant. He might

take a ball or two, but he could be gone while she luffed in coming about.

Barring that, he would have next preferred a storm—a downpour with shifting winds in which he could put *Faith* under tow and creep out past the blockading vessel, exchanging fire as he could, but with a good hope of breaking free.

What he had to work with was neither of these, but fog, and he was content. The vessel in the mouth, by her posture there, clearly was hunting. He had to assume he was the prey. He would try his hand at stealth.

Faith had good water under her keel now, and lay ghostly in the moonlight as the wall of dark silver strode across the Sound and enveloped her. As soon as she was fogged in, Dalton lit a dim lamp and had Victory Locke carry it forward. By the time the seaman was amidships, Dalton could no longer see the point of flame. He cupped his hands and called, "Maintop watch!"

The voice came down through the fog. "Aye, Sir?"

"Does the fog top out?"

"No, Sir. Fog in the crosstrees, Sir!"

Kilreagh came astern, rubbing his eyes, followed by Charley Duncan reporting that all hands were ready to make sail.

"Very well, Mister Duncan. But silently, if you please. By call, not by whistle." He loosed the tiller. "Up anchor, Mister Duncan.

Duncan hurried away toward the bow. Cadman Wise replaced him in the stern. Excellent, Dalton thought. If we live long enough I'll have a crew here yet. He listened to the squeak of tackle and felt the tremble in the deck as the ship's makeshift anchor was hauled up and secured. "Hoist stays'l and jibs'l, Mister Wise." The bosun's mate hurried off. "Did you bring up the small sandglass, Mister Kilreagh?"

"Aye, Cap'n."

Duncan returned, and Dalton felt the tug at the bow as canvas at the ship's nose took the offered bit of wind. "Hoist your fores'l, Mister Duncan."

Grommets rattled as the spencer gaff was hauled upward on its bridle. He heard the big midships sail flutter, then snap full as the north wind caught it. "Close haul aport," Dalton called, and *Faith* heeled and began edging forward. Dalton tested the wind. He made it fifteen knots and steadying. Counting to himself, his fingers sensing vague life in the tiller bar, he waited. Except for a hooded lantern astern, it was pitch dark in the fog. The sounds they made were muted, the movement ghostly. Finally there came the whisper of water past her hull. Dalton counted again. "Now turn the glass, Mister Kilreagh. Set it there by the lamp and tend it for me, please."

It was a half-bell sandglass, measured to time a precise quarter hour. Dalton eased *Faith* a degree to port, then held her steady. A spirit ship in darkness, she crept blind through the obscuring fog. A heavier gust hit the sails. *Faith* rolled a trifle and the whisper of water alongside rose in pitch. "Haul closer on the spencer," Dalton ordered. As the sail was pulled in tighter, the water sound subsided to a whisper again. Dalton had never navigated by ear before, but he saw no reason it couldn't be done. He wondered idly how he might feel about it cold sober. Nonetheless,

171

the shakedown yesterday had given him *Faith's* song, and he knew it by heart.

Minutes passed, the silence aboard evidence of the tension the men felt, most of them still slow from their rum and moving blind in the darkness. Dalton played the tiller by inches and half inches, his head cocked aside, intent on the sound of the water. More minutes passed, and in the distance ahead there was the muted sound of a bell. Kilreagh straightened, peered into the gloom, and turned, but Dalton hushed him and bent his head again to the water's tone.

Kilreagh watched the glass intently. As the last drop of sand ran out he said, "Now, Sir." Dalton swept the bar over and brought *Faith* hard about. Her bow swung to starboard, through the wind. "Close haul for port tack," he called forward, and heard the foresail luff and flutter as it was sheeted to his right. *Faith* felt dead still in the water. He hoped he had read it right. There were sounds now from his left, close by in the mist, a querulous voice, a response, muffled calls, and the creak of tackle. The sloop *Wolf* must be within a hundred yards, by the sound of it. Another minute and he would have rammed her. Judging by the calls, they had heard the approach of *Faith* and were coming alive over there. Well, he would be gone before they could make sail and come probing into the darkness.

The ship's swing was undetectable except for a slight veering of the breeze as her nose edged further past it. The ragged flutter of the foresail quickened, seemed to drum, then snapped as the sail filled. By pure sound reckoning, Dalton allowed she should now be aimed due north. And out there somewhere was the broad mouth of the bay. "Take the tiller, please, Mister Kilreagh. I am going aloft. Keep her sail full and by the wind, as close as she'll make it."

"Aye, Sir." Kilreagh's voice was strained. This was far beyond any kind of sailing he had ever done . . . or heard of. "Sir? How do you know where we're going?"

Dalton buttoned up his coat against the chill. "Dead ahead of us is either the point, the mouth of the bay, or a hostile vessel. I wager it is the mouth of the bay. We shall soon know." Going forward to the mainshrouds, he swung up on them, found the ratlines with his feet, and climbed. When he reached the masthead, forty feet above the deck with the topmast towering above him, the gloom was less. He could see ahead to the foremast in a moon-silvered mist.

From just above and a few feet ahead a voice called, "On deck!"

"Hush, lad! I'm here at the maintop."

"Aye, Sir. Fog's topping out, Sir. I can see the moon."

Grasping the maintop shrouds he climbed again. A few feet and he could make out the dark form of the man in the fore crosstrees ahead. Even as he reached the top tackle high in the main rigging, where the topgallant spar was cleated in, he broke out of the mist. The fingers of his masts stood clear and stark above the moon-silvered sea of fog. And directly aport, fifty yards if that, was the probing topmast of the British sloop.

From below and aside, from *Wolf's* deck, he heard

a call, "Ahoy the ship! Who are you?" No one answered. Peering hard across the night, Dalton saw a figure move atop the sloop's mast. "I see her, Sir! She's right there!"

From below, "Right where?"

"Right there, Sir!"

"Damn it, Paul, I can't see where you're pointing. Say it out!"

"Aye, Sir. She's hard aport of us, Sir, starting to move astern!"

"Make sail! Make sail!"

The man on the topmast called, "If you're going to shoot her, Cap'n Farrington, you'd better hurry! She's moving!"

"Port guns ready, Sir!"

"Ahoy the schooner! Will you strike?"

Dalton's order of silence was holding. No one aboard *Faith* made a sound. Dalton held his breath. Don't shoot blind, you fool, he thought.

"Fire port gun and swivel!"

Cannons roared and the mist below Dalton was ablaze with their flame. But Dalton felt no tremor, no slightest shiver, in the mast he held. He shook his head. "I wish you hadn't done that," he muttered. The cannon's roar reverberated across the water and echoed from far shores. He had half hoped he might catch the vessel at the bay's mouth asleep.

Slowly the sloop's masts slid astern. He could hear the agitated activity on her deck as sheets were hauled and see the sway of her topmast as sails caught the breeze. She was no longer aground.

When the sloop was more than a cable length astern, Dalton turned his entire attention to the fore.

The fog bank seemed to flatten to windward, and ahead he could see the ragged line of dark treetops that marked the neck of land blocking the bay. Standing with one foot on the topmast stay block, a leg and an arm wrapped around the mast itself, he pulled his glass from his coattail pocket and squinted through it in the moonlight. Dead ahead, a mile away, a single, tall mast jutted above the silver mist. The unknown vessel lay precisely in the center of the break between treelines that indicated the mouth of the bay.

Dalton blinked his eyes, rubbed them, and peered again. The moonlight was confusing, dimmer than its silvering of the fog bank indicated. But he was sure there was only one mast, and it had high spars. The ship would be a cutter, then, as the pressedmen had said, "Long and skinny and lots of guns." One tall stepped mast and vast amounts of sailcloth—a lithe, fast, and deadly vessel, smaller than *Faith*, but heavily armed. And she would be a colonial privateer. He knew of few cutters in the Atlantic fleet, fewer so far in the colonial navies. This would then be a mercenary, one of those dreaded sea wolves that haunted the shorelines and inlets of the American coast, taking their toll in British naval vessels and merchantmen alike. His mind raced. *Faith* with her four little four-pounders would be no match for the cutter in a standing fight. Nor could she outrun or outdance the sleek little pirate. And there was scant chance of slipping past. The sloop's cannon fire would have her alerted.

"Therefore," Patrick Dalton told himself, "I need a stalking horse."

Twisting around on the cold topmast, careful not to lose his precarious footing on the cleat, he squinted back the way they had come. The sloop *Wolf* was just finishing coming about, making a ragged job of it, but heeling now as she put on sail, following her lookout's signals to make chase after the fugitive schooner. He saw her topmast dip sharply once, and then again. Mainsail and foresail both, he nodded, and in this pea soup, and at night. "Audacious," he murmured his approval.

"On deck!" he called, and the answer came up from gloom below, "Aye, Sir?"

"Two points off, Mister Kilreagh! Let her luff just a bit!"

"Aye, Sir!" Dalton felt the nervous quiver through the spar as *Faith* lost the fine edge of the wind. He waited. Minutes crept by. *Faith* was moving, her bow aligned now on that point of trees that was the end of the peninsula, but the *Wolf* was moving faster, coming on. He wished he had asked young Mister Caster whether the sloop carried a bow chaser, but it was too late now to worry about it. Slowly *Faith* closed on the mouth of the bay, creeping in the fog, drawing nearer the waiting privateer, while *Wolf* came on astern. He heard the victorious shout of the sloop's lookout, a bare cable length behind now and closing. Still she had not fired. Either her master was supremely confident or he had no bow chaser. Dalton suspected the latter. He put his glass away. The fog was flattening out, the ranges were closing. Swiveling back and forth, he estimated distances to the ship before and the one behind. The cutter was now almost abeam and he saw her mainsail rising. Sounds of orders came clear from her deck, still wreathed in fog. There was a lookout on her masthead looking across at him, calling signals to her deck. If the light had been better he could have made out the man's features.

Faith was on course to pass the cutter a hundred yards out. *Faith* was also on course to run aground on the end of the jutting spit. He glanced around. The sloop was so close now he fancied he could feel her bowsprit probing at the seat of his britches. He braced himself, cupped his hands, and called, "Mister Kilreagh, smartly! Aport four points and take the wind!"

Faith heeled sharply. Dalton clutched the mast top against her sway as she turned toward the cutter. His breath hissed through his teeth. It was going to be awfully close. He heard a shout from behind him as the sloop's lookout saw the schooner's turn. He glanced back and saw the *Wolf's* mast sway as her captain heeled her to follow. The crosstrees aligned again, then went beyond, and the sloop, with its speed up in the fog, dove directly between *Faith* and the cutter as they came abeam. "Aport two points!" Dalton shouted, barely ahead of the roar of multiple great guns almost directly below him. *Faith* heeled and for a moment Dalton was face-to-face with the sloop's lookout across a short stone's throw of empty space above burning red fog. "Hoist mains'l, Mister Kilreagh!"

Instantly winches sang, grommets rattled, and the big spanker's gaff rose beneath him. Bless the old seaman's heart, he had read his mind. The mast he was on quivered and thumped as the big sail was sheeted home and the wind billowed it. *Faith* leaped like a racehorse and Dalton clung for dear life. He had a glimpse of his own foretopman frozen in the crosstrees watching him. The man's mouth hung open. Dalton rode the pitching spar.

From below a'port, turmoil resounded up through the mist. To starboard the line of trees raced down on him and passed abeam, and *Faith* bumped and shuddered as her keel nudged across the bar, then found good water and lifted her nose to crest her own bow wake. In a moment the sound of battle was behind and *Faith's* staylines sang in the freshening wind of the open Sound. Dalton breathed deeply and relaxed, and his foot slipped off the cleat. Flailing, he caught a spar with one hand, slipped off as it sagged, felt his boot hit the maingaff hawser, and waved his arms for balance as he slid down it. When his feet hit the gaff boom he flipped over, forty feet above the deck, and grabbed desperately at the air. His arms wrapped around the boom and he clung there, winded, dangling at the windward side of the great sail. Distantly through ringing ears he heard the fore lookout shouting, "Lower the mains'l, deck, lower it! The captain's fallen!" As the gaff bucked against him he thought he heard someone scream below. Then he was dropping . . . dropping.

When the mainsail gaff came down they had to pry him loose from it. They lay him on the afterdeck and lit a lantern. He lay stunned, eyes open but unfocused, blood flowing from a gash on his head. They gathered around him, but Constance shooed them away. She wiped his face, tore a strip from her shift to wrap his head, hovered over him. "Patrick," she coaxed, "please. Wake up, Patrick. Please look at me."

He trembled at her voice, drew a breath that burned in his chest, and tried to focus his eyes. The voice seemed distant, but he struggled toward it. His hand lifted, touched warm flesh beneath a thin shift. He shook his head, trying to clear his vision. His mouth worked and he said, "Molly?" Vaguely, it seemed odd to him that she might be so close and yet not answer. With a moment's lucidity, holding away the darkness, he said, "Mister Kilreagh, the spanker is down. Please raise it."

Then the darkness would wait not longer. It closed in on the heels of Kilreagh's. "Aye, Sir."

Triumph still swung lazily on her stern kedge, her prow in the mist pointed into a bay empty of ships. No one aboard, not even the topman who had seen above the mists, was clear as to what had occurred, except that where there had been two vessels at bay, now there were none—and Triumph was abruptly the worse for wear.

"Pair of high masts, clear as day," the topman said. "Seen 'em fair, I did, makin' right for us. Topman there on the fore, lookin' back at me, an' another man on the main but above th' maintop, like he was standin' on th' to'gallant block an' clingin' to th' topmast. Clear as day I saw him, an' clear as a bell I heard him, callin' orders to his deck like he was captain."

"The man is mad as a mudhen," Shelby Jones allowed.

"Or as a fox," Isaac Purdue hushed him. "Go on, Tully. What then?"

"Well, Sir, then there was another mast astern of him, comin' up fast like to overtake, an' I swear it must've near put its jib right up his mizzen afore he wore a'starb'd an' let it pass. Fair bit of close-haul work that was, Sir. Anyways, th' second one—th' sloop, it must have been—hauled right in atwixt us an' taken our fire an' returned it, then they both headed into th' Sound."

Purdue shook his head in exasperation. Two prizes in the pen, one aground at last sighting and one patching its hull, and he had blocked the only exit to wait for shooting light. A fugitive schooner and a Georgie sloop, neither a match for *Triumph* in either speed or firepower. Yet now they were gone and all he could hope to do was mend his shot rigging and try to overtake one or the other somewhere up the Sound.

"What's the damage, Mister Jones?"

"Mostly rigging, Sir. One shroud line shot away, two deadeyes fouled . . . we don't know what else yet, Sir. May have to makeshift some stayline if we want a fast job of it."

"That is exactly what we want," Purdue said. "I want this vessel under sail in one hour, whatever it takes. We are going after that schooner."

"You think that's the one the Georgies are after, Sir?"

"Of course it is, and I have a keen urge now to find out why."

* * *

On the fog-dark waters of Long Island Sound, master and crew of the limping sloop *Wolf* gathered wide-eyed in shrouded lantern-glow to stare at the wreckage of their midships deck. Port gunwales were shot away in two places, fore and aft of the shroud channels. Iron balls had smashed into the high wales at deck level, taking out great gouts of timbering as they passed. Bulwarks, sills, and even toprail were gone from yard-wide spans. Stubs of shattered decking lay twisted and split, blackened by the flare of powder from the gaping mouths of cannon.

Lewis Farrington held a lantern close while William Moweth leaned into the hole to peer at the structures beneath. He withdrew and looked up, squinting against the light. "God's wonder, but we're still firm. They missed the knees and beams. How did he do this, I wonder?"

"It wasn't the schooner. I don't think he fired at all. It was the other ship, the one coming in." Farrington chewed at his lip. "Which guns did we fire, then?"

"Port railers, two rounds. That's all there was time for. I don't know whether we hit anything or not."

"So we didn't volley the schooner at all? We made chase on the schooner and then exchanged fire with someone else?"

"That's how it seems, all right."

"And no casualties."

"Just me, Sir," Roger Bradley held up a wrapped hand. "I took a bit of splinter, but it wasn't much."

Farrington turned to his topman. "Tommy, how much clearance would you say there was between those two vessels when we went through?"

Moss considered it. "About one sloop's worth. I guess, Sir. I know we grazed channel against the one a'starboard. Like to shaken me out of the tops, that did. But I saw the topmen on both of them. Had we been out on spars I could have shook hands and said howdy-do with either one of them."

"You said there was another man up there, too?"

"Aye, there was, but he wa'n't in the trestles, Sir. He was back on the mainmast gallants, just sort of standin' there."

Farrington wiped a smudged hand across his eyes. The whole thing defied description. "How are we headed now, then?"

"Out," Moweth shrugged. "We haven't turned."

"Well, then, let us turn at once. I have no desire to go to Connecticut. Let's see if we can't get that sail the rest of the way up, and all the canvas on the fore. Make northeast for a time. I would like to at least have a glimpse of the devil that did this to us."

"He's back there, Lewey. Probably still in the bay or just coming about."

"No, not that one, the other one—the schooner. I should just like to see whether his hull paint really does match the scrapings on our shroud channel."

With quickening wind, the fog bank had flattened, mists drifting and tumbling in the busy air. "Line banks," William Moweth muttered as he helped cleat a sheet line to trim the jib topsail. The canvas boomed hollowly in response, taking the breeze. Those who sailed the sound knew the line banks of fall—great tunnels of shrouded mist where the fog moved and lifted with the wind, and fell back upon itself to move again. "Wind tunnels," some called the line banks. Good wind for sailing, but no visibility at all within the great worms of fog that lay upon the water. Good sailing, if a man didn't care to see what lay ahead.

Wolf was badly gouged aport, but her legs were unimpaired. With wind in her sails she clove the waves and drove smartly northeastward on dark waters where only Tommy Moss, high on the mast top, could see even a bit of what was around her.

Near dawn she cleared the fog for a time, and Farrington corrected course to run within a mile of the dark shoreline to his right. Then they were in fog again, a fog that glowed pink as first sunlight hit its top.

Half a bell later they were in clear morning, with yet another fog roller visible ahead. But Farrington was pleased. Even blind, they had maintained their course—in sight of Long Island, but far enough out to avoid shallows and shoals. He turned to his charts. There were channels ahead, somewhere. They reduced sail and crept into the next line bank, blind again in a world of bright mist.

Bradley had tea brewing over a little fire in a sand tub when they heard a shout, then another, nearby and angry. Tommy Moss came scrambling down the ratlines and dropped to the deck. "We better halt ship, Lewey," he said. "There are people around us in boats."

"I heard them. Who are they?"

"Fish trawlers, looks like . . ."

Through the hull of *Wolf* they heard a scraping, keening sound, moving from fore to aft. Then Moweth swore and wrestled with the tiller. "Sail down, Lewey!" he shouted. "Our rudder's afoul."

He wasn't the only one swearing. Harsh words echoed back from the mist beyond both rails.

Farrington strode to the starboard rail. "You people out there!" he called. "What have you done to my rudder?"

A querulous voice answered, "We don't know about your bloody rudder. Who are you and what are you doing here?"

"His Majesty's sloop *Wolf*," Farrington called. He turned to Moweth. "Can you see what's wrong?"

Moweth was doubled over the stern rail, head down. "I sure can," his voice came. "We've picked up a fishnet."

Farrington clenched his teeth until his jaws hurt. Into the faceless fog he shouted. "What are you people doing trawling a ship channel?"

After a moment's silence, a placeless voice asked, "What ship channel? This is the fishing banks."

Clearing the rudder was several minutes' work by sloop crew pushing boathooks and fishermen rowing around *Wolf's* stern, salvaging webbing. It was a pained and silent sloop of war that crept north then for almost three miles, with William Moweth on its stem working a sounding line. But finally there was clear depth under their keel, and they turned northeastward again.

Still, when next they cleared the fog, Tommy Moss came down form the tops and handed Farrington his glass. "There's a sail off yonder," he pointed. "Hull down, but her yard's in sight."

Farrington squinted through the telescope. "Is it the schooner, do you think?"

"It might be."

"Then let's try for a closer look."

One hundred miles away, in the open sea off Montauk Point, five bells sounded on the fog-shrouded quarterdeck of the frigate *Courtesan*. Second officer Jack Liles, on the morning watch, had his helmsman ease another point to starboard to keep good wind in the big warship's spritsails, then waved the helmsman away and took the helm himself. A bosun's mate turned the watch glass and entered the turn in the deck log. *Courtesan* crept, with barely enough way to send ripples purring along her hull, a tall, dark shadow in the sun-topped mist, riding smoothly on the swells of running sea. Jib and sprit sails were up and close-hauled. A fore-and-aft spencer curved behind her foremast and a gafftop spanker took wind on her mizzen. Except for these, all the frigate's many sails were furled as she beat slowly northward on port tack.

A lookout in the maintop called, "On deck!"

Liles cupped his hand to his mouth. "Lookout report!"

"Sir, the fog is flattening out ahead. I can make out the point."

"Whereaway, lookout?"

"Hard off the beam, Sir. Half a league."

Liles felt a slackening in the big ship's way and eased yet another point to starboard. "Bosun's mate, dress that spencer a bit."

"Aye, sir."

Liles rubbed his eyes. An hour and a half remained in his watch, another hour and a half of dark fog and lantern light, of long tack to windward in shrouded darkness where the only eyes that could see were those on the masthead, above the mist. He rubbed his aching eyes and felt the ship balk as a vagrant north wind took the billow from her cloth. He spun the helm a half turn to starboard, his shoulders bunching as he willed the rudder to bite. Slowly, raggedly, *Courtesan* answered the helm and crept forward again, now sixty degrees from the wind.

"Very sloppy, Mister Liles." The captain's acid voice at his shoulder startled him. He hadn't been aware that Hart had come onto the quarterdeck.

"Aye, Sir." He looked around, snapped a salute, and turned his attention back to the helm. "Good morning, Sir."

"An officer whose attention wanders is a poor officer, Mister Liles. Report our location and bearing, please."

"Montauk Point is two miles off port beam, Sir. We bear northeast, forty or fifty degrees, at about two knots."

"Forty or fifty degrees? Really, Mister Liles. Which is it? What is our heading?"

Hart stood directly over the boxed compass, but he held his head high, arms behind his back, looking off into the fog, disdaining to look at the compass. Liles leaned and peered through the misted glass. "Forty-six degrees it is, Sir. I'm trying to keep her full and by, close to the wind as she'll tack, but it's hard sailing, Sir."

"It is not hard sailing, Mister Liles. You simply are having a hard time of it."

"Aye, Sir." Liles's jaws tightened and he stared straight ahead into the fog, the aurora of the mizzen lamp making his eyes ache even more.

Bosun's mate Buster Willis appeared in the lantern light below the taffrail. "Spencer's dressed close, Sir, but the new tack has it rippling a bit. Shall we re-trim?"

Liles eased the helm back aport until he felt the tiny surge of the ship taking good wind. "Leave it be, Mister Willis, go and rouse the cook, if you will, and tell him it's two bells to breakfast."

"Aye, Sir." Willis turned and went through the companionway leading below. At the foot of the ladder he met his midwatch counterpart, Clyde Serrey, rubbing sleep from his eyes as he lighted a lamp.

"Heard the captain going on deck," Serrey yawned.

"Aye, he's there, and in a fouler temper than yesterday, by the dressing down he just gave Mister Liles."

"Well, he ain't the only one, I warrant. Plenty of grumbling going on in the gunroom before deadwatch. The lads are none too happy, Buster. Shore leave cut short an' all, to go chasin' after booty we'll have no share in, that ain't right."

Willis didn't comment, but he nodded. Jonathan Hart was not a popular captain among his officers and crew. He was cold and strict, with a capricious temper that kept the entire company on edge. Rarely did a Tuesday morning pass that someone didn't feel the lash, and his sentences were often harsh. Every man aboard had seen what a hundred strokes of the cat could do. They had buried poor Sam Hankins at sea with scant ceremony after his punishment. Scuttlebutt had it that Hart had once, in a rage, had a swabber keelhauled for some minor infraction. Not a man aboard ever wanted to witness a thing like that.

On the other hand, the prizemaster produced royalties for them and every man aboard, officers down to the lowest tar, kept track of his shares in the prizes taken. Not a captain in the fleet took so many prizes as Hart. His warrant was direct from the Court of King George, and it took an Admiralty order to bind him to fleet business. Thus while other ships of the fleet were doing naval duty—tiresome blockade runs and flag missions against colonial privateer packs—*Courtesan* went her own way and took what she wanted. Just in the past year *Courtesan* had captured five vessels in the North Atlantic and along the American shore.

As each was delivered to Crown registry, the officers and crew computed their shares and added to their tallies. Two had been colonial warships rigged for fighting, and would be assumed by the Crown, with royalties paid to Hart. The others had been fat merchantmen which would go on the auction block in England, and these would produce prize shares . . . divided in decreasing twentieths among captain, ship's officers, bosun, quartermaster, chief gunner, navigator, carpenter, sailmaker, captain's clerk, and sergeant of marines, and finally among able seamen, gunners, ordinary seamen, and marines.

Any man who could complete a tour with Captain Hart might go home wealthy.

But of late the men had felt cheated. Two of the ships they had braced proved to be neutrals, and the captain had let them go. One was that Dutch contract packet off the Carolinas bound for New Spain. Hart had boarded her himself and had come back with a private prize, that beautiful Spanish girl. Any man aboard *Courtesan* might have done the same, but it rankled them that only the captain had benefited in the slightest from that excursion . . . and there was a fair chance that their prize shares might suffer if the Crown received enough pressure from the Spanish to cause a penalty to be levied on the *Courtesan*. Taking the woman off a neutral ship had been an arrogant and unwise move.

What upset them most was the schooner. Hart had taken *Courtesan* into Delaware Bay in search of privateers. He had found the bright schooner at anchor. Not a shot was fired. They boarded, put the guard over the side, put a prize crew aboard, and set sail for New York. A right pretty prize. Twenty thousand pounds, at least, on the block. Then Hart decided not to register her. He would keep her. Dreams of shares dissolved and the grumbling began.

Willis made his way through to the fore galley, shook the cook awake, and started back through the gunroom and the maindeck lofts. Hammocks were slung here five deep and fourteen inches apart, most of them filled with sleeping men. The closed space was thick with their odors and their snores. As he passed a hand reached out and tapped his arm. "Mister Willis?" The voice was a whisper.

Squinting, he made out the face of young Foss. "Aye, Terry, it's me."

"Mister Willis, they say it's the same little ship we're after. The one the captain's claimed for himself."

"I wouldn't know, Terry."

"Aye, Sir. But if it is, there's several here missed shore leave for her who won't take it kindly."

Willis frowned. "Mister Foss, you had best keep your thoughts to yourself. We all do as we're told, nothing more."

"Aye," the youngster was chastened, yet angry. His whisper became thin and strained. "Just seemed to me you might want to know, that's all." He turned over in the hammock. Willis went on through to the companionway. Clyde Serrey waited there. "Now you see what I mean," he said.

On the quarterdeck Captain Jonathan Hart straightened his hat and buttoned his coat higher to keep out the chill. "Keep her on course, Mister Liles. Full and by through the watch. The fog will pass by the forenoon."

Jack Liles kept his eyes straight ahead in the graying darkness. His pride still stung from the captain's words a few minutes earlier. Liles was accustomed to ship's discipline. He expected it. But he had never become accustomed to insult. He was a capable sailor and a good officer, and he knew it.

Inside his waistband was the message that had

come during the first hour of the morning watch, flashed from the shore. He hauled it out. "Message from shore, Sir." He glanced at the captain's face as he read it, and suppressed a smile. The Navy wanted Hart's toy destroyed.

XIII

Trailing skirts of the fog bank hung at deck level, mist-pink frosting on dark water as the morning sun touched spars with a brightness which crept down onto rounded sails. The sky was bright above and a fine northwest wind blew pine-scented from the Connecticut coast below the port horizon.

Patrick Dalton noticed these things even before he became aware of the throbbing in his head and the ache in his chest. He shifted in the midships hammock and groaned, hearing the sounds of angry voices.

Abruptly he became aware that a tumult had awakened him. His eyes took a moment to focus in the early light and he sat up, held his aching head in his hands for a moment, then swung down and stood. *Faith* sailed on a port reach in open water. Spanker, spencer, and jibsail belled out, driving her through mist-hung running swells. Clarence Kilreagh was at the tiller, several hands were at sheets and fife rails, and all were staring forward, where a pushing, cursing mass of figures struggled at the forepeak.

Shaking the dizziness out of his head, Dalton hurried forward. Seven men were on the foredeck, six of them standing. One lay sprawled and groaning against the forehatch cover. Four men had two others backed against the rail over the port cathead. They crowded in wielding belaying pins. Dalton shouldered men aside and pushed in between.

"Belay that!" he shouted. "All of you! What is going on here?"

The four backed off a step and the two crouched at the rail, weapons high. They were Delaware men. Their assailants were tars. Dalton turned full circle, his eyes blazing. "Well? Speak up! What is going on?"

"It's them, Sir." Virgil Cowan, one leg up on the cathead, pointed at the four assailants. "They attacked us. They already decked Jubal Foster over there, now they're after the rest of us."

"We didn't start it, Sir," Victory Locke asserted from the British line. "We was doing fine until they started callin' us 'Georgies.' We asked them to quit sayin' that, Sir, but they kept on, they did."

"Georgies?"

"Aye, Sir." Purdy Fisk nodded. "Georgies is what they called us. I don't take to bein' called any such thing as that, Sir."

"Especially not," Claude Mallory added, "by a bunch of strakes."

"There they go again," Virgil Cowan roared. "They started callin' us 'strakes' before ever we called them 'Georgies.' "

As Dalton stared around him in disbelief, the combatants backed off a bit more, cowed by the captain's presence. Charley Duncan hurried up, sleepy-eyed, drawn by the fracas. Dalton said, "Mister Duncan, please relieve these men of their belaying pins."

"Aye, Sir." Duncan went the rounds, collecting the heavy clubs.

When he was finished Dalton ordered, "Mister Duncan, assemble all hands amidships. And I mean all hands. Roust them out."

"Aye, Sir."

Irritated and still a little dizzy, Dalton strode along to the afterdeck. "Did you see that, Mister Kilreagh?"

"Aye, Cap'n. But I didn't know what they were about."

"Neither do they, Mister Kilreagh. Where are we?"

" 'Bout off Field Point, Sir, bearin' east-northeast an' makin' four knots by log an' line."

"How long have I been indisposed?"

"Just a while, Cap'n. It's just sunup. I took her into the Sound an' headed up, just stayin' between th' horizons, ye might say. An' I'm sorry, Sir. I couldn' likely turn back for the lads we left, wi' all that goin' on back there. We barely squeaked out as 'twas."

"What lads?"

"Why, them that was out wi' the jolly boat, Sir. They never come back aboard. There was Mister Coleman an' two of th' colonials, the Cranston boys, they was. But they can make it on their own from there, I allow."

"Aye. But we've lost the jolly boat. Well," he shrugged, "has there been sign of those ships back there?"

"Not yet, Sir. Wi' a bit o' luck they'd have sunk each other."

"That's much to hope for, Mister Kilreagh. I've called a muster of hands. If you'd tend the watch until I've finished, I'll take it from you then."

"Aye, Sir."

By twos and threes Charley Duncan turned them out and squared them up amidships, in ranks facing aft. Dalton's eyes went from face to face. Seven of the men he ranked as able seamen—six now, with Samuel Coleman gone. John Abernathy, Brevis Grimm, Martin Smith, and Victory Locke wore the pigtails of Royal Navy sailors. Virgil Cowan and Michael Romart were shaggy colonials, but able seamen nonetheless. Another six were ordinaries, and a motley lot they were. Ishmael Bean and Claude Mallory were Londoners gone to sea. Purdy Fisk was from Liverpool. Both of the Cranstons, now beached somewhere back there, had been ordinaries. Jubal Foster was another colonial.

Ranked among the seamen were the pressedmen, William Moses from Virginia and Peter Tarkington from Southampton, a beekeeper.

Ranged alongside were Charley Duncan and Cadman Wise, his bosuns, Solamon Grimm, Guy Neely, a sour-looking Robert Arthur, and Billy Caster.

Arthur bore a livid bruise on his half-bearded face

and scowled curiously at the bandage wrapped around Dalton's head.

"Beggin' pardon, Sir . . . did I do that?"

"Of course not, Mister Arthur. I fell from the topmast."

The big man tipped his head to look into the distant heights, then stared dumbly at Dalton for a moment before a glimmer of insight lit his eyes. He winked hugely then, grinned, and a hand went to his painful face. "Aye, I believe that's what happened to me, too."

Dalton spread his feet, crossed hands behind his back, and scowled at them, letting the silence build. Suddenly he roared, "All those loyal to the King, let's see your hands!"

It was so sudden that Bernice, the ship's cat, grooming herself on the low companionway top, jumped and disappeared down the hatch. Every hand in the ranks shot up.

"Very well," Dalton nodded. "Now, those who are free men, let's see hands!" Again the hands went up. Even the two pressedmen, who had not known freedom since the day they were pressed into service, raised their hands high. Dalton raised a clenched fist. "Strike for liberty and honor!"

The roar of voices drowned him out. "Huzzah! Hear! Hear!"

In the silence that followed, Dalton nodded in satisfaction. "Do you know the origin of the cry you've just echoed, lads? It's a battle cry of the rebels in Jersey. And it was a cry of the Irish before them— and of Bonnie Prince Charlie's band before that. Are you rebels, then? Or are you just free men?"

On the British side Victory Locke raised a tentative hand. "I be no rebel, Sir, but the cry is one I'd follow." Several of the others voiced agreement.

"Aye," Dalton said, "and do you know what they call those who follow it? Strakes, that's what they call 'em. It seems every man aboard this ship is a Strake, and proud of it." Several of the Englishmen cast sheepish glances at the colonials across the way.

"Now, you Victory Locke, you are a subject of the King?"

"Aye, Sir."

"Then what is the King's name, Sir?"

Locke scratched the stubble on his chin, concentrating. From behind him came a harsh whisper, "It's George, ye idiot. George."

"The king's name is George, Sir."

"Very good, Mister Locke. You colonials . . . you, Mister Romart . . . what is the name of the American general who held Manhattan Island last year?"

"General, Sir? You mean General Washington, Sir?"

"Exactly. What is his given name?"

"Why, it's George, Sir."

"And do you support General Washington, Mister Romart?"

"Aye, Sir, I suppose I do."

"And are you a subject of the King?"

"Aye, Sir, I reckon I am."

"And you are a colonial?"

"Aye, Sir. I was born near Ox Cross . . . ah, that's in Delaware, Sir."

"Do you know what a Georgie is, Mister Fisk?" He swung an accusing finger at the ordinary seaman in the front of the British rank.

"Aye, Sir," the man's face colored and he glanced around. "But there's a lady present, Sir."

Dalton had not noticed until this moment that Constance was at the stern rail watching the proceedings. He glanced at her, then back at his men. "Obviously, then, you do not know what a Georgie is, so I'll tell you."

To a man, their eyes swung toward the woman and every face in the ranks turned bright red.

"A Georgie," Dalton pressed on, "is one who supports King George . . . or one who supports George Washington. Whatever else you might have thought it meant is wrong!"

The faces before him showed relief. The men had expected to be acutely embarrassed before the lady.

"Now that we have settled that," he said, "if any man here has complaint against any other, let him step forward and state it."

There was silence in the ranks, but Brevis Grimm's hand went up tentatively. At Dalton's nod he said, "Not a complaint, Cap'n . . . just a question. Are we British or American? Which side are we on?"

"We're on neither side, Mister Grimm. *Faith* is a fugitive ship. We may go as far as New Spain."

Puzzled glances shot back and forth through the ranks. Victory Locke raised a hand. "Then are we Spanish, Sir?"

Robert Arthur hunched massive shoulders and furrowed a puzzled brow. "Beggin' pardon, Sir, but I took it . . . considerin' yerself an' all . . . I took it we was Irish."

Dalton willed a straight face. The pain in his head helped. "We are the schooner *Faith*. As fugitives, we are without nationality. Now you men who were fighting, I'll see all of you shake hands before you leave these ranks. And you, Mister Arthur, I'll be wanting to talk with you directly after you've prepared breakfast. Dismissed!"

Relief swept over them. There would be no floggings. Some gazed at the Captain in awe and wonder. "Long live King George!" someone shouted and they all took it up. "Long live King George! Long live George Washington! Huzzah for Georgies an' Strakes! Up the *Faith!*"

"Hands to the watch!" Duncan bawled. "Lookouts aloft! Look alive, there!"

Constance Ramsey frowned. "What was that all about, Mister Dalton?"

"Ship's discipline, Miss." He squinted, trying to drive away the ache in his head. He took the tiller and watched Clarence Kilreagh stump off along the deck. "It may be I owe you an apology, Miss."

"Whatever for?"

"Last evening . . . this morning . . . whenever we were talking, I believe I had taken a bit too much rum. It strikes me my tongue may have been loose. I may have offended."

"Why, not at all, Sir. Some of what you said actually was quite flattering."

"It was?" For the life of him he couldn't remember exactly what he had said. But he pressed on, "And when we sat together under the quilts . . ."

"It was quite cool."

". . . and my elbow was poking at you . . ."

"Not all that uncomfortable, really."

200

". . . I'm afraid that wasn't my elbow, Miss Constance."

She blushed furiously. Dalton hurried on, "And did I suggest you might, ah, call me by my given name?"

"You did suggest that."

"I must withdraw the suggestion, then. It could lead to laxity aboard ship, you know."

The light of the rising sun struck shining water beyond her. New pains shot through his aching head. He frowned. At the scowl, Constance's blood went cold. All she had allowed herself to imagine, in those eldritch moments in the dark of morning, dissolved. She returned his frown with one of her own.

"Then as long as we are speaking frankly, Mister Dalton, I accept your apology, and no such thing shall happen again."

Dalton felt something shrivel inside him. Apparently everything he had felt—the closeness, the attraction, that aura of tenderness and warmth, was a fiction of a besotted brain. He had fantasized like a schoolboy. He cleared his throat and turned away. His voice was thin. "Naturally not."

But she wasn't through. "You said something about New Spain."

"It is a possibility."

"I have no intention of going to New Spain. I want to go back to Delaware."

"I expect we can put you ashore somewhere, then, Miss."

She stamped a small foot. "Put ashore, nothing! This is my ship."

Dalton sighed. "You lost your ship to an act of

war, Miss. A crown vessel preempted it. I, in turn, as a fugitive, have preempted *this* vessel from the naval yard at Long Island. It is mine now, by possession. As far as I am concerned, we are discussing two entirely separate ships."

"That is pure piracy!"

"No, Miss. That is survival. And right now my major concern is to remove this vessel and all aboard her from harm's way. We can discuss niceties at another time."

Blazing, she turned away and he noticed how her hair caught the sunlight. He looked away.

Rising sun off the starboard quarter washed its blaze through the distant fog bank. It angled from abeam to distant dead ahead. *Faith* ran in a broad trough of clear sky between opposing distant cliffs of bright mist ahead and behind. Good water, Dalton mused, confining his thoughts to the moment. Good water and clear sailing. The aches in his head and chest dimmed at the bright pleasure of a good sea at morning.

He read the chill in the wind, the subdued amber of the hazing sun. Through his boots he read the running sea. His ears heard the whisper of parting waters, the mewing of gulls kiting above *Faith's* wake. He read the day as he had off Belfast as a boy, slewing a balky old boat through autumn swells on trimain and jib. The deep sunglint in the fogbank ahead was precisely the color of Constance Ramsey's hair. A weariness came over him. Enjoy the day, he told himself. It will not last.

Kilreagh came to stand at the rail. "I make yon a

true line bank, Sir. A roller. We'll be in fog again soon, but with wind."

"Aye. The birds will leave us when it closes."

Arthur's roar from the companion hatch announced breakfast, and Wise took charge of sending the first shift below. Billy Caster came up with his supply ledger. "Captain, we're running short of just about everything. Can we put in somewhere for provisions?"

"I thought we had ample provisions aboard, Mister Caster."

"Well, no Sir. Not with all these people to be fed. And cook's tally was short because of that short pantry bulkhead in the galley, so . . ."

"Let me see the inventory, then."

There was food for another two days, at most . . . water and tack for a day or two beyond. He handed it back. "Thank you, Mister Caster. Go below and have your breakfast."

Dalton's lip curled in frustration. He turned again to the fore. The sun was a hand above the looming fog bank now, but frozen there as *Faith* drew nearer. The wind was easing. Soon it would begin to gust, but for the moment *Faith* whispered along through gentle swells and there was that delicious sensation of flight. Flight in a stolen craft. Escape. Escape from Belfast, he thought. Images . . . a young man in a stub-masted scow, flying away across misted waters. A lad in a corner, betrayed . . . the irony of it intrigued him. What happened once came back to happen again. Fly away . . . escape.

Short pantry bulkhead? He shook himself awake. "Mister Kilreagh, take the tiller."

He sprinted to the companion hatch and dropped below. The galley was packed with hungry young men. Without ceremony he flushed them mug and scupper and confronted the big cook.

"Now, Mister Arthur, show me where you found the rum."

Arthur chewed his lip. "I didn't mean harm, Sir. It was jus' there an' I tasted it an' . . ."

"Where, Mister Arthur? Where was it?"

"Why, right here, Sir." The cook turned to the pantry head and heaved bales and parcels aside. Shelving covered the new-timbered wall. "Down here, Sir." On hands and knees they peered into the shadows below the bins. A rough trap opened into darkness. "It was in that hole, Sir. I slid it out to see what it was."

Dalton brought down the lantern and squinted into the hole. Beyond was a solid rank of stacked kegs. One had tipped above, blocking the top of the hole, leaving a space. He stood and rehung the lantern.

"Mister Arthur, fetch a line. Take it to the companion hatch—the aft frame—and run it to the top of this bulkhead. Knot it there and bring it to me."

"Aye, Sir."

Dalton went on deck. "Mister Wise!" He caught the bosun's attention. "Please bring a lantern and hand line to the midships hold."

Drawing the grate, he dropped into the hold. In dimness, he looked about at the cargo. Bales of shingles were stowed forward, lashed to cover the entire bulkhead with its timbered crawlway to the fore hold. Crates and kegs rode high on both beams. The after bulkhead was a solid wall of lashed kegs. As Wise's lamp flooded the hold with light, he could read the markings. Nails, oil, wax, tar . . . one of the nail kegs was open and he dipped a hand into it. Nails.

With a perplexed Cadman Wise holding a knotted line at the hatch frame, Dalton ran the line aft to the bulkhead, between nail kegs. He knotted the line where it touched timbers. "Thank you, Mister Wise. Let's go on deck, now."

Robert Arthur was waiting with a piece of knotted line. The curious crew looked on as Dalton laid out his line from the cargo hatch aft, then laid Arthur's line from the companionway forward. The marker knots fell ten feet short of meeting. He whistled. No wonder *Faith* ran heavy amidships. He looked around. Constance Ramsey was huddled at the after rail, a quilt drawn about her. She looked small, frightened, and guilty. "Miss Constance!" His shout was imperious. "Attend me, please. Now!"

Sailors cleared a path for him. The captain had a stormy look. He checked the schooner's trim, lashed the tiller, and cleared all hands out of earshot with an angry glance. "Now, Miss Constance, would you care to explain the false hold in this vessel?"

The conversation lasted for a time, observed by curious eyes all along the deck and in the tops. Finally, the small figure in the bulky quilt whirled away and went below.

They were closing on the now-stalled fog bank when Dalton regained the tiller. Clarence Kilreagh came aft to stand near him, by the rail.

"Liquid gold," Dalton told him. "Pure Jamaican rum. Four hundred kegs of it, or more. A fortune, Mister Kilreagh. Enough rum there to buy a regiment—or drown one. It's no wonder the wench came searching for this ship!"

Kilreagh frowned. "Still, you might have been more gentle, Sir. It appeared to me she was weeping."

"Hang her weeping! She could have told me about it before we fought an ill-laden ship through that damnable channel!"

"An' if she had, would ye have jettisoned it? A fortune? You said yerself—enough to hire a regiment. After all, Sir, the lass's father *is* a rebel."

"Phaw! I warrant he's a hypocrite, nothing more. A smuggler! Small wonder he's ill. Apoplexy, no doubt, from losing his rum."

"Now there's an interestin' point, Sir. Supposin' Cap'n Hart knows what we've taken from him? Do ye suppose he knew of the rum?"

"Apparently not. She thinks not. Besides, if he did he'd have half the fleet after us by now."

"Seems to me half the fleet *is* after us, Sir."

"Aye, but that's politics. Those gunners back there were out to sink us, Clarence, not capture us. And the sloop in the bay, he told us so."

"Aye, that's so."

"On deck! On deck!"

They craned their necks. In the maintops Purdy Fisk was waving wildly. "Sail ho, Sir. Starboard astern an' comin' on!"

"Take the tiller, Mister Kilreagh." Dalton got out his glass and braced himself at the after rail. For a moment there was nothing, then he found her—a small, sleek craft cutting through tendrils of hovering mist, a light hull with a full suit of canvas, combs of spray breaking off her rising prow—a cutter, fast and deadly.

Dalton put away his glass. "Mister Duncan! All hands to stations! Up stays'l, up jib tops'l, up fore and main gafftops! By the numbers, Mister Duncan!"

"Aye, Sir!"

"Mister Kilreagh, bring her over for broad reach. Dead into the fog bank yonder, sir."

"Aye, Sir. Ah, Cap'n . . . yonder somewhere is shoals, Sir. In the fog we'll be blind."

"In the fog he will, too, Mister Kilreagh. Broad reach, if you please. Mister Grimm, keep that woman below!"

"Ah, Sir . . . Mister Grimm? With the lady?"

"Quite right, Clarence. Belay that, Mister Grimm! Mister Caster? Where are you? Ah, there you are. Please keep Miss Constance below, Mister Caster."

"Aye, Sir."

Faith shook out her kinks and climbed the running swells as high canvas took the wind. The bright mist ahead stood taller.

"On deck!" There was panic in the cry, and Kilreagh shoved the tiller hard a'port. "Holy mother, look at that!" Dead ahead, a hundred yards at most, a huge ship lumbered out of the fog. Great skymasts carried billowing cloth hauled hard to catch the wind on short tack. *Faith* scudded hard into a swell, throwing spray across the deck as the rudder took. Agonizingly, she swung her nose to the right, closing on the hull of the big ship. For a frozen instant she was jib-to-prow with the frigate, then she slid past barely ten feet off the banked gunports, shivering in

207

the instant's lull of the big ship's lee as she passed. They heard shouts, and a belated cannon thundered somewhere astern. Then *Faith* had her wind again and they flew into dimness that turned bright and thick as the fog closed around her.

"Steady her, Mister Kilreagh! You'll lose your way!"

Kilreagh hauled the tiller back to keel and *Faith* settled again into her long stride.

"What in God's name was that?" Charley Duncan slid to a precarious stop by the stern rail.

"That was a frigate, Mister Duncan." Dalton wiped a sleeve across his brow. "You have seen frigates before."

"But so big, Sir?"

"I know her," Kilreagh said in a voice that came tight from his throat. "That's *Courtesan*, Sir. The devil's own fighting ship. That back yon is Captain Hart."

XIV

Aboard the privateer *Triumph*, Commander Isaac Purdue watched his quarry close on the standing fog and cursed. "He will try to evade us when he's in cover, Mister Jones. How do you read him?"

First Officer Shelby Jones pursed his lips. "There's a shoal between channels off there, Sir. I guess he'd know that, and quarter about when he's out of sight."

"A full quarter, you think? With all his canvas up? On a full reach a gust could put him keel-up."

"But a gust is unlikely in the fog, Sir. You see how it stands."

"Aye. And the man is a sailor, I'll grant him that. Very well, then, when we lose him, we'll lean a bit and see if we can outthink him in the fog."

"We can always catch him when he comes out, Sir."

"If we know where he's coming out, Aye. Otherwise it could be a long chase."

With its narrow hull nose-high, water curling at

its bows, the cutter paced the swells. The rattle of hastily mended port shrouds was a discordant sound, distasteful to Purdue. Two more shroud lines cut and he would have lost his mast. The fore-shroud was coupled with a tied-off grapple sealing a broken span of cable too wide for a turnbuckle. The ball that had taken out his shroud lines had left evidence also on the starboard deck, where planks were smashed and a railing breeched. That ball and another had reduced his crew to eight men. He had put the injured one ashore at a settlement on the island.

Commander Purdue still had no idea how the schooner had done what it had done. His lookout had seen it all above the fog, but the report was unclear. There had been two ships. One had pursued the other. The schooner had luffed or veered at the last minute, in the blind mist, and the second ship had run between. In was that second ship he had fought, rail to rail. He knew he had hulled it, but it had hurt him too. And to this moment he didn't know who it was. It had limped on past him in the fog, out of the bay, and by the time he got underway, both it and the schooner were gone.

Well, he would have the schooner. From two sightings he knew its course. It might duck and hide, but it could not outrun him. *Triumph* might be small—barely more than a racing hull with a double suit of sails—but she was all legs and teeth. Purdue turned to look back, then turned again when he heard Jones' explosive curse: "By the good Lord, Sir. Look!"

The schooner was nearing the fog bank. They were close enough to see the two figures standing in her stern. She was hull-up and running. Then, ghostly, a shape appeared in the fog directly ahead of her and a great ship was there, coming head on, almost on top of her. As Purdue and Jones gaped at the sight, the schooner heeled sharply to the right and skinned past the big ship, where chaos had erupted on deck. A cannon barked, and then the schooner dived into sun-shimmered mist and was gone. *Triumph* bore down on the frigate.

"Hands to sheets!" Purdue roared. "Hard a'lee!"

The sheets were eased by frantic hands, gaffs swung about, and he hauled the tiller to him. *Triumph's* hull boomed as she skidded broadside into a swell, sheeting water out before her.

"Sheet home a'port!" Half about in the water, the cutter took wind in her cloth and heeled to the left, coming hard about, almost doubling back on her wake. Purdue breathed a prayer of thanks that the patched shrouds were on the port side. They would never have taken the strain on the starboard.

The frigate had begun to veer, but now it adjusted course and came on toward them, slow and lumbering on its full tack but well within gun range. Purdue gritted his teeth and knotted his shoulders, willing the cutter to greater speed. He counted, the syllables hissing between his teeth, ". . . four . . . five . . . six. . . ." He felt *Triumph* picking up way. The rudder began to respond. ". . . Eleven . . . twelve. . . ." Now. He eased the tiller to starboard and felt *Triumph* answer, her bow easing to port. Behind him was thunder, and a ball threw water off his starboard beam. Twin chasers? Probably. He eased a' starboard and knew he had guessed right. The second shot plowed the sea to his left and skipped off ahead before sinking into its final splash. He held his tiller and ran.

Beside him Shelby Jones and one of the men touched fuse to the cutter's stern chaser and its roar deafened him for an instant. The smoke rolled off aport.

"By damn, Sir, I think we hit him!"

Purdue glanced back. On the receding frigate there was a scramble of men in the fore, and one of the jib stays hung loose below the sweeping spreader at her nose. Even as he looked, a boat hook thrust out from the deck and caught up the dangling line.

"For all the good it did," he said sourly. Faced with a frigate, the best thing *Triumph* could do was get away as fast as possible.

"Damn, but she's big," Jones allowed. "Do you know her, Cap'n?"

"Hart's *Courtesan*. It has to be."

Another minute and the agile cutter was beyond range even of the warship's guns. When he was satisfied, Purdue eased her over into an easy reach and looked back again. On the frigate's tall masts, spars were hauling around as the ship made about in a great circle to port.

"He's going after the schooner, Sir." Jones breathed. "Damn, but I'd not like to be aboard that schooner with that monster behind me and the wind at its tail."

"Nor I." Purdue rolled his shoulders to relieve the tension in them. "Take the tiller, Mister Jones. When the frigate is out of sight you can bring us about. Set her a full reach with the wind on port beam."

"Into the fog, Sir?"

"Of course into the fog. That's where our prey went, isn't it?"

In stilling wind the autumnal fog bank lay dense and bright-shouldered, three miles across and a hundred long, bridging Long Island's Atlantic face, all of the Sound and off across Rhode Island into Massachusetts, a mist-white mole of mixed-wind blindness under the hazy morning. In its belly sailed vessels.

Aboard the schooner *Faith*, Patrick Dalton pulled his coat close about him and strode to the stern deck. "Come about to port, if you please, Mister Kilreagh. Let's get some wind on her beam, and I'd like it quiet aboard, Sir."

The frigate *Courtesan* was swallowed in the murk, and Captain Jonathan Hart stood, arms folded, scowling into blindness. Finally he told his helmsman, "Steady as she goes, Mister Serrey. The fugitive can hardly fail to use this cover to throw us off, but he will make for open water and we'll find him there." The great ship plowed on, directly across the bank, its broad, stacked sails capturing every whisper of the breeze.

Commander Isaac Purdue of the cutter *Triumph* knew these waters better than any of them. This was his home territory. With his first beside him, he took the tiller and veered the swift little ship gently, broadly, to starboard, his ears probing the mist.

When the muted song of timbers and tackle reached him, he tilted his head, catching its every note. "That's the frigate," he whispered, and First Officer Shelby Jones turned his head to the right to listen. "She's ahead of us, moving with the wind. A bit more a'starboard now . . . that's it." Triumph cut the frigate's wake and edged away. Out of earshot Purdue told Jones, "Let's get a line over and read for shoals. There's an island over there, and I'm betting we'll find a pretty little ship lying in its lee.

An hour later Perdue found a pretty little ship. Creeping around the crag-end of the island in a failing wind, still mostly shrouded by fog, *Triumph* came about dead still on the leaden swells, relying on the tide to keep her off the island's shoals. Her sail was just rattling down when a shout came from the misted foredeck. There was a grinding crash a'starboard and Purdue heard the unmistakable chewing crunch of grapples biting his railing. An instant later armed men poured onto his deck and he was confronted by a young, ruddy, and embarrassed face. The stranger held out a hand.

"Good morning, Sir. I am Lewis Farrington, commanding His Majesty's sloop *Wolf*. I've taken your ship, Sir. Now I wonder if we might rig a line. I seem to have gone aground here."

Lying out on *Faith's* jib, Victory Locke hauled in his sounding line from beheath the schooner's keel, looped it and prepared to sling it again. "An' a quarter, six," he called over his shoulder, and heard the signal relayed from midships to stern. *Faith* carried

214

her full suit of sails, spreading her wings to catch the fitful wind, creeping blind into her second hour of dead fog.

Amidships some of the crew coiled lines, some stood at the rails holding rifles and fretting under the critical eye of young Billy Caster who forbade their shooting the fine weapons unless there was something to shoot at. The rest were below, taking their shift at an interrupted breakfast. On the after deck Patrick Dalton and Charley Duncan shared a pot of tea. The tiller was lashed, sails were set and as long as the breeze held *Faith* would tend her own course up the tunnel of fog.

"An' a quarter, six," came the sounding.

Dalton nodded. "Open water, Mister Duncan. Open water, and a provision port somewhere ahead."

"Provision port, Sir?" It was the first Dalton had said about where they might be going.

"The Rhode Island colony, Mister Duncan. At the last I heard, the King is not at war with Rhode Island. Therefore we should be able to put in there with some caution and take on supplies. Mister Arthur's pantry is running bare."

"But the fleet holds Newport, Sir. And Narragansett is the slave lane. I've heard there's pirates and runners and . . . and all sorts of thievery about off Rhode Island."

"We should fit right in," Dalton nodded. "Let's not forget, we haven't a man aboard who isn't a fugitive from a stockade, a court-martial, or a hangman."

"Aye," Duncan compressed his face in a worried frown. "But ours are all good lads, Sir. No real harm in any of them, don't you see."

With a sardonic glance, Dalton asked, "How many men was it Mister Arthur laid out before they got him stockaded back there? And Mister Wise and Mister Smith in the thick of it with him, by reports."

" 'Twas only a brawl," Duncan protested. "They meant no harm."

"And the brothers Grimm, Mister Duncan?"

Duncan grinned. "Those two *do* like the ladies, bless 'em."

"I gather some of those ladies didn't consider themselves blessed."

"Matter of attitude, Sir, so to speak. What I meant was, our lads may be high spirited, and maybe in a bit of trouble at the moment, but no . . . no real bad ones among 'em. No berserkers or thieves or bludgeonists, you know."

"I take your point, and I agree. But *my* point is, good intentions or not, we are all fugitives at the moment. By the way, why were you in the stockade that first time, Mister Duncan? I mean before the mayhem business."

Duncan's freckled face turned bright red. "They said I took something that wasn't mine, Sir."

"Ah. A bit of thievery, Mister Duncan?"

"Oh, no, Sir. What they said I took didn't really belong to anybody. It was just a helm."

"A helm?"

"Aye. The helm off the brig *Thurette*. A fine, twelve-spoke wheel with ivory inlays. A real beauty."

"Off the *Thurette*? You stole the helm off the Vice-Admiral's flagship?"

"So they said, Sir."

"My. I wonder what a wheel like that would bring at the thieves' market on Manhattan Island."

Duncan grinned crookedly at him. "I got four pounds seven for it, Sir."

"When we reach Rhode Island, Mister Duncan, I believe you may join me in our provisioning expedition."

"Aye, Sir, I'd like to." Duncan looked at him curiously.

"You see, Mister Duncan, despite some valuable cargo, we have almost no money. We may just have to make do."

Hannibal Cranston awoke to a rocking motion and the scraping of a light keel against the gravel bottom. Morning had come, and with it the misery of awakening after a long and foggy night with very little sleep at its end. He rubbed his eyes, wishing that his head would stop throbbing so. He untangled his legs from those of Samuel Coleman, asleep in the jolly boat's damp bilge, and raised his head to look around. Bits and pieces of the night before came back to him, and he groaned and shook his head, then wished he hadn't as new miseries pulsed there.

The rum keg sat stolidly amidships in the little boat, one of Coleman's arms around it. The tar was smiling in his sleep. Echoing the dull chop of waves against the boat's side was a smaller sound . . . whatever rum remained in the keg gurgled and sloshed happily as the boat rocked against gravel. Beyond the keg Hannibal's brother John snored against a bench brace.

There had been fog, Hannibal recalled—darkness and a blind fog that gave no hint of direction. They had sipped at the rum to ward off chill, and somehow the more they had sipped, the less they cared where they were or where their ship might be. Between darkness and plentiful rum, time had passed pleasantly and it hadn't really mattered that they were all sitting in a small jolly boat somewhere in a fog-enshrouded bay where ships made ready to shoot at one another. They had, in fact, quite forgotten about all that after a while.

To pass the time, they had taken turns rowing, first one way and then another, and he recalled having seen lantern glow and the shadows of ships . . . one or two ships, possibly even three, at different times. Or possibly they had seen the same ship two or three times. They had talked about that, but had not been able to reach a concensus, so they had sipped a bit more rum and changed the subject. They had talked of politics for a time, then had agreed to stay away from such subjects. There wasn't room in the jolly boat for a brawl, and none of them really wanted to be put over the side.

Then they had talked of ships and sailing. Coleman the Englishman, for all his experience on king's ships, had never set foot aboard a merchantman. And neither of the Cranstons—until most recently—had ever been involved with navies. Coleman had explained to them the fine points of life aboard a man-of-war, with emphasis on the ports of call and the proper spending of shore leave. They had explained to him the workings of trade harbors and commercial vessels, with emphasis on the delights to be found along Delaware waterfronts, provided a man knew where to look.

Then they had talked about women.

In all, it had been a pleasant evening until the cannons began firing.

The men didn't know what had happened, but there had been the thunder of guns across the bay. And they had lost one of their oars.

Hannibal turned full around, studying what the morning presented. Then he slouched on the little boat's bow seat and nudged Samuel Coleman with the toe of his boot. Coleman groaned and opened his bloodshot eyes.

"The schooner is gone," Hannibal told him.

Coleman lifted himself from the bilge and slowly scanned the view all around. Finally he nodded. "It's gone. Where did it go?"

"I don't know. I didn't see it."

"Well, where are we?"

"Aground," Hannibal said. "On this beach."

"Well, I can see that." Coleman sat up, sighed and rubbed his temples. "Oh, mercy. I've felt better than I do right now." He glanced around at John Cranston. "Is he dead?"

"I don't think so. He was snorin' a minute ago."

After a time they brought John around, and the three of them waded ashore. They hauled the jolly boat further up the beach, and looped its lanyard around a tree. Then they inventoried their possessions. Two rifles, a horn of powder, one oar, and a quart of so of rum.

"Didn' we have a lantern when we set out?" Coleman squinted.

John Cranston studied the boat from end to end. "Seems like we did. Wonder what became of it."

"I know we had three rifles," Hannibal said. "We had one each."

"I lost mine," Coleman admitted. "After we lost the other oar, I was usin' it for a paddle and it got away."

"What were we supposed to be doin' out there, anyway? What did Mister Kilreagh tell you?"

"He said for us to lay off in the jolly boat and patrol around the ship."

"Did we do that?"

"Best I can remember, we did."

John squinted across the water and pointed. "Look out there. Is that us?"

In the distance, almost at the west end of the bay, sails arose on high spars. Coleman shaded his eyes. "No. That's only got one mast. It looks like a cutter."

"Do you suppose it's friendly?"

"Probably not. I think it's a colonial."

"Colonial is friendly," Hannibal stated. "It's England we're at war with."

"Not me, you bloody Whig," Coleman rasped. "I *am* English."

"Well, so are we . . . I guess. Delaware's a crown colony."

"But Delaware is revolting."

"I think Mister Neely was right," John decided. "I think we're all a bunch of fugitives."

Across the bay the little ship was moving, but not toward them. It was heading out into the Sound. Coleman picked up the keg and shook it, listening to its contents. "Probably make more sense if I felt better," he said.

"There was a town over here someplace," Hannibal recalled. "The place where they lit the bonfire. Let's go there and see where we are."

"Bunch of Whigs, most likely," Coleman tipped the keg and tasted the rum.

"Probably Tories, the way they acted," Hannibal said. "Let's have a share of that rum, if you don't mind."

Eventually they found the village of Northport, and traded the remainder of their rum for a meal at the tiny inn on the waterfront. They saw few people about. The fishing boats were away, and in the fields above the little town, the harvest was in full swing. Those people they did see, though, glanced at them furtively and stayed apart from them. Coleman blamed this on the rifles the Cranstons carried. The Cranstons blamed Coleman's tarred-canvas hat and his pigtail. "You look like a sailor," Hannibal pointed out to him.

"I *am* a sailor!" he snapped "An' what's wrong wi' that, then?"

"You look like an English sailor," Hannibal clarified. "Maybe there's been trouble with sailors up here."

"An' of course th' two of you would pass unnoticed in these parts. With yer Delaware boots an' Pennsylvania rifles, I suppose you look right in place hereabouts."

"Maybe it's because your mates volleyed the town last night," John suggested. "Maybe they think we're from that same ship."

221

"Well, we *are* from that same ship, but we haven't told anybody that, have we?"

They walked along the quay below the town, looking out past the little harbor toward the open Sound. The only vessels in harbor were an aged ketch under repair and a produce scow. They saw no sign of troops or patrols, no sign of fighting ships.

"I don't think they'll come back for us," John Cranston said after a while. "There are people after them, you know."

"Aye, and after us too, if they knew who we were."

"I guess when we mined those ships down there with Greek fire, that must have upset everybody."

"Sinking gunboats probably didn't help, either. I don't know," John squatted atop a pier beam and gazed at the distant waters of the sound. "I guess we should try to get back to Delaware. Miss Constance has her ship now, so we've done what we came for."

"Be best for me," Coleman said, "If I could get passage to Newport or someplace. I could find a ship an' sign on. Maybe nobody'd know about any of that, was I on some ship."

"We'd best not go back the way we came," Hannibal decided. "Somebody back yonder might have seen us. We might cross the island, though . . . maybe find a trader that's goin' south. . . ."

Out in the sound a sail had appeared, a coastal packet coming around to enter the harbor. The Cranstons watched it gloomily while Coleman looked at the village on the rise with the bay beyond.

"I sort of miss the *Faith*," Hannibal said. "Even if most of them aboard was Englishmen . . ."

"Down," Coleman rasped.

"What?"

"I said, down!" he whispered hoarsely. With a long stride he grabbed them by one arm each, spun them around and dragged them off the pier head, down the slippery bank beyond. They huddled then beneath the pier, raising their heads slowly to look over its top.

"Yonder," Coleman said. "Up there in the fields. See?"

In the nearest cornfield, harvesters were scurrying away as a line of red-coated figures marched toward the town, led by a captain of marines on horseback. Sunlight glinted on muskets and bayonets.

"There's what those people's bonfire brought them," Coleman hissed.

"Are they looking for us?" John Cranston's eyes widened.

"Do you see anybody else around here that's done recent mayhem on His Majesty's fleet?"

XV

Throughout that brisk day *Courtesan* stood blockade off Montauk, securing the mouth of Long Island Sound, roving the lanes with lookouts in all the peaks. With mid-afternoon, a freshet sprang up, rolling back the fog moles and the overcast, putting caps on wavelets where the tide coursed over the banks and shoals. Visibility broadened and the sea was empty.

"He has escaped us, Sir," Jack Liles remarked to his captain, then recoiled under the furious glare that fell on him.

"He is hiding, Mister Liles. He has found a hole and crawled in, but I doubt he can remain where he is for long. He must make his run, and I'll be waiting. Put fresh lookouts into the tops."

"Captain wants his play-toy, he does," was whispered in the midships.

"Captain wants revenge, matey. He's never been snooked ere now, an' it's got him riled."

Three bells into dog watch the mizzentop called, "On deck! Masts off port beam, hard down!"

Hart read the wind. "Aye, he's a slick one. Come out where his rig has advantage, will he? Down sail, Mister Liles, then run up fore-and-aft cloth on all masts. Trim to tack close-hauled on the port."

Heavy, ponderous, and underpowered on her small laterals, the big ship came about and began to move, quartering into the wind.

"Fore batteries, load chain and cannister!"

Four bells sounded, then five. Minutes later the foremast lookout called, "On deck! I make it two craft, Sir, both single masts. One's luffing, Sir. She's crippled."

Hart swore under his breath, but held his course. Nearing six bells, and they had closed to a mile. Fore lookout identified. The lead vessel was a cutter, the second a crippled sloop. Hart's eyes went hard. A cutter. A hound for the chase. He could use a cutter.

The wind freshened and veered. *Courtesan* put on more speed and closed. The sloop ran up her colors: Royal Navy. On the cutter, a prize flag rose on its halyard. Men waved cheerfully from both decks. Jonathan Hart stood scowling on his quarterdeck as they closed.

"Put a shot across that cutter's bow, Mister Liles."

"Sir, that's a prize vessel and its attendant."

"You heard my order, Mister Liles."

"Aye, Sir."

As *Courtesan* closed, a chaser thundered and its ball sang across the cutter's nose. There was frenzy aboard both small ships as sails came down and they sat dead in the water. A launch cast off from the sloop and skittered toward the frigate, now standing abeam a hundred yards from the two little vessels, guns poking from their ports. When the launch drew near, Captain Hart strode to the starboard rail.

"Stand off, there! Who are you?"

A ruddy young man stood in the bow of the launch, agitation plain both on his face and in his movements. "Lewis Farrington, Sir, commanding His Majesty's sloop *Wolf*," he gestured back toward the sloop and almost lost his balance. "The cutter is a privateer, and it's in my custody. We're bound for the naval yards, Sir."

Hart stood a moment in bleak silence, his eyes riveted on the sleek cutter. A fine hound for a hunter, he thought. Then he cupped his hands again. "I'll take your prize off your hands, then, Commander. Remove your crew from her and I'll put mine aboard."

"I can't do that, Sir." The young commander's voice was strained and determined. "She's my prize. I will take her in."

"I have need of the vessel, Commander! Remove your crew and go about your business."

"Respectfully, Sir, I refuse."

Hart turned. "Mister Liles, fore batteries to bear on that sloop. At my command, sweep her deck with chain and hole her at the water line."

Lile's face was ashen. "Captain, that's a Crown vessel, Sir. What you're doing is . . . is . . ."

The hard eyes bored into him. "Don't say it, Mister Liles. I am in command here. You heard my order."

"Aye, Sir."

On the launch Farrington's face blanched as he heard the order, and he watched in shock as the big ship's guns were run out, almost overhead. He shouted, waved his arms, and was ignored.

Hart pulled his hat down tightly on his head. "Open fire."

In the hell of smoke and thunder that followed, Farrington dived into the sump of the launch and his oarsmen heaved to bring the boat around. They heard the banshee wail of chain, heard the crashing and screaming from their ship, heard the thump of collapsed hull. Smoke roiled on the water, swirling in the breeze, hanging in the frigate's lee.

The launch raced toward the wounded *Wolf*. Hart pointed. "Guns four and five amidships, put a ball in that launch."

Eight-pounders erupted. A gout of spume rose alongside the small boat, shunting it aside. Men dived overboard. Then the second ball tore through gunwale and keel and the boat exploded into kindling.

From the deck of the captured *Triumph*, William Moweth watched in horror, then whirled on his captive. "Captain Purdue, let's get these sails up!" Purdue and his colonials already had the sheets in hand. Moweth and his three Britons joined them.

"That's a madman over there," Shelby Jones breathed, cleating a line. Sails flew up the cutter's mast and Purdue and Moweth raced for the tiller. Agile and quick, the little ship took wind and came alive. Purdue held the tiller, his teeth clenched. Moweth stood at the after rail, his fists clenched beside him. "Move, ye scutter, move!"

Water rippled at *Triumph's* bow and became a keening along her hull. Her rudder bit water and the broad sails tautened. Painfully, seeing and dreading the lapse of water-smoke, they began to pull away . . . slowly, too slowly. Behind them lay the wrecked and shrouded *Wolf,* and there was screaming aboard her. James Mudd pointed. "They've seen us, Mister Moweth!"

The frigate bulked huge in the searing smoke, coming about, bringing guns to bear. Purdue cursed and Moweth prayed as *Triumph* leapt into bright water. A cannon spoke and cannister shot whined above. The smooth swell beyond them broke into tattered spray. Another roar and chain howled into their wake, then the cutter had spray in her teeth and was rising, running, singing.

"Aboard *Courtesan* Jonathan Hart howled in livid rage, hastened forward, and grabbed his senior lieutenant by the collar of his coat. His hand smashed into the man's cheek, withdrew, and smashed again. Jack Liles, released, tottered backward and slumped against a fife rail, blood at his lips. Seamen around them stared in horror.

Hart clenched his jaws, bringing his rage under control. "Report, Mister Liles!"

Through battered lips, Liles said, "We missed her, Sir." He stood shaken, eyes downcast, dripping blood. But in his words Hart heard a strange tone. It might have been satisfaction.

He looked out at the diminishing cutter, then up at his own masts through a haze of fury. The orders he started to give died in his throat. With a fresh wind and open water, the great ship could not catch a dashing cutter. Along the frigate's starboard rail, seamen gathered to gape at the sinking wreckage of the little sloop drifting away off the beam, the bobbing bits of a shattered launch now flotsam on the swells. A bit of color fluttered at tilting masthead out there, the ensign of the Royal Navy. Her decks were awash and there was no movement aboard. Clyde Serrey, bosun's mate, stood ashen and shaking. "That was a King's ship. It was a King's ship."

Passing him, Jonathan Hart overheard and laid hand on the man's shoulder to swing him around. "I saw no King's ship!" he bellowed. He looked around at staring faces and straightened his shoulders.

"We have engaged a privateer under false colors. You'll all bear witness to that!" Towering in his anger he turned slowly, staring them all down. "This day we have destroyed a hostile in Crown waters. It will be so entered in the logs, and no man will say otherwise." He nodded and stalked away.

"Mister Liles," he called, cool now. "All hands to make sail, if you please, due northeast the course. We have a prize to recapture."

By the time he reached his quarterdeck, the prizemaster's rage had dissipated. He felt no regret at the destruction of *Wolf*. He was content that the sloop had indeed been a hostile under false colors. But he regretted the loss of the cutter. He would find the schooner *Faith*, no doubt of that. But finding it and taking it essentially undamaged were two different things. The fox was more agile than the hunter. Still, if the hunter had a hound . . .

Jonathan Hart regretted losing the cutter. And regretting it, he turned his thoughts to where he might find another fast vessel to serve him as a hound.

Carrying two rifles and a stolen oar, two Delaware rebels and a beached tar made their way through seeping ditches and foul tidal sumps until they were well past the village of Northport. As they rounded the crest of the rise beyond which was forest, John Cranston glanced back at the little town . . . then ducked into shelter. There were redcoats in the streets, searching.

"Come on, then!" Samuel Coleman hissed. "Look alive, now. They'll be comin' to have a look at the bay, you know."

Ducking and running, they skirted the ways of the bay fishers and the little beach that backed the village. Once they were in the forest, Hannibal Cranston led the way. They had learned early on that Coleman had no skill at navigation on dry land. They had spent the better part of an hour lost in this very strip of woods earlier in the day.

"If somebody has found the jolly boat, what then?" John muttered.

"In that case, we have a long walk ahead of us," Hannibal said.

But the little boat was where they had left it, still tied to its tree and floating high now with a risen tide. Coleman loosed the halyard and they waded out and climbed aboard. The oar they had stolen was a trawler sweep, longer and wider of blade than the jolly boat's remaining oar. But it was the best they could do.

For a time they rowed along the shore, south and west away from the village, until the bay's opening was clearly in sight just a few miles away, northwest. Then they headed straight out onto broad waters. By the time Samuel Coleman had learned the art of rowing with mismatched oars, he was about used up. John Cranston spelled him, and the little boat zigged and zagged helplessly for several minutes before he got the hang of it.

At the sternpost Hannibal squinted into the distance, watching the east shore. There was movement there now, people coming down to the bay. Among them were bits of red, the coats of marines, and he glimpsed the captain tall upon his horse.

"Get this thing to moving, Johnny," he said. "They've seen us now for certain."

Slowly, grudgingly, the jolly boat crept toward the distant inlet with its flanking spit of forested ridge.

"Volleying that town was a mistake," Coleman said to no one in particular. "Still, they *were* putting out to come and look at *Faith*, 'an the captain wouldn't have wanted them around."

"I wish we had that launch now instead of this bedamned jolly boat," Hannibal muttered.

"All I wish," John panted, "is that we had a proper pair of oars. Why didn't you take two while you were about it?"

Hannibal shrugged. "I thought we only needed one."

They were in mid-bay when Hannibal tensed and pointed. "They're coming after us."

Distantly on the east bayshore, they saw a boat being put into the water, redcoats clambering aboard. A scrap of sail rose on a stubby mast, lateen-rigged, and took the breeze. Seaward from the beach, other men were quickstepping toward the end of the spit, with the mounted marine leading them. And above the beach, three or four redcoats led a band of motley farmers, heading around the other direction.

"Tories," Hannibal growled. "I told you those was Tories."

When John's breath was a rhythmic, exhausted panting, Coleman had an idea. "You take one oar," he told Hannibal, "And I'll take t'other. Then let's both pay each other no mind whatsoever, but just both push as hard as we can as fast as we can as long as the boat keeps its heading."

Hannibal agreed and drew the short oar. "You push hard," he said. "I'll push fast."

It seemed to work. The little boat picked up way and sliced ahead erratically. Slowly the cut drew nearer, as did the lateen sail behind them and the horseman on the spit to their right. He was spurring his mount, urging it on, outdistancing the foot troops behind him.

John looked to the load of his rifle and freshened the charge in its frizzen pan. "If he gets to that point before we do, I'll have to shoot him, I guess."

"Shame we can't just spike his cannon," Coleman growled. "That's the civil thing to do, ye know."

"In the meantime, Johnny," Hannibal suggested, "You might stoke up that other rifle and see if you can't discourage those folks back there in that sailboat. They're comin' on."

The lateen rig, its hull crowded with burly marines

from gunwale to gunwale, bayonets glinting like spines on a hedgehog, was three hundred yards back—still well beyond musket range. John reprimed the second rifle, then edged down until he could rest its long muzzle on the sternpost for sighting. He held on the following boat, hesitating as the jolly boat dipped into a trough and rose again on a foot-high swell, then aligned his sight on the mast of the lateen, just where it showed between red-coated shoulders, and touched his trigger. The rifle barked and smoked, and he saw a gout of white water at the boat's prow, just at the waterline. A marine on the forward brace lurched backward into his comrades and went down, and an instant later a bloody boot was thrust over the railing. The lateen trawler slewed off at an angle.

"That's one way to discourage people," Hannibal allowed. "Shoot 'em in the foot."

"It's this damned reground cannon powder," John apologized. "It shoots low." He set to reloading. "I put a double charge in the other rifle. I'll do this one the same."

Before he could set his ball, Hannibal interrupted with an oath. John glanced around. They were approaching the narrow cut, but so was the mounted marine officer. He was near enough for them to see his face, and charging down on the end of the spit. He was shouting, waving his sword. Hannibal and Coleman redoubled their strokes and John picked up the charged rifle. Then he put it down again.

"Shoot him, Johnny," Hannibal swore. "Before he shoots us."

"With what?" John grinned. Fifty yards away the

horse skidded to a halt hock-deep in tidewater, and the officer gaped at them . . . then at the useless sword in his hand. John Cranston grinned at him and waved as the jolly boat skimmed past, heading into the Sound.

Hannibal gawked at the redcoat. "Bedamned," he muttered. "What was he chargin' down like that for if he didn't have a gun?"

Coleman shrugged. "Habit of command. Seen it many's the time. Man gets so used to takin' the lead and still havin' others do his shootin' for him that if it don't come out even, then just nothin' happens."

On the spit the mounted officer stared at them and returned John's wave halfheartedly. His face was nearly as red as his coat.

"Let's come about to starboard an' get some shoulders into this business," Coleman suggested.

Hannibal glanced at him. "Where we going?"

"Back to Northport. If we can get there ahead of all these people, I'm a mind to hail that mail packet that put in a bit ago. I don't care if it does go all the way to Boston, I'm a sailor, not a rower, and I'm a mind to fetch us a ride."

XVI

In late afternoon Seth Underhill lay flat on his belly in the ragged sedge that topped a battered cliff overlooking the strait off Montauk. His brush-whipped old fowler lay at one side of him and Uncle Joe at the other, his tongue lolling out of a long mouth and his tail brushing lazily in the salt grass. A brace of fresh teal, strap-tied, lay where Seth had dropped them. He had come a long way from home this day. The weather had been bad for hunting until well after noon.

At the moment teal, fowler, purpose, and Uncle Joe were forgotten as Seth squinted through his little brass-bound telescope, peering out over the waters of the Sound. Thunder rolled back from the bright distance. White smoke squatted on the far water where ship masts stood. Even in the light of day he could see the orange eruptions of cannon fire. Agape, he watched the only naval battle he had ever seen. There were a big ship, towering and dark, and two little ones. Beyond that, he could tell little of what was happening. He wished Pa were here. Pa would know and could tell him.

Again there was fire in the smoke, and he saw sailcloth rise on the single mast standing seaward of the rest. It began to move, outward and away. As he watched, there was more fire, more smoke billowed from the big ship, and when the long delayed thunder reached him across the water, its hollow roar was blended with a faint, eerie squeal that made him shiver. The littlest ship was moving now, breaking away from the conflict, and he trained his glass on it. At this distance, with a little glass, he could barely make out its low deck, but he saw sunlight strike its sails as they filled and he saw it rise on a swell as it cleared the drifting smoke and took the wind. Straight out it headed, into the open sea, coursing fast across the wind.

His open eye tearing, he strained to see detail as the ship bore away, edging to the right to get better wind in its sails. It might have been a ship he had seen before, farther down the Sound, but he couldn't be sure. Compared to the hulking warship standing out there it was hardly more than a sailboat. For long moments he watched. The little ship continued to veer right, out toward Plum Island, distant now, scarcely more than a sliver of sail away and beyond the banks. As westering sun found its full sails, they shone golden.

He brought the glass back to the north. The smoke had rolled away, and he saw the big ship making sail, going about, beginning to move away. That left one, and he studied it. It drifted still in the water . . . its mast partly down, hanging by its shrouds. It looked dead—a shot duck in a marsh pond, its feathers all askew.

The big ship was tail-on and heading away. With sudden resolution Seth stood, pocketed the glass, picked up fowler and birds. "Come on, Uncle Joe."

Pa might tan his tail for him, he thought as he waded into the little brushy cove to haul out his skiff, but he could see the swell was smooth, the waves slight; and there was still a good bit of afternoon remaining. No telling what might be floating out there that could be salvaged.

There might be dead men, too. Floating dead men. He stopped. No, dead men would sink away. He hauled on the painter, cleared the skiff, and scrambled into it. Uncle Joe leapt and paddled to the boat and hauled himself aboard. Seth set oars and willed himself not to speculate on what might be out there. He would just go see. It wouldn't be the first time Seth Underhill had ventured beyond the shore, but of course Pa didn't know that. Probably. With sturdy young shoulders hauling them, the oars drank deep and the skiff plowed water, out of the cove, through the light, bucking surf, and into the swells of the Atlantic's mouth. Uncle Joe curled up by Seth's feet and dozed.

Lewis Farrington clung to a shard of timber and coughed salt water. He didn't know how long he had been under, but when he broke surface, the timber was there and he hid for a time in its screen, getting his senses back. Now he dared a glance over its shattered top. The frigate was bearing away. He eased down again until only his face was above water and coughed some more. After a time he began kicking his feet, paddling with his free hand, raising himself a bit to look around him. A sickness came over him. Across a swell littered with wreckage he saw his sloop. *Wolf* drifted, dead and shattered, her spars a shamble of broken wood, her deck awash. Coaxing the timber around in the water, he kicked out toward the little ship. H heard a sound off to his left and edged that way. A swell lofted him, and in the trough beyond he saw his cook, Roger Bradley, fighting a tangle of rope caught on a boat plank. He struggled toward him.

Bradley was near-drowned, clinging for his life as tangled line tried to pull him under. Farrington held the man's blue face above water and got him untangled, then helped him get both arms across the floating keel timber. Bradley tried to speak and went into a fit of choking. He coughed up water and struggled to breathe. Farrington righted the timber again and headed for what had been *Wolf*. At the near rail he clambered over, hoisted Bradley after him, and stood unsteady in ankle-deep water on the mid-deck. She was down by the stern, and he dragged Bradley forward to lay him on dry planking in the bow. Then he looked around. Three men had been aboard the *Wolf*, after he and Bradley and Sykes had put off in the launch. Moweth, Williams, Toke, and Mudd were on the taken cutter.

Back in the sunken stern a body, face-down, washed lazily between the rails. He waded down to it, slipping and stumbling. It was Tommy Moss. He felt shock beginning to set in, and held it at bay.

There was no time. The wash crept forward on the deck. He went to the forward hold and raised the hatch. Black water stood a foot below the coaming's bottom edge. Nothing was visible down there. He couldn't reach the cabin and galley. They were under the stern. He went back to Bradley, who now was up on hands and knees, heaving.

Courtesan was a tall, diminishing shadow on the northwest horizon. There was no sign of *Triumph*. To the south lay the low shoreline of the point, two miles away. Farrington looked away, then looked back. In the middle distance was a small boat. He shouted and waved his arms.

When *Faith* cleared the fog, Dalton gave the helm to Charley Duncan and went up into the shrouds with his glass. A pair of hours on beam reach had brought the schooner well up into the Sound's mouth, out of sight of Orient Point and within view of Fisher's Island. But there they had lost the wind and sat rocking in the swells for an hour more before a freshet rolled back the fog and cleared the day's waning hours.

First he took a full view around and saw no sail. Then he laid glass on the storm-hewn island off his starboard quarter and studied it. There were fishing craft working the banks in the distance, but no ships nearby. Far beyond, on the edge of the world, he thought he saw sails. But it could have been just sun-fairies on the horizon.

Due north, within hazy view, was the Connecticut coast. Downcoast New London sprawled around its harbor, and he felt a desire to head there and put in to rest. But no, that would be a trap for a fugitive. New London was a rebel base and the King's fleet watched it closely. The *Faith*, neither colonial nor royal—neither fish nor fowl—would be open game in New London. Better to find neutral ground, however unreliable, for a quick stop, and then be gone. Newport, at the breaks of Narragansett Bay, was held. But between, opposite Fisher's Island, was Little Bay. The Rhode Islanders had not jet joined their neighboring colonies in declaring for independence. They had fought early, then petitioned the Crown directly, and had achieved for the moment what the seaboard colonies were fighting for. Rhode Island, until such time as the King had pause to reconsider, was an independent freehold. Lawless, unreliable, and dangerous, it yet was the nearest thing to a neutral port where a man's colors didn't matter as much as his money.

Northeast would be the night's course, to Fisher's Island, avoiding the trade lanes off Block Island. With a fair wind he could raise Little Bay and the settlement of Westerly by tomorrow's afternoon watch. He put away his glass and clung for a while to the ratlines.

In the companionway Clarence Kilreagh stooped from the galley, reached to hoist himself through the deck hatch, and changed his mind. Swinging around the ladder he rapped on a bulkhead. "Miss Constance? Be ye awake?"

The curtain parted and she peered at him, then backed away. "Come in, Mister Kilreagh."

"Thank you, Miss. I thought if ye have the time, we might talk a bit."

"Delighted." She sat herself on the bunk. "What shall we talk about?"

Kilreagh had never been one for small talk. He pursed his lips, squinted at her as though a change of light might unravel mysteries before his eyes, and asked, "Be ye witchin' the Captain, Missy?"

She tilted a pert head, not sure she had heard right.

"It does seem to me," he said, "that yourself an' the Captain had begun to get on flamin'ly, up to just now, and of a sudden there's a coldness between ye. Why is that?"

"Mister Kilreagh, I don't know what you're talking about."

"Oh, come, Miss. When the talk is of men and women, women always know what it's about. And since I am old enough to know that, I'm old enough to talk straight wi' a lass who's equipped to do considerable mischief should she set her mind to it. No, just you set an' listen a bit . . . there's a good lass."

He hitched his good leg over his stumped knee and crossed his arms. In the tiny space, their faces were barely three feet apart.

"I mind when I was a young rooster, Miss, an' I'd hit port wi' my jib a'pokin' an' my blood asurge. There was two things I was bound to have. A tot an' a totsie, in no particular order. The one was to trim my sails proper, t'other for a port to ship my cargo. An' I did have me a weather eye for a fair port, I did. Many's th' proud prow an' nimble stern I'd overhaul, shadow alee an' have at wi' me high primed fairin' piece. Not to cause ye discomfort, Missy . . . I'm not, am I?"

She shook her head, wide-eyed. "I don't believe so."

"Good, because I'd not want to. All that's just to say I do know how it is to be a young man, ye see."

"I see."

"Now Captain Dalton, though of a far finer trim that this rough ol' hulk ever was, he's yet a full man through an' through, an' he carries more fotherin' on his keel than a man his age should have to. Three times in his life to my certain knowledge he's had his hull holed by those he trusted an' had to hoist an' fly. Once, as a wee lad in Belfast, 'twas a faithless cousin set the press gangs on him. Th' latest time was his own King's court, wi' their devilish warrant for treason . . . an' him th' one than whom there's been no loyaler. It's hulled him to the bilges, Missy, to have to flee from his own flag.

"But th' middle time, scant few years ago, was th' worst hurt of all. She was a lass named Molly. Molly Fitzgerald, it was. She batted her fine eyes at him, twitched her rudder jus' so an' lured him to a lee shore, then had her father—th' damned ol' fool—put the Carls on him an' bid him gone. He's never right got over that. But here's th' point of it, Missy. Ye be, in some ways, th' spittin' image o' that lass Molly, ner even better I'd say, an' ye have the power to tear out the poor lad's heart if that be yer way."

Her chin came up. "Fine chance of that, Mister Kilreagh, when your captain won't even exchange the time of day with a person unless he's besotted with rum."

"I told ye, th' Captain's hull's been holed by those he cared for. Do ye think he's anxious to take such a batterin' again?"

"Mister Kilreagh, I do believe you have the soul of a matchmaker. But you're in the wrong waters this time. Mister Dalton is aboard this vessel for his own reasons, and I for mine. There certainly is nothing between us, Sir, nor likely to be."

"Missy, this old tar has been at sea too much not to know a true current when he sees one. An' I'm askin' ye . . . should Patrick ship alongside an' offer ye his helm, either accept it or don't but don't chart one course an' then sail off on another. He has been betrayed too much already."

Her eyes flashed. "You are presumptuous, Mister Kilreagh. And your concerns are wasted. Your good captain is no more likely to look twice at me than at a turnip. If he is smitten with any 'proud prow and nimble stern,' they're those the builders put into this schooner. He has eyes for absolutely nothing else."

"Ah."

"Ah, what?"

"Ah. As I said, Miss, I'm old enough to have a knowin' of the fair gender an' its ways. An' at my age it is a mixed blessin'. But yes, I see. It's *Faith* herself, is it? Aye, I knew it was somethin'."

"That is absurd. Everything you've said is absurd."

"There was a Frenchman had a fine galley an' a fine house an' a fine comely wife, an' when he was gone each summer on his tradin', she'd wring her hands an' go gaunt an' swear she hated him for bein' gone so much, but when he'd ask her to go wi' him,

245

she'd refuse. It was because she hated his ship. She saw him lovin' it better than her. She never understood, the poor thing, that he loved it as a ship an' her as a woman, an' in his mind there were no conflict there atall."

"Very philosophical. What became of them?"

"Nothin' much. Moors caught him, cut off his extrany an' threw him to the fishes, an' took his galley."

"And I suppose she longed for him throughout her poor life and wished he would come sailing home in his galley?"

"Aye, now," he marveled. "An' wouldn't that ha' made a fine tale? But, matter of fact, she had already gone to whorin' some time since and paid no mind atall. But that was them. We're talkin' about yerself an' Captain Dalton, Miss."

Distantly, down through the companionway, came the lookout's call, "On deck!" Kilreagh hoisted himself to foot and peg, ducked under the lintel, and turned back.

"I'd best see what's amiss, lass. But I'm pleased we understand each other."

Heaving himself to the deck, he saw Fisher's Island due ahead.

As evening drew down on the whispering sea, young Billy Caster drilled his rifle company on *Faith's* forward deck. The company was six men, all English, all fascinated by the rifles the colonials took so much for granted. Brevis Grimm and Martin Smith took handily to the long weapons. Cadman

Wise, Purdy Fisk, and Ishmael Bean were methodical and reliable. The errant Victory Locke dearly wanted to be a rifleman.

Purdy Fisk chipped a floating twig at a hundred yards. Four others volleyed it and Victory Locke volleyed the jib topsail. Billy swung on him. "I expect, Mister Locke, that if you set our sails afire, the captain will have you keelhauled."

A mixed chorus of British and Delaware watchers hooted and cheered until Charley Duncan dispersed them. "Leave 'em be," he ordered. "Captain wants them drilled to stand guard when we make port. There may be pirates about."

Jubal Foster bowed his head. "Heaven help the pirates."

Billy stowed the rifles, finished inventory, and went below to light a galley lamp and enter the day's events in his running log:

September fourth, 1777. Fog in morning, wind north and turning. Banks and troughs. E/NE gen. Captain recovered from fall. Ship's discipline called. Captain discussed politics. False hold found, full Jamaican spirits, logged in manifest. Cook report two days provisions. Encountered hostile cutter. Encountered hostile frigate. Entered fog. Rifle drill, Mister Locke must repair sail. Wind at evening west. Bearing E/NE. Island sighted.

Later he would rewrite the notes "in fine" into the ship's log. Captain Dalton preferred such things neat and precise. He did not care for laxity aboard his ship.

After supper Constance Ramsey came on deck and leaned for a time at the rail. When Dalton came aft to relieve Cadman Wise at the tiller, she watched him covertly for a time before he turned and caught her eye.

"Good evening, Mister Dalton," she said casually.

"Good evening, Miss Constance. I have been wanting to discuss something with you."

"Yes?"

"It . . ." he hesitated. "It's a bit personal, I'm afraid."

She waited.

"Miss Constance, do you have any money?"

"A very little. Why?"

"Well, I have had Mister Caster tally a list of provisions we will need. I am estimating only, of course, but our needs will come to something on the order of two hundred fifty pounds sterling at the only port we might safely enter. My own assets fall a bit short of that amount, as do Mister Kilreagh's. And no one else aboard has any money to speak of."

"How much do you have?"

"Between us, about thirty pounds . . . maybe a bit more. Most of that is Mister Kilreagh's."

"But I have only a few pounds, Mister Dalton. I spent most of what I had on the launch and provisions. It was very costly."

"Ah-hum. That leaves us quite short. I suppose we may have to trade cargo."

She gazed at him levelly. "Why not just steal what we need?"

His brow furrowed. Such a straightforward suggestion from such a pretty face was startling. "First, I suppose, because despite appearances, I an not a thief. And secondly, even if I were, the place we are going—Little Bay—is blessed with much more competent and better-armed thieves than any of us could hope to be. We will be fortunate to get away from there with our skins, Miss Constance, even if we do not attempt any crimes."

"I wouldn't want to part with my father's legitimate cargo."

"Nor would I. The lot of it wouldn't bring enough to provision us for a week. I had in mind the illegitimate cargo. The rum."

"That is quite valuable, isn't it?"

"It is liquid gold, Miss. On the market, possibly three thousand pounds. Something less at a pirate port, of course, but near."

"Mister Dalton, why should I agree to finance your provisions?"

"You have said it is your ship."

"You have not admitted it."

"I have not denied it is your cargo."

"I suppose selling the stuff would be the best way to get rid of it."

"The best by far."

"Then if you can find a buyer, Mister Dalton, I will talk with him."

XVII

Jonathan Hart stood at his quarterdeck rail and looked down at the grappled deck of the little coastal packet snugged alongside *Courtesan*. Its crew and passengers, six men in all, had been brought aboard *Courtesan* and Mister Liles was boarding the boat with a prize crew.

Caper was no cutter, but she would do for what Hart had in mind. She was fast and cutter-rigged and had some small armament—enough to play the hound to *Courtesan's* hunter when the schooner was found.

"You will stand off Fisher's Island," he told Liles. "You will remain in close sight of my signals. The fox must pass. If he turns south, you will follow as best you can while I close on him. Should he try to break upwind of me, you will push him back within my range. Herd him, Mister Liles. Keep him for me. I want him downwind when I catch him."

He gazed out over the open water of the mouth of the Sound, then back down at the little packet. In a way, *Caper* might be better than a cutter. She could keep the fox busy as long as need be. And he wasn't sure he would trust Jack Liles with a full cutter. The man was becoming increasingly sullen of late.

Amidships the six taken men had been read off. A bosun's mate brought Hart the report. He read it casually. Three of them, the packet's crew, were small-boaters out of Massachusetts. Two of the passengers were Delaware men with some experience as ordinary seamen. Brothers, it seemed. Hannibal and John Cranston. The other was a pigtailed sailor, an able seaman named Samuel Coleman. He had crewed warships. He handed back the report.

"Read them their articles of war," he said. "Put this Coleman in the foretop crew. The brothers Cranston can handle sheets amidships. The other three can serve as holystoners."

"They've been read their articles, Sir," the bosun's mate said. "But this one—this Hannibal Cranston—he put his hands over his ears. He said he'll not serve aboard a King's ship."

"So." Hart scowled and fingered his chin. "Then it is time for an example, Mister Mace, and no time like the present. Lash this Cranston to a grate and flog him. Twenty strokes of the lash will do. Hands on deck to witness punishment and make sure that his mates are in the front rank. Carry on."

Hart turned back to the rail. Liles and his prize crew were aboard *Caper*, casting off. Hart watched critically as the five men fumbled with the little vessel's unfamiliar rigging, raising jibsails and spanker. The boat reacted quickly, scooting off across the swells like a cork on the water. Hart watched until

Caper came about at a chain's distance, then turned to watch the flogging of Hannibal Cranston.

A half-hour later, as *Courtesan* stood for Cape Cod with *Caper* dancing along behind, Hannibal Cranston lay half-conscious on a table in the orlop deck, groaning as a surgeon treated his back with vinegar and brine. John Cranston and Samuel Coleman crouched in the reeking dimness of an open sail hold and watched between beams. They had crept here to see if Hannibal was still alive after the beating he had taken.

"They didn't have to give him twenty," John Cranston whispered, tears on his cheeks. "He didn't do anything to deserve that."

"Hush, Johnny," Coleman silenced him. "This is a warship, lad. And the captain must be a hard man. But your brother will live. You can see he's comin' around."

"But they didn't have to do that. Captain Dalton wouldn't have done that."

"No." Coleman mused on it, and a fire caught in his eyes. "No, Captain Dalton's a fair man, Johnny. He saved our lives, you know. Both of us . . . all of us. My mates an' me, in the stockade, we'd have gone either to deck crews on ships of the line, or to prison hulks. An' you an' your mates, you'd ha' been caught an' hanged had we not had a captain the likes of him to spirit us away."

In the lamplit galleyway on orlop deck, Hannibal Cranston stirred and groaned loudly. In the dim crawlway behind the beams John Cranston sighed, easing the tension in his shoulders. "I guess he'll be all right."

" 'Course he will. He's a stout lad. Did you hear what ship this is, when they read us our articles?"

"No."

"She's the *Courtesan*. The very same."

Johnny looked at him blankly.

"The *Courtesan*, lad. Jonathan Hart's frigate. The prizemaster. The one Mister Kilreagh said we took the *Faith* from."

"Oh."

"An' that's got me to thinkin', Johnny. Could be this ship is out lookin' for *Faith* this very minute."

"I hope not. I hope they get away."

"Aye. I hope so, too."

The Rhode Islanders had started and finished their war with the Crown almost before the other colonies began. As a consequence, the old Williams colony and its obstreperous offshoots around Narragansett Bay now held a fuzzy truce with the empire, providing the Royal Navy a base right in the midst of the Massachusetts and Connecticut fleets and providing the Rhode Islanders tentative freehold status that remained subject to the whims of the King.

Newport and the mouth of the bay were a British stronghold. The upper bay ports and settlements went about their business blithely ignoring the hostilities around them. And at the far southwest corner of the little freehold, separated by Indian lands and wilderness, was the Westerly settlement on Little Bay where slavers, freebooters, common pirates, privateers, Tory hellions and the rabble of the seas mingled with sharp-eyed landsmen who were there like and their equals.

Licensed merchantmen, ships of warrant, and commissioned fighting vessels alike stayed clear of the place.

Ramshackle docks, quays, moles, and guarded stores backed against cabins, cottages, and a few substantial houses along the little harbor.

Cannon-loaded and ready, Dalton brought *Faith* to midbay and dropped anchor. Billy Caster's rifles stood at the rails, all primed except Victory Locke, who was forbidden to prime until necessary.

A brig and a sloop lay above, heavily guarded and showing no colors. An odd, box-ended vessel lay sheer of sail in the top of the inlet, bristling with cannon and new timber. At the quay an armed snow rode its hawsers next to a merchant slaver.

Dalton took Duncan and four oarsmen and went ashore with the launch. "This place is a powderkeg," Duncan said. "Let one shot be fired and think of the powder set to be burned the next minute."

As the launch stood off to await them, they climbed to the shelf above the gravel beach. Dalton adjusted his sword belt and felt the reassuring weight of pistols in his coattail pockets. Duncan had buckled on a cutlass and shoved a pistol into his belt. Evening was chill on the low, rugged coast. A steady wind swept cold from the hills above and there were few people about. At the top of the rise a wizened man approached them, his eyes shrewd and careful. "Yon schooner on the bay, how is she called?"

Dalton answered easily, "She is mine, Sir. The

Gladys, out of Chesapeake. We come on peaceful trade."

"*Gladys*, aye. A comfortable name, without bounty attached to it. Be glad she isn't one called *Faith*, though her appearance does fit, Sirs."

"What of this *Faith?*"

"Oh, a famous vessel these days, Sirs. Seems as every tar an' man-jack be out to get her. The Georgies, they wants her sent to the fishes. The rest has a terrible curiosity to see into her holds, an' the prizemaster—one Cap'n Hart—he sets a right high bounty on her capture, he does."

"Aye, most uncommon," Dalton turned away, but the man scuttled in front of him and doffed his hat. "Ezra Cunnningham, Sirs, at yer service. I might be of use to you."

"And what is it you might do, Ezra Cunningham?"

"Ye be strangers to Westerly. Might be ye need one as knows his way around?" He grinned a wrinkled, crooked grin. "There's some as attends me an' finds me comments worth a bit."

Duncan growled, but Dalton stilled him. "A man who knows his way can be valuable, indeed, Sir. But whose colors might you fly?"

Cunningham's chin went up. "My own , Sir, and those of them as hires me. Never any other."

Dalton dug into his purse, found a silver, and handed it over. "A token, Mister Cunningham. We seek provisions, and have but a short time here. Can you show us a chandler one might trust?"

"Aye, a chandler. The best, o' course, is Henry Lee. Some trust him an' some don't, both wi' good enough cause. But he's a fair man when he has to be, I reckon." He squinted at Dalton's thin purse. "Be ye dealin' in cash or custom, Cap'n?"

"Custom, Sir, and right handsome custom for a man who'll deal me fair."

"Then we'll go to Henry Lee. But have an eye to yer dealin', sir. Remember, he's as fair as he has to be."

The chandler was a square, bulky man, potbellied and shrewd, and the store in the front of his big, guarded warehouse was well stocked. Hooded-eyed men lounged in the shadowed corners of the place. Henry Lee would not be troubled with brigands.

While Duncan wandered about the store and bins, under the careful eyes of Lee's men, Dalton outlined what he needed. Lee nodded placidly. "A fair amount of tack, Cap'n. It'll cost you a pretty penny."

"The Cap'n will deal in custom," Ezra Cunningham said.

"What sort of custom?"

Dalton pursed his lips. He wished he knew more about the man.

"Let's start with these items," he said, drawing a written manifest from his waistcoat.

Lee read it through and snorted. "It won't tally up, Cap'n. A pound a bale for shingles, three if they're good. Five a keg for the nails. I might make an offer for the beeswax and oil. You can keep the rooftrees."

Dalton nodded. The prices were shrewd, but they were fair. "Then how about rum, Mister Lee?"

Lee's eyes narrowed. "How much rum might you be talkin' about?"

"Maybe four hundred kegs, or a bit more. Best Jamaican. If a man had that, would it interest you?"

"It would interest me a good bit, Sir. *If* a man had it. I might go, say, six a keg for what could be had."

"Then there'd be none to be had. It's worth more than seven a keg."

"Of course it is," Lee agreed readily. "Just take it to Providence or New London, and you can get your seven . . . maybe even eight. But Cap'n, if you wanted to go to the regular ports, you would hardly have put in here."

"You have the money?"

"If you have the rum, I have the money."

"Then let's fix a price, Sir."

"I'll want to see the cargo before I call in the money for it, Cap'n. Why not put it ashore on my dock out there, then we can talk."

"I'll not do that, Sir. But if you'd care to send someone aboard my vessel to inspect . . . ?"

Lee thought about it. He moved away and huddled for a few minutes in conversation with one of his men. Dalton began to feel nervous. At sea he felt a match for any man. But ashore he was vulnerable, uncertain.

Lee returned. "I will go with you to see the cargo. I've just left my man there to mind the store."

As they went out Ezra Cunningham plucked at Dalton's sleeve. "Watch yerself, Cap'n."

Charley Duncan had disappeared. Dalton looked around, then decided the red-haired seaman could take care of himself. He called the launch in and he and Henry Lee boarded.

Canvas hung over the prow and fantail of *Faith*,

obscuring the escutcheons. *"Gladys,* you say?" Lee asked as they approached. "A mighty fair vessel, she is. Could carry any of a number of good names, I'd reckon."

Aboard, Dalton introduced Constance Ramsey, "the daughter of my consigner, Mister Lee. She'll approve any bargain."

"Of course," Lee bowed. "Mighty nice to meet you, Missy." His eyes on her were contemplative, appreciative.

Constance reacted with aloof directness. "Maybe we should discuss business, Mister Lee."

"Mister Kilreagh," Dalton called. "Have some of the lads bring up a few of those kegs, please. How many would you like to see, Mister Lee? We have four hundred and forty. Rather, we have four hundred and thirty-nine."

"Four hundred and thirty-seven," Constance corrected him, and he shrugged.

As the casks came up, Dalton looked around the ship, then got Kilreagh aside. "Where are Jubal Foster and Virgil Cowan? Where's Michael Romart?"

Clarence looked worried. "I don't know, Sir. Right after you left, Miss Constance sent them ashore in the skiff. She said she had your leave, Sir."

"My leave?" He strode back to where Constance and Lee were watching kegs come up. "Miss Constance, where are . . . ?"

"Not now, Mister Dalton." Her tone was commanding. "We will discuss the crew later. Right now, Mister Lee is checking cargo."

Lee picked up the eighth keg to arrive on deck and tapped out its bung. He sniffed it, tipped out a bit into a cup, and sampled it. Then he turned to the rail and raised his arms twice. Dalton's hackes rose. Out there was the armed snow he had seen at the dock, but now it was adrift on jibsails and jigger, standing off *Faith's* beam. Hand at his sword, Dalton grabbed the merchant's shoulder and swung him around. "What are you doing, Mister Lee?"

"These are trying times, Captain Dalton. One must do the best one can, and a man deals best from strength. Do you see that snow there? There is a man aboard with a glass, watching my signals. On a moment's notice, that vessel can move in and take your ship, Sir."

"You are a thief, then?"

Lee looked hurt. "Not a thief, Cap'n. I aim to pay for your goods, but only at my own price, you see."

"The snow would move at jeopardy to yourself?"

Lee shrugged. "Sadly, Sir, it would not be a useful force any other way."

Dalton knotted his fist, but Constance caught his arm. She looked up at Lee. "That certainly is a convincing argument, Mister Lee. But you should consider all aspects of it." She pointed. "Do you see that man there, by the mast?" Guy Neely stood at the main mast, holding a lanyard. "He has an ensign affixed to that rope. And I have men ashore who have already signaled to me. If that flag goes up, Mister Lee, your warehouse will burn down almost instantly. It seems to me, Mister Lee, we are in position to negotiate."

In the fading hours of daylight a line of boats plied between the schooner and Henry Lee's dock, carrying rum. The snow had returned to work dock.

When the last kegs were gone—except two which Constance insisted on keeping aboard— Dalton supervised the loading of boats with provisions. He needed fresh meat, salt meat and onions, salt and vinegar, tea, coffee, dried fruits, juice of lemons . . . the list was long. The last trips were made by lantern light. Lee stood about, fuming, and his toughs appeared worried. Far back in the main bins, Jubal Foster sat on a tar vat, casually swinging a lighted lantern in his hand. An open barrel of fuel oil stood before him, and several other barrels had been tipped over, their contents seeping and saturating through the warehouse.

When the transactions were complete, Dalton demanded the difference in coin, and Henry Lee came up with it. It was a vast amount of money.

"We are even now, Mister Lee. Neither of us has cheated the other."

Lee scowled at him. Dalton turned away, his helpers carrying the sacks of coin. Everything else had been loaded aboard. They strode from the store, all eyes on them, and down to the dock. Their launch was waiting, and they could see *Faith's* lights in the bay.

When they were gone, Henry Lee cursed and two of his guards turned toward the back of the warehouse, weapons in their hands. The lamp was still swinging. They hesitated.

"At least that one can't get far," Lee said. "As soon as he sets down that lantern, we'll be on him."

In the back of the main bins, just out of sight from the store except for its swinging light, a lantern hung suspended on a string from a rafter, waving in the wind from an open loading hatch.

Dalton climbed aboard *Faith*, ordered the launch cleated up to its stern davits, and supervised the transfer of the money to Constance Ramsey's cabin. He was eager to be away. They were no longer welcome in Little Bay. He became aware of something bumping against *Faith's* hull, and heard voices on deck. He hauled himself up through the hatch. There were men at the fore-rail, and as he neared he heard Charley Duncan's voice from overside.

"Douse that lantern, damn it! Now get an anchor line down here, quick. And another on starboard!"

Chain rattled as the lines dropped. Dalton peered over the rail into darkness, shouldering the others aside. "Mister Duncan? Is that you? What are you doing?"

"We have to hurry, Captain . . . there, I've got it secured. Sir, have the men get this line on the capstan and haul away about eight feet of line, then cleat off. And stand by for another line a'starboard, same thing . . . Sir. Please."

There was no time to argue. Dalton gave the orders. He felt *Faith* quiver as the lines came taut, one after another, and heard the cursing of men on the capstan hafts. "What'n hell is that?" one asked. "It weighs a ton."

As first one line and then another hauled up, they heard the *chunk* of something solid snugging against the chain chutes. Astern, the launch was hauled up, and a moment later the skiff came alongside. Excited colonials surged up onto the deck, hauling the boat after them.

"On deck!" It was the foretop.

"Aye, Mister Abernathy?"

"Deck, there's a furious lot of activity over by that warehouse, Sir, and that snow is castin' off from the dock."

"Hands to stations," Dalton called. "Hands to make sail!" He raced for the tiller. The wind was strong and crisp. When her wings went up, *Faith* would fly.

"Mister Kilreagh, douse bow lights! Is Mister Duncan aboard?"

"Aye, Sir. He just came on."

"Are all hands aboard?"

"They damn well better be, Sir, beggin' pardon, Sir, 'cause that snow is movin'."

"Make sail! Make sail!"

Grommets rattled and *Faith's* mast shook. Jibs first, and she swung her nose. "Up anchor! Look lively there!" There was a howl from the winches and a sullen rattle of heavy chain. *Faith* veered free. Spencer went up with its loose sheet lines and the schooner heeled and made way. Spanker followed, booming taut as the wind took it and four strakes of the port beam went into dark water. "Sheet home!" She steadied. "Topmast lookout, signal the channel, please!"

"Aye, Sir. In sight."

Dalton looked back. The snow was coming on. By the light of its bow lanterns he could see men at its foredeck. *Faith* plunged ahead into the choppy bay, feeling sulky and abrupt. She picked up speed, but the bow wake she threw stood out from the rails. She plowed the water, but did not climb it. Dalton swore.

What the devil had Charley Duncan hung on her nose?

"Douse all lights," Dalton called. "Mister Caster, where are your riflemen?"

"Coming up, Sir."

"Get them aft, please!"

They swarmed past him to the stern rail, priming their pieces as they came. There was a flash and a sharp crack. Billy Caster's adolescent voice rose in exasperation. "For Christ's sake, Mister Locke, will you shoot at them and not us!"

"See if you can keep those people away from the snow's bow chasers, Mister Caster."

"Aye, Sir. Mister Locke, reload! Misters Grimm and Mallory, hold on that ship's bow . . . ah, Captain Dalton, Sir?"

"Yes, Mister Caster?"

"It looks like that ship doesn't have any bow chasers, Sir. There are mounts there, an' a lot of people around them, but I don't see any guns."

Dalton shook his head. "Mister Duncan?"

From foreward, "Aye, Sir?"

"What size bow chasers would you say that snow had, Mister Duncan?"

"Long eights, Sir. A pair of 'em, real beauties they are. We'll need to clean 'em up when we hoist 'em aboard, Sir, but they're right nice guns."

He knew now why *Faith* was nosing the chop as she was. Two twenty-two-hundred-pound cannons dangled from her bows. "Fore stays'l up!" he called. "Jib tops'l! Rig a double sheet up there, Mister Kilreagh. Let's get her nose up, if you please."

"Aye, Sir."

A chain length behind them, the snow veered to port, bringing her forward starboard guns to bear on the roll. Rifles cracked and people howled across the water. Two cannons thundered, but they had missed their timing. The balls cut wavelets in *Faith's* wake and sank short of her fleeing tail.

"On deck! Channel aport!"

He eased the tiller over. *Faith's* bow answered heavily. Her spanker boomed.

"Hold true, Sir!"

The snow had run up courses and was sweeping out on *Faith's* stern quarter as the bay mouth came into in the moonlight view. She was gaining by weight of sail. A volley from foreguns thundered behind them and a ball ripped through the spanker sail right over Dalton's head as a second went wide.

Constance Ramsey scurried up through the hatch with a smoldering piece of slow fuse on a striker stick. "Shoot at *Faith*, will they?" Before Dalton could react, she was at the aft four-pounder, two men hauling its lines for her as she sighted. She crouched to peer along its notches, judged the roll, steeped back, and touched fuse to touch-hole. The gun erupted.

Off the stern quarter they heard a resounding crash. Clarence Kilreagh peered over the rail. "By the holy mother, Sir, she's cut the damn thing's jib right off. Blew it to smithereens, she did."

Dalton glanced back. The snow was suddenly no longer in pursuit. It was wandering off into the shallows, out of control, with too much way for its rudder to overcome. He looked ahead again. He could see the mouth of the bay and held for it. Broad, rounded triangles of sail stood high on the schooner's jib, taking the wind, bringing her nose up a point or two. Dark waters sang and she took the spray in her teeth, seeking the solitude of the open sea.

XVIII

On moonlit sea off Fisher's Island, *Faith* crept southeast at four knots on jibrig and reefed spanker while the business of stepping great guns aboard proceeded on her deck. By shifts men worked to mount the cannons and went below for a fresh-meat supper provided by a ragged-tempered Robert Arthur from stores not yet sorted and shelved.

The great cannons hung from anchor chutes on both bows. The foremast was sheered of sail and put into function as a hoist, its yards swung to cleat in tackle.

Timbers creaking, halyards straining, a gun was hoisted clear of the deck and released from its anchor line. Then a halyard was affixed to tackle on the mast and taken in, swinging the heavy gun inboard as the spar tackle was eased. Guy Neely and his helpers worked by lantern light to rig skids fore and aft.

Dalton told Duncan, "One day I'll want to know how you did that."

The foregun was eased into its cradle of rooftree timbers, and trimmed in place with quoins for elevation. The aftergun was swung carefully by alternating tackles from bow to foremast to mainmast to spanker gaff to stern deck slides.

With the guns in place, one across the bow rail aport of the jib and the other across the stern rail astarboard of the tiller, *Faith's* balance was restored and the schooner sailed as her makers had intended. Gone was the midships weight of hidden cargo. Gone was the bow weight of dangling cannon. *Faith* raised her nose, took moonspray in her teeth, and schooned cheerfully into the false dawn.

"Now she does sing," Dalton told Kilreagh. "Just listen to her music."

"First light will find us off Port Orient, Cap'n. If they've blockaded for us, it's there they'll be."

"Then we'll outdance them, Mister Kilreagh. There's no deep-sea warship can catch *Faith* in open water. Not so long as we stay upwind."

"Running downwind one could."

"But once past the shoals we don't have to go downwind. We can go where we please."

"Once past the shoals," Kilreagh nodded. Dalton glanced around curiously. It was still too dark to read the old man's face. But something in his tone made "once past the shoals" sound a very long way indeed. "What are you thinking, Clarence?"

"Oh, just thinking. You don't know Jonathan Hart, do you, Cap'n?"

Dalton frowned. "I know enough of him. He cost *Herrett.*"

"When we passed the frigate back there, it was

the *Courtesan*, Cap'n, certain I am. So I says to myself: Clarence, how does it come that the prizemaster is way off up here? An' the only answer to hand is that he wants his schooner, y' see."

"Be that as it may, I've no intention of turning it over to him."

"No. But I've got an eerie feelin', Sir. I'll be just as glad when we stand off the point with a world of open water beyond us."

"Are the little people whispering in your ear, then, Clarence?"

Dalton turned his attention back to the tiller. "We'll have dawn soon. Please put fresh lookouts in both tops. And see to it all guns are swabbed and loaded."

"Aye, Cap'n."

Dawn was pink-bright in a clear sky swept clean by a fresh northwest wind. Block Island's cliffs lay abeam and the shoal-froth of shallows was a bright line on each horizon.

The sea was clear. And then, with the sun just up from the starboard quarter, it was not.

"On deck! Sail ho, a'starboard!"

Dalton came up from the companionway, tea mug warm in his hand. "Mister Duncan, what is the sighting?"

Duncan, at the tiller, was squinting off toward the point. "I don't make it, Sir. Try your glass."

In the glass it was a speck of brightness just off Plum Island, laying out from its south point. But even as he watched, it grew. Sails, tall enough to clear the view even at this distance. Dalton wiped the glass, blinked the fatigue from his eyes, and looked again. Royals, pink in the new sunlight. Topgallants, topsails, main courses just becoming visible. She was flying all her canvas, running east on the wind, a course to intercept.

"She flies her royals," he breathed. "She's in pursuit. Mister Duncan, let's shake her out."

"Aye, Sir." Duncan grinned. Then he bellowed, "Hands to stations! Hands to make sail!" They scrambled. "Topsails and all, Sir?"

"Topsails and all. Let's see if we can make open water ahead of her."

"Topmen aloft!"

Kilreagh was beside them at the stern rail, resting elbows on davits to steady his glass. "Colors, Cap'n. By the Lord Harry, it's *Courtesan*. He was layin' for us there!"

"So he was. How do you read the wind, Mister Kilreagh?"

"West-northwest, Sir. Twenty knots an' freshenin', she is."

"More to his advantage than ours, Mister Kilreagh. Still, he'll need an hour to intercept us."

Kilreagh looked pale, staring off across bright water at the white speck that was *Courtesan*. Dalton glanced at him and then away. There were long miles ahead, and on this course *Faith* was disadvantaged. The frigate could close on them. With the wind off its aft quarter, *Faith* was fast. But the frigate, running full with the wind in its square sails, was faster. It could use its massive spread of canvas to full advantage. He peered again and calculated . . . an hour. When they closed, his only evasion would be to tack hard into the wind, to run back the way he had come. No, his chance was now. The chances he would have later were far less.

It was no good. "Bring her about to port, Mister Duncan. New course east-northeast. Let's make for the channel north of Block Island."

Faith lost some of her way as she took the new course. Her sails were less efficient in a leeward run.

"Shall we try wing and wing, Sir?"

"Not now, Mister Duncan. We don't have to chance it yet. Just set her full and by for the coastal channel."

At the end of an hour the frigate was closer, but staying off to the south, not on a closing course. Kilreagh was puzzled by it. "He doesn't seem to be trying to overhaul us, Sir. There, you see, he has furled his royals. And his topgallants as well! Look! What do you make of it?"

For a time Dalton made no answer. He held *Courtesan* in his glass.

Duncan asked, "Would he be playing cat-and-mouse, do you think?"

"Not Hart, no. I don't think so. But look . . . he's matching pace with us, laying back, like. Why would he do that?"

Dalton put down his glass. "He's pushing us, Mister Kilreagh. For some reason he wants us to go the way we're going."

"Herding us?"

"Like sheep. You see, as he stands we can neither slip past him nor tack back around him—not without going back into the Sound. What's ahead of us, Mister Kilreagh?"

271

"Block Island, the Narragansett channel, Cape Cod, and some islands beyond."

"Mister Duncan, come to due northeast."

"Aye, Sir." *Faith* heeled, her billowed sails took good wind, and she picked up way. Dalton held his glass on the frigate. The big ship reacted quickly, adjusting its course to follow, still remaining southwest of them.

"Very well, Mister Duncan. We'll just play his game for a while. Bring her back to course."

"Aye, Sir."

"As *Faith* put over, the distant frigate responded, resumed its flanking course.

Nearing Block Island, the frigate eased closer, barely two miles away, cutting off any possibility of a dash around the island and south. Dalton was tempted to come about when the island was between them and beat back up the wind to outflank the frigate. But *Courtesan's* master was shrewd. Courses were reefed and the frigate stayed back, cutting off retreat until the schooner was in the clear. Then the warship came on under full sail, resuming its flank course.

Constance Ramsey came on deck, glanced at the strained faces of those about the tiller. "Mister Dalton, what is the matter?"

He pointed, and heard her breath catch in her throat.

"Can't we outrun it?"

"We can if we tack, but we'd only run up on that coast over there."

"Then can we run around it?"

"No, Miss . . . he's not giving us the opportunity."

"Then where are we going?"

"Apparently just where he wants us to, Miss. Right into the funnel."

"Can he catch us there?"

Dalton was busy, ciphering. "I think not. If we maintain our lead, we should clear that big island up ahead before he can overtake us. The funnel is just beyond—a channel between islands. Once past it, we will be clear. We need open water to outdance a frigate. He's denying us the south route, but there's all the room in the world past the Cape."

"It'll be a close thing at best," Kilreagh muttered.

"Course due east, Mister Duncan."

"Aye, Sir."

"We'll stay south of that big island if he'll let us. I am going below for some breakfast. Let me know if the frigate changes his position."

In the galley Dalton sat alone, puzzling. Why had the frigate not tried to close on *Faith*? Why did he stand out there, two miles back and to the south, flanking? Why was he pushing?

It was, of course, *Courtesan*. There was no mistaking the great, dark frigate with its new sails, polished brass and varnished spars, its ranked rows of gunports. It was the prizemaster. But why so reluctant to close? Hart wanted the schooner. Why did he not come? His mind went back to *Herrett*. the doughty brig with its fierce commander had closed on two armed snows like a pit bull to the kill. But *Courtesan* never closed. Hart had stood off exercis-

273

ing his ranging guns while *Herrett* did his slaughter for him.

He had won without putting his ship in harm's way.

In the dark of puzzlement came a glimmer of light. A time before, in Belfast, there had been one—a heavy-shouldered, rough-faced man with pig eyes; others cowered before him. Cantry had been feared. But Cantry never fought, never took the punishment of hurting those he intimidated. Sometimes he had others do it for him. He was threat and bluster, but when caught off his own ground, braced by a determined rival, he turned and ran, Dalton knew.

Was this also Hart's way? When Kilreagh came below, Dalton asked him, "In the time you've watched at Long Island Yards, has *Courtesan* ever come in damaged?"

The old sailor considered. "No, Sir, can't say as I recall that. No, I've never seen a mark on her."

Dalton nodded. Not that it changed things much. With forty-four guns, *Courtesan* could do about as Hart pleased. The question remained, What would he please? Certainly he would not just keep following. Once in open water *Faith* could turn, if not south, then north. Across the wind the schooner could escape. Hart knew that. What, then, was the prizemaster waiting for?

When he had eaten he came back on deck, somewhat refreshed. The sun was high and *Faith* whispered smugly along, leaving a neat wake behind her. Her big spanker thrummed to the following wind.

Topsails and topgallants stood full on her upper masts, and the three great albatross wings of jibsail, jibtop, and staysail swelled above her stem. Behind and a quarter a'starboard in full view on the near horizon stood the tall, stacked sails of the frigate, a little closer now. Vineyard Island was ahead.

"That frigate is closing a bit, Sir," Duncan said. "He is still on reefed shrouds, but it seems like the further we get from Block Island, the closer he comes . . . and he's more directly behind now, as you see."

Dalton nodded. Of course. Hart would take no chance on a sudden tack and dash that might let *Faith* escape by circling upwind. *Courtesan* was holding just the distance and attitude to make that extremely difficult.

"Anything else?"

"Aye, Sir. Another sail. You see out there, off the port beam, just in the shallows? We thought at first it was a cutter, but it's just a coaster, Sir—packet, most likely."

Dalton studied the little vessel pacing them a mile to the north. Duncan was right: the boat was cutter-rigged, but smaller. It was no fighting ship, no ship at all, just a little mail carrier. He turned away, then looked back. The coaster's broad forestaysail was reefed high. It was just matching pace with *Faith*.

"How long has that been there, Mister Duncan?"

"Can't say, Sir. Maybe an hour, maybe less."

"Abeam all that time?"

"Aye, Sir."

"On deck! Land closing ahead."

Duncan pointed. "Funnel's end in sight, Sir. That's the Vineyard aport, and beyond to the right, that's Tuckernuck and Muskeget, with Nantucket below. Beyond Great Point is all the ocean a body could want."

Two hours, Dalton thought . . . three hours at most. He looked back at the frigate. With his glass he could see its dark hull above the swell. Two hours . . . three at most. "Very close work," he muttered. "Very close indeed."

Billy Caster sounded the bell and Clarence Kilreagh relieved Duncan at the helm. Dalton paced the deck, watching, listening to the song of *Faith*, his glass often in his hand.

"On deck!"

He looked up into the foretop where Martin Smith was pointing to port. He turned his glass there. The coastal packet was just vanishing beyond the western point of Vineyard Island, heading into Vineyard Sound. Its forestays'l was no longer reefed. Dalton relaxed a bit. That boat out there, pacing him, had been a worry.

An hour passed. Green coastline crept by on the port horizon, above a thread of bright beach. Tuckernuck's long point and little Muskeget grew ahead. The wind was better than twenty knots now, and held steady a quarter astern. A square-rigger's wind. A traveling wind, but not the best for a schooner. *Faith* keened, but she was nowhere near her hull speed.

Masts and spars were visible on the pursuing frigate, dark threads between banked sails. And when she crested, a swell, he could make out the shape of her driving forecastle. Even as he watched, a patch of white blossomed beneath the warship's jib. A spritsail .. he hadn't seen one used in years. *Cour-*

tesan was no longer flanking. She was in full pursuit. The man behind them was holding nothing back.

The point grew before them. Off to the left was the end of Vineyard Island . . . the final funnel. Closer by half than the frigate behind.

Kilreagh's dour visage eased. "We're going to make it, Sir."

"On deck! Sail ahead!"

The little coaster hove into view around the point of Chappaquiddick Island and veered toward them on a close tack, its cutter sails beating into the wind. It angled directly for *Faith's* path on a collision course. Even as Dalton took the schooner's tiller, the coaster's swivel gun spoke and a two-inch ball sang through the rigging. Splinters flew from the foremast. The boat came dead on.

"On deck!" Solamon Grimm was in the foretop. "She has a cannon as well, Sir!"

"Man the guns! Mister Kilreagh, take charge forward. Mister Duncan, aft guns! Mister Caster, muster your rifles, please!"

Faith bore down on the little coaster. Dalton held the tiller steady, watching the cutter sails grow beyond the schooner's bow. He held his sprit in line with the coaster's mast and waited, expecting another shot. Instead the coaster veered off, and Dalton eased the tiller away. An instant later they passed beam to beam, and one of *Faith's* starboard fourpounders thundered. Even as they cleared, Dalton saw the light coaster coming about tightly, its sails taking the wind.

"I tried for the mast," Kilreagh called from forward. "But I missed."

Charley Duncan and a gun crew of Cadman Wise and Jubal Foster were hauling at the hawsers of the stern chaser, trying to get the big gun lined up as the coaster slipped astern. But as its sails filled, the little ship came about, dashed away to the side, and doubled back on *Faith* at a fast beam reach. Its swivel gun barked again and the starboard cathead collapsed on *Faith's* rail, splinters flying. Ishmael Bean grabbed his head and collapsed by the capstan. As the boat closed Dalton could see its name lettered on its bow: *Caper*. Kilreagh unleashed the second starboard four-pounder . . . too early. A gout of water erupted just ahead of the boat's bow. *Caper* veered slightly, its crew hauling sheets for best trim. One of them was ramming a fresh load into the swivel gun.

Billy Caster swarmed out of *Faith's* companion hatch, followed by Claude Mallory and Purdy Fisk, all carrying rifles, pouches, and horns. The coaster moved in, on a collision course with *Faith*, heading for her bow. Charley Duncan swore, "Th' madman's tryin' to block us with his hull! He's sacrificin' his vessel!"

"Of course he is," Dalton muttered, looking back. The hulking frigate was closing rapidly, now only a quarter mile away, and as he watched, he saw the first smoke-rose blooming at its bow. A large ball scudded into the swell ten yards from *Faith's* fleeing nose. Spray sheeted over her foredeck. *Courtesan* was testing for range, firing high. That was no proper way to test, he thought, and the significance caught him. *Courtesan* didn't want to hull the schooner. Hart wanted her as little damaged as possible. That meant the men on the coaster had their orders . . .

bracing his shoulders he hauled back on the tiller. *Faith* responded, leaping toward the little boat now directly ahead. He saw the frenzy aboard *Caper* as they hauled over, losing way. *Faith* sheared past, her bow wake breaking over the coaster's deck. As they passed, Billy and his rifles opened fire, a sharp volley of three. When Dalton peered down over the rail at the passing boat, one of the men aboard was crumpling, toppling overside. He righted the tiller and brought *Faith* back to her trim, still driving east. He felt, rather than saw, another great ball from the frigate's chasers passing overhead. It traveled the length of *Faith*, arching twelve feet above her deck, and spumed fifty yards beyond. A gaping hole appeared in the spencer.

Courtesan was closing rapidly, now directly astern, running true with the wind, two cable lengths away. Wide spray-whiskers sliced from her bow. He could see men on her foredeck, could imagine he heard the howl of her bosun's whistles. A banshee wail drowned out all other sounds, and chain screamed through the upper rigging. A stayline parted with the crack of a rifle-shot, and he heard a protesting spar creak. Things were falling amidships—scraps of tattered canvas, a running block, splinters . . . the body of a man thudded into the decking half over the mainhold hatch and lay motionless.

Dalton gritted his teeth. Next would come cannister. He had to keep moving, keep her on course, dead away from the frigate. If once he lost way, the warship would close and turn for broadsides. It would be the end. From the corner of his eye he caught movement. The little coaster was moving in again, dashing past *Faith* for a run, coming up to pass astern. Charley Duncan was swearing and sweating at the big stern gun, trying to bring it into action against the frigate. "The boat, Mister Duncan! Bring down the coaster if you can!"

Duncan reversed his lines, hauled the eight-pounder about and depressed it, then set match to frizzen as it came astern, nearly point blank. The flare and the smoke completely engulfed the coaster. But then it reappeared. Its spanker fluttered from a smashed boom, five feet of its breadth out of use. But still it sailed, and bore in on the schooner. Dead ahead now was the tip of the final island. Beyond was open sea. Gambling, Dalton steered to the right as the coaster closed, careening it away on his wake, forcing it off his beam, then righted course. He had lost more lead, but the coaster was still behind him. He heard more banshee wailing to the left . . . chain from the frigate again, but wide this time. His veer had saved him from a hit. Duncan and his man were struggling to reload.

Dalton cupped a free hand to his mouth. "Miss Constance! On deck!" God save me, he thought, I've just called on a woman to do my fighting for me.

Constance appeared immediately, her skirt tied up between her legs, her hair banded. She hurried past him to the stern gun.

"Let her fire, Mister Duncan. The little vessel, Miss Constance. Slow it down!"

She darted a glance at him. "I can hit the big one."

"Forget the damned big one! Take out the little one!"

She shrugged, knelt by the long-eight, and gave orders. Duncan hauled on its lines. Holding her slow fuse just above the touch-hole, the girl sighted, paused, and sighted again. Thunder rolled from the closing frigate and cannister shot whined into them, riddling the spanker. Dalton heard sickening sounds ahead. What was the woman waiting for? "Fire, damn you!" he roared. Still she hesitated, and then as *Faith* topped a swell, leveling for an instant, she fired. Smoke rolled over them. Then Duncan cheered.

"By God, Sir, she's took its friggin' mast right off at the stump, she has!"

Dalton risked a glance back. The little coaster drifted, a tangle of down canvas and rigging flopped over a rocking hull, directly in the path of the frigate. He looked to see the big ship swerve and his eyes went wide. *Courtesan* veered not a point. Its great sails full of the rising wind, it crested a swell, leaped down upon the hapless little vessel, and ground it under timbered keel, and kept on coming. Dalton felt sick. There had been men aboard that coaster. Hart's own men.

Sails leaking and tackle fouled atop, *Faith* had lost way. The frigate was close . . . too close. Even as he looked, he could see a scramble at the bows, men shoving others aside, snugging double long chasers to sight right down *Faith's* deck. "Below!" Dalton screamed. "Get below!" Holding the tiller with one hand he ducked under its bar, grabbed Constance around the waist, and hurled her toward the companion hatch. Charley Duncan and Claude Mallory dumped her down it and followed. It was too late for those amidships and in the fore. And it was too late for Dalton. He steeled himself for the ending impact of cannister shot that would blast through him.

Nothing happened. After a moment he glanced back. The frigate's fore guns were manned, but un-fired. There was turmoil there. He saw an officer break into the bow and kneel over one of the guns. Men were holding a struggling man.

Muskeget slid past off *Faith's* starboard beam. Chappaquiddick was far astern. The water was dark.

"Hands to the sheets," he called, and men appeared about him and amidships. "Port tack! Ease those sheets . . . cleat . . . haul . . . now! Sheet home! Sheet home!"

He shoved the bar far over and *Faith* heeled four strakes into singing waters as she made about. He brought her stem a full quarter-turn and heard rifles popping from the midships rail. For a moment she was sullen, and he could hear the muffled thunder of the frigate's hull riding down upon him. Then *Faith* took her wind and surged. She whispered, she crooned, she hissed in a swell and found her pace. She sang.

Due north he held her, and hell erupted close behind. Wild-fired balls, chain and cannister howled and hissed all around. Something thudded amidships and a rail collapsed. Rent sails crackled. Then she was away.

Dalton looked back and the frigate was receding, trying awkwardly to come about on his tail. He increased his tack, heard the schooner's sailing song rise in pitch. Shaking a fist in the air he shouted in exultation, his voice lost on the wind. "Now she schoons, you bastard! Now I have my open water!" Squaring his shoulders he eased her a trifle to starboard for trim and for the first time looked about to assess damage.

"Mister Duncan, all hands on deck, if you please! Mister Caster, stow the rifles! Mister Kilreagh, I'll need a . . ." His voice died away. Clarence Kilreagh couldn't hear him. The old seaman lay amidships, peg leg jutting above the hold hatch. Just beyond him a piece of chain hung imbedded in the red-spattered foremast.

XIX

It was a grim and bloodied schooner that fled north-ward toward the Cape, the man at its helm wrapped in silent, cold fury. Those who approached him took one look at the set jaw, the tight lips, the hard eyes, and turned away. Constance Ramsey huddled white-faced by the after rail and stared out across bright water, trying not to look forward.

They brought fresh canvas to cover the bodies of Clarence Kilreagh, Solamon Grimm and Martin Smith. Ishmael Bean with his gaping splinter wound and William Moses with his shattered arm were taken below for tending. But no one had yet washed away the gore and debris that littered *Faith's* deck.

Dalton held north, cross-wind, angling more and more westerly as *Faith* bore away from the pursuing *Courtesan*. By the time the Cape was in clear view, the frigate was a speck three miles astern and Dalton brought the schooner about to tack southwest. Then as the frigate lumbered to intercept he put her to a broad reach and ran down toward the Vineyard. Another hour passed. *Faith* had looped two hundred and forty degrees through Nantucket Sound, and Dalton watched coldly as the great frigate fought against a still-freshening wind in an attempt to intercept. He had a thing in mind, and though common sense told him to abandon the game, each time his eye fell on the shrouded forms amidships, his resolve returned. When *Courtesan* was a mile away on a converging course, he called Duncan to him.

"Mister Duncan, please go into the main hold and bring up two of those casks of nails."

With the nails on deck, he had the men pull the loads of the long eight in the bow and all of the four-pounders, and reload them with nails and wadding. Charley Duncan grinned cruelly as they set to it.

Constance looked dully out at the distant frigate, now a quarter aport and creeping into the wind. "They won't catch us again, Mister Dalton. We will be long gone before they get here."

He turned to her and she shivered at the coldness in his dark eyes. "Not if we go to them, Miss Constance."

"But that would be madness. We have won. We have escaped."

"Aye. Madness." He stared for a moment at the dead men amidships. "We have the options now, Miss Constance. I can choose to hold this course and we will pass far ahead of the ship. Or I can come aport and we will pass behind him . . . but somewhat more closely. Either way, we will leave him behind. But I intend to give Captain Hart my regards in passing—for Clarence. Tell me, would it please you to operate the eight-pounder over there?"

She looked then at the shambles to the fore, the shrouded bodies. When she looked back, the color had returned to her cheeks. "Yes, Captain Dalton, I believe it would."

As the courses closed, Dalton eased mainsails, letting them luff in the wind. Hart would have a glass on *Faith*. Let him see her limping.

As she lost way the range between the vessels closed more and more. The frigate was making poor time on a tack-and-tack course, trying to intercept. Dalton eased once imperceptibly to port, and then again.

With a half-mile between them the schooner luffed and limped on ill-set sails, having a hard time of it, playing duck-in-the-water for *Courtesan's* benefit. The range continued to close.

Dalton waited until they were nearly in gun range, studying *Courtesan* through a glass. He saw something he had not seen before. There were hanged men at two—no, three—of her yardarms, their dead bodies turning and dangling beside the ship's courses.

"Now, Mister Duncan. All four-pounders to the starboard rail. Two men to a gun. Give Miss Constance two men forward to help her with the long eight."

When the guns were readied he brought *Faith* about, full downwind, spanker and spencer spread wing and wing. Her surge as she leapt into the new course made sailors grab lines to keep their footing.

It was so abrupt and unexpected that *Courtesan* had no time to react. *Faith* raced dead at the frigate, nose-to-nose, and was on the big ship in moments. No cannon fire came from the frigate's bow. Dalton had expected none. When they were fifty yards aport, Constance touched off the bow gun, and through its smoke they heard the sounds of hell from *Courtesan's* forecastle. With a touch of the tiller, *Faith* veered left. Dalton shouted, "All guns, fire as she bears," and as the frigate's beam ran past, the four-pounders volleyed, their charges sweeping her rails. In an instant *Faith* was past, and the belated fire of the frigate's chasers fell short. As the smoke rolled away, Dalton called hands to sails, trimmed the mains, and set course for Muskeget pass and the open sea beyond.

Constance crouched beside the great gun in the bow, awed at what she had done. Nearly forty pounds of nails had swept the frigate's decks in space of seconds. She tried to imagine the effect. Then she tried even harder not to think about it.

Charley Duncan came astern, his face ashen. "Cap'n, Sir, I saw men hanging at her yardarms as we passed. Two of them I saw close. They were the Cranstons, Sir. Hannibal was hanged from the fore-yard and John from the main."

Dalton lowered his head. "I know, Mister Duncan. I saw them. How they got aboard that ship we'll never know. But they saved us back there in the chase. Somehow, those lads managed to spike the frigate's bow chasers."

"Then the third one . . . ?"

"Was Mister Coleman. He was with them."

Admiral Lord Richard Howe stood square and solid before the blazing hearth in the parlor of Forsythe House above Staten Island's east point. The admiral was a judicious man, seldom given to wrath, but those cowering before him now felt the whiplash of his words.

Vice Admiral Sir Walter Jennings' pink cheeks and portly belly quivered as he tried to meet his senior's intense, dark eyes. Post Captain Roger Mercer and Guard Officer Croney did not try. They stared fixedly at their own feet. None of the three had ever seen "Black Dick" Howe in a towering rage. They were seeing him so now.

"Among you," he told them, "you may have scuttled our last chance of putting an early and peaceable end to this uprising in the colonies. Know you that while you and Captain Hart have been playing your little games here, I have been in meetings with some of the more reasonable leaders of the colonies, trying to reconcile their differences with the Crown. They have given me certain guarantees, gentlemen, and I in turn have given them certain guarantees—made, I might add, in perfectly good faith and based on my estimation that in my absence, my officers here were keeping things under control.

"One of my guarantees, to an honorable and conservative gentleman of the town of Wilmington, was the return of his private vessel, the schooner *Faith*, taken without warrant or cause by a vessel commissioned to the Navy."

"Captain Hart has letters of—" Mercer ventured.

"Captain Hart is authorized to capture and claim privateers and hostiles, *not* to enter harbors and confiscate the vessels lying there! The man has overstepped himself this time, and will be dealt with. But the ship I agreed to return is no longer available, is it?"

Croney raised his eyes, nervously. "It was the traitor Dalton, Sir, him and his incendiaries . . ."

"Phaw! Patrick Dalton is no more a traitor to the Crown than I am, Mister Croney. There are as many fools in Whitehall as it seems there are in this command. Read your own reports, gentlemen! Dalton could not have had a hand in the sabotage of this harbor. He was not ashore here long enough, nor in touch with any who could have done the deed. Coincidence. Nothing but coincidence.

"But he fired on ships of the fleet, Sir," Jennings insisted. "He did considerable damage. He has put two of our warships out of action, and those gunboats . . . the reports do substantiate that, Milord Admiral."

Howe's dark grin was wicked. "Aye, that he did. Two first-rate cruisers and the best of our harbor vessels. And he did it all with a small civilian schooner barely equipped for its own defense. Gentlemen, the man should be decorated for demonstrating to us our own weaknesses. And by the way, who fired first? I gather it was not him. And now, to top it off, you gentlemen have sealed the *Faith's* fate with your general order to seek and destroy her. Surely you must have been out of your minds!"

"Possibly we were hasty. It can be reversed . . ."

"It *has* been reversed. But what are the chances that *Faith* still sails? With the fleet after her, not to mention Captain Hart and *Courtesan*, it is most likely that schooner has already been destroyed. And if so, our chances for an amiable discussion with at least one rather influential colonial are greatly reduced."

Guard Officer Croney cleared his throat. "With reference to that . . . ah . . . particular influential colonial, Sir, ah . . ."

"Mister Ramsey. Of Wilmington."

"Yes, Sir. John Singleton Ramsey. The information I have, Sir, is that the man is hardly more than a scoundrel himself, albeit a wealthy one. They say he isn't above a bit of smuggling now and again to avoid Crown taxes. . . ."

"We are not here to collect the King's taxes," Howe pointed out, "at least not at the moment. There is a full-scale rebellion under way among these colonies, Gentlemen . . . as I am sure you have noticed. It is a rebellion that the Crown has little time to deal with right now. Our task is to contain the situation by whatever means are expedient. Lord North himself has directed that I attempt to negotiate a reasonable solution, providing I can find reasonable colonial leaders who are willing to talk. Which, in addition to planning a campaign up the Hudson, is precisely what I have been attempting to do."

"But, Sir, dealing with smugglers and the like . . ."

"However he conducts his business, Squire Ramsey could be of assistance to us, provided we could see our way clear not to offend him. He may be a rebel himself, for all I know. But he is first a businessman. One of his close associates is Patrick Henry of Virginia."

"A firebrand and known rebel," Croney noted.

Howe glanced at him, his dark brows lowering. "Of course he is! Who do you expect I should negotiate with, if not rebels? Tories, for heaven's sake? That's preaching to the choir."

By last light of evening Faith sailed on a broad reach due south on the open sea, strong wind in her tattered sails, rolling dark water rising to meet her martingale.

Sails set and tiller lashed, she tended her own course while Patrick Dalton assembled his company amidships. With no real sailmaker aboard, they simply wrapped the bodies of their three mates in canvas, strapped them tight, and weighted them with shot. Dalton read over them. Then strong hands lifted them over the rail and consigned them to the sea. Tears streaked Brevis Grimm's face as he saw his brother disappear into the sea. Martin Smith followed and then, after a pause, Clarence Kilreagh. Standing apart, Constance Ramsey turned to watch the featureless swells where the old man's wrapped form had gone. Wind whispered in rent sails aloft, and again she heard his voice . . . speaking to her, telling her about Patrick Dalton, telling her wisdoms that no book had ever imparted.

When the burials were done, the men huddled amidships at the rail. Wrapped in coats and quilts against the chill wind, they said their private prayers. Motley group that they had been, they were all Faith's now and had lost six of their number on this day.

Billy Caster took lanterns and log below, to enter the day's record in rough:

September sixth, 1777. Morning clear, wind freshening west. Course easterly. Frigate sighted, gave chase through the morning. At Nantucket small craft *Caper* intercepted and engaged us. Maintained course through engagement. Frigate gave chase. Our lady dismasted *Caper*. Frigate engaged, heavy exchange of fire. Captain turned north and outdistanced the ship, identified as *Courtesan*. Losses three dead and two injured, item below. In afternoon came about to southerly, Frigate moved to intercept, we engaged, swept *Courtesan* with forty pounds of good two-inch drawn nails from cargo, value estimated two pounds ten. Sighted three of *Faith's* crew lost the fourth inst. now hanging from *Courtesan's* yardarms. Item below. Captain said they spiked the frigate's bow chasers.

Item: six men deceased. Clarence Kilreagh, HMRN able seaman retired, first officer of *Faith*, killed by chain. Solamon Grimm, late HMRN able seaman incarcerated, navigator and second boatswain's mate of *Faith*, shot out of the foretop. Martin Smith, late HMRN able seaman incarcerated, able seaman of *Faith*, hit by cannister shot. Samuel Coleman, late HMRN able seaman incarcerated, able seaman of *Faith*, hanged aboard *Courtesan*. The brothers Cranston, of Delaware, ordinary seamen of *Faith*, hanged aboard *Courtesan*.

Item: two men injured. Ishmael Bean, ordinary seaman, head wound from a splinter. William Moses, pressedman, arm broken by falling tackle.

Wind at evening bells west and northering. Near thirty knots. Bearing due S. No land in sight, no ships sighted. Misters Kilreagh, S. Grimm, and Smith buried at sea. Memorials for Misters Coleman, Cranston, and Cranston.

He paused, fingering his quill. Then he dipped ink and added: Damage to *Faith* mostly rigging. Counting the captain and the lady there are eighteen of us now. God save the souls of the six.

Mister Arthur's cat Bernice appeared from somewhere and leapt onto the galley table to sit licking herself by the lantern. She had spent most of this long day forward in the chain locker, hiding among the stowed kegs of Greek fire. In hammocks in the companionway, Ishmael Bean and William Moses slept, their wounds bound. The air about them smelled strongly of rum.

Billy put away quills and ink and closed the log. A stray tear ran down his cheek and he rubbed it away with his sleeve. Had there been a home for him to go to, he would have wished it.

On deck Charley Duncan, now acting first officer, led a crew in mopping and swabbing decks, clearing away the gore of the day's engagements. He pushed them hard and pushed himself harder. It would be a good thing to be very tired when they sought their hammocks this night.

Cadman Wise stood watch at the tiller, respecting

the brooding silence of the slim, quilt-hooded figure seated at the after rail, staring out across darkening north waters. The captain had been hit hard by the deaths of his people, and those around him knew it. It was a thing to be pondered. Most aboard *Faith* were experienced seamen, and most had served on warships. Sentiment was not a thing one expected of captains. But then, they knew Patrick Dalton had never been a captain before taking command of *Faith*. He had been first officer on two King's ships, and had brought one home wounded when his captain was shot away with the helm. But Captain Dalton was hardly what any tar expected in a captain. Though he demanded a trim ship and said he abhorred laxity, there was more than a touch of democracy in the way he commanded. And none aboard had yet felt the lash.

In evening gloom Guy Neely, Virgil Cowan, Michael Romart, and Jubal Foster hesitantly came astern and stood waiting until Wise asked what they wanted.

"Word with the cap'n, if we may," Neely rasped.

Dalton shook himself from his distant thoughts and turned to the delegation. "Yes?"

"Cap'n Dalton, we come to petition ye. We took a vote, Sir."

"You took a vote? Who?"

"The four of us, Sir. We voted on . . . whether we might ask ye to take us home."

At the tiller Wise drew his breath sharply, but Dalton hushed him. "Mister Neely, all of you have signed articles on this vessel, just like everyone else."

"Aye, Sir, an' we'll abide by them. But we wanted

you to know how we feel . . . where we stand, so to speak. All the rest of the crew is Englishmen, an' Navy sailors. But we're Americans, Sir, and there's a difference. We've done a bit of sailin', the lot of us, but only around the bays an' down to the Indies a time or two. Virgil an' Michael here, they've done a bit of gunnin' too, aboard merchantmen, but we ain't none of us Navy, so to speak."

"What is your point?"

"Well, it's that we took a vote, like I said, Sir. An' we'd like it if you could take us home . . ."

"That's hardly a . . ."

"Moment, Sir." Neely held up a pleading hand. "We'd like you to take us home long enough for us to see Miss Constance safe to her family, an' then go talk to the Cranston boys' ma. We know her, Sir, and it would be a comfort to her to hear it from us before she hears it from strangers. Then we'd all four come back aboard *Faith* an' give ye our best in the fight comin' up. We'd like that, Sir."

Dalton stared at them. "Mister Neely, I can hardly take *Faith* into Delaware Bay. We are a fugitive ship, fair game for anyone who'd recognize us. Don't you know those of us who are . . . were . . . King's men are liable to be taken off and shot?"

"Only if we was recognized, Sir. Maybe you hadn't noticed, but *Faith* don't look much the way she used to, what with the big guns fore an'aft, an' the stern braces on her now, an' that tackle rigged up for gaff-top sails. An' then there's the patchwork along her hull, an' the batterin' we've took from them ships. . . . *Faith* isn't what you might call neat right now, Sir."

" 'Bout the only thing on *Faith* that looks like *Faith* is her escutcheons, Capt'n," Jubal Foster added. "And those wouldn't be hard to replace."

Dalton shook his head. "There would be some who'd know her."

"With them as did, we'd speak for you, Sir. All of us would. I wager even Miss Constance'd speak for you if you was to ask. It ain't like she ain't got her money for cargo."

"What fight?"

"Sir?"

"You said 'the fight coming up.' What fight, Mister Neely?"

"Why, Sir, we just thought . . . after what that frigate done to us, you know . . . well, we calculated if he didn't come after us again you might be inclined to go after him. That's why we took a vote, Sir. If that's what ye have in mind, we'd be pleased to join ye."

Dalton was nearly speechless. "You thought . . . against a man of war? A first-rate with forty-four guns? With this?"

"Aye, Sir. If anybody could pull a thing like that it would be you, Sir. An' it does sorely need doin', considerin' what he's done."

"Mister Neely, that is absolutely preposterous! This is no fighting ship!"

"Seems to us we've done right well so far, Cap'n."

Dalton turned away. After a moment the delegation wandered off, their shoulders slumping. Cadman Wise stood by the tiller, his mouth hanging open. Finally he closed it, lashed the tiller, said, "Goin' ahead, Cap'n, Sir, right back," and headed off past the lantern into the murky reaches amidships. He went looking for Charley Duncan.

In settling darkness Dalton stood alone at *Faith's* stern rail, considering what the Americans had proposed. The sheer novelty of their idea . . . the ridiculous, impossible audacity of it . . . had shaken him out of the black gloom that had dogged him through the waning day. He felt alive again. The memory of Clarence Kilreagh, of Solamon Grimm and Martin Smith, of those poor hanged men, would be a long time going away. But those lads, with their knot-headed ideas, had turned his mood. He was grateful.

A hand touched his arm and he jumped. He hadn't noticed Constance coming on deck. She was wrapped in a quilt against the chill. A tray sat on the coaming beside the lamp, the pot on it steaming.

"Mister Dalton," she said hesitantly, "I am sorry." The words were gentle. He knew what she meant.

"Yes, Miss. I'm sorry, too. About everything."

"I've brought hot tea, Mister Dalton. You might catch the vapors, brooding up here."

"Thank you. I am no longer brooding. Your lads from Delaware have seen to that. They have comforted me immensely."

"They have? Well, I am glad. May I sit here a while? We might talk." She nodded toward the bench. "There is room for both of us. And the wind is quite chill.

"I believe I'll stand, Miss Constance, thank you. I cannot abide laxity aboard ship, you know.

"Oh, pooh!" She stamped her foot. "One moment, Mister Dalton." She turned away to the coaming and busied herself in the lantern's light. Dalton wanted to look away, but found his eyes bound by the vision of warm light through wind-rippled auburn hair.

She turned with two steaming mugs and handed him one. He raised it and heady vapors filled his passages, almost choking him. The hot stuff was more rum than tea.

"Drink it," she ordered. "It's good for you."

When Cadman Wise returned, Charley Duncan was with him. "Word with you, Cap'n?" At Dalton's nod he said, "We got some of the men below and we took a vote, Cap'n."

"Another vote, is it? Who voted this time?"

"Just about all of us, Sir. We think it might be all right if we was to put into Delaware Bay, if we kept our wits about us. We could be *Gladys* again, like at Rhode Island. That way the lady could go home, Sir. Then we could go find that frigate if that was what the cap'n wanted to do, Sir. We would all be agreeable."

"That's enough, Mister Duncan."

Duncan lowered his head. "Aye, Sir. Beggin' the cap'n's pardon."

"Voting is not accepted procedure aboard ship, Mister Duncan. You know that. A ship goes where its captain says it goes. Nowhere else."

"Aye, Sir."

"Now get below, all of you. I'll tend the helm for a while. I want you men rested. We need our escutcheons replaced and our rails raised fore and aft. We need a deck house built amidships . . . we can use timbers and shingles for that, I believe. There is sail to patch and rigging to mend and a hull to smear with tar. And all that must be done smartly if *Gladys* is to put into Delaware Bay on our arrival there."

Duncan and Wise fought to keep their faces straight. "Aye, Sir."

Behind them in the gloom Billy Caster erupted, "And maybe we could build fighting tops. Nothing'd change a ship's looks like having fighting tops."

"Further," Dalton intoned, "I suppose a tot of rum would be beneficial to all hands before turning in. We wouldn't want anyone catching the vapors."

As they disappeared forward, Billy's voice came clear. "Fighting tops, Mister Neely. Platforms, like, at the mastheads. Where riflemen can stand to shoot. Far less difficult that building a barn."

On a moon-bathed sea *Faith* keened along her tiller-lashed course as Dalton and Constance sat cozy and content beneath layered quilts. The pot was empty and they were full of rum.

"Mind your elbows, Mister Dalton," she said, drowsily. Then after a time, "May I tell you something about yourself, Patrick Dalton?"

"Of course. What?"

"You are pompous, overbearing, and in all respects an irritating man. But only when you're sober."

XX

The wind held, and *Courtesan* made a slow voyage down the Atlantic slope to New York Bay. Every hammock on the orlop deck held sore and bandaged men. Twelve were dead and thirty-seven were wounded from the spray of nails across her crowded decks. The men remaining, still nearly two hundred, were sullen. Hardly a watch passed those two days that did not see a fight break out somewhere aboard. With the death of Second Officer Jack Liles, something had gone out of *Courtesan*. He had, in a way, been the buffer between the captain and officers and the crew. Now there was no buffer, and no man came within sight of Jonathan Hart without a scathing. Nor did any man have immunity from the lash.

Buster Willis, bosun's mate, was passing through the near-deserted gunroom during first dog watch when young Terry Foss accosted him. "Mister Willis, can we talk a bit? You should know what some of the men are sayin', Sir."

301

"I know what they're saying, Terry. No need to tell me."

"Aye, but about some of 'em jumpin' ship when we make port, Sir. There's some are right serious about that, Sir. They aren't just talkin', like. You know?"

"Then I'd suggest they keep their talk from the captain, Terry. He's of a mood to flog or worse, these days."

"Aye, Sir. We all know."

"Ah, Terry . . . just supposin' some of your mates *did* have a thing like that in mind. It's never a bad idea to stay with your mates, Terry. Remember."

The captain's mood blackened through the final hours out as he fed on his rage. He came upon some of his marines belowdecks, huddled in whispering merriment, and their guilty glances at his approach made it clear what they were enjoying. *Courtesan* had been humiliated—outsailed, outgunned, and outrun by a civilian schooner. It was unthinkable. And some aboard were enjoying the humiliation of it. What loyalty he had come to expect aboard his ship was gone. In retaliation he ragged and lashed his officers, coercing them into pushing the men, seeking satisfaction and finding none. It just made matters worse.

This was the state of affairs aboard *Courtesan* when the frigate reached Long Island Yards. He anchored her in midchannel and had bunting run up, requesting leave of hospital, yards, fitters and provision dock. "When they respond, Mister Mace, take us in. I'm going below to change my shirt."

But minutes passed and there was no response.

302

When Hart returned to his deck, Mace was still at the glass, waiting.

"They're not answering, Sir."

"Then fire a salute, Mister Mace, to get their attention. Must I tell you everything?"

"Aye, Sir." At the first officer's call one of the port-side guns thundered a salute. The bunting was run down and run back up. Still nothing happened. Hart began to swear quietly under his breath.

"Ah, there they are, Sir. Coming up now. Wait . . . no . . . here, Sir, you might want to take the glass. I might be misreading the signals."

"I shouldn't be at all surprised." Hart wrenched the glass from his hand, leveled it toward the ensign staff ashore. He read the flags. Permission to dock denied. Hospital boat would come alongside for wounded. Captain was requested at headquarters, promptly. White-faced, he put down the glass. "Lower my launch, Mister Mace. I'm going ashore."

"What's the meaning of this?" Hart thundered at the post captain, without waiting for the door to close behind him. "I need repairs, provisions, access to the yards. I demand it now!"

"Orders, Captain." Mercer's face was bland.

"Whose orders, Captain?"

The door behind Mercer opened and Admiral Howe stood there, his dark gaze level. "My orders, Captain Hart. Come in, please." He stepped aside.

Still glowering, Hart strode past him into the inner office. Inside he paused to look around. Vice Admiral Jennings sat in one corner, inspecting the palms of his hands. He recognized three others as masters of ships of the line, officers of the admiral's fleet. The two remaining were clerks. Maps and papers were spread over the center table.

As the door closed Hart turned, saluted the admiral, said, "Milord," and nodded to the others present. Admiral Howe looked tired. He needed a shave, his wig was askew, and his waistcoat was open to the fobchain.

He returned Hart's salute absently. "Captain Hart, I sent for you because we have a problem . . . one of many, as you can see." He waved a beefy hand at the table. "This uprising among the colonials has gotten quite out of hand."

Hart had little interest in dealings with colonials. "Milord Admiral, if I may, my ship requires provisioning and fitting, and I need access to the yards. I have very little time."

"Oh?" Howe's brows raised in polite interest. "That has the sound of hot pursuit, Captain. Something of essential nature to the Crown, I trust?"

"A private matter, Milord. If you would just be so good as to . . ." His voice trailed off as the admiral's look turned to cold steel. In the corner, pudgy Vice Admiral Jennings was smirking.

"A personal matter, Captain?" Howe's voice suddenly was as cold as his eyes. "Another prize, perhaps? I'm afraid it will have to wait, Sir. There is fleet business at hand. *Courtesan* is required . . . once we have clearly understood each other."

"Sir, it cannot wait. It is a matter of honor. Now by your leave, I seek access to yards, provision dock . . ."

"Captain Hart, I said *Courtesan* is required for fleet duty."

Hart straightened his shoulders and met the admiral's gaze. "Is it general orders from the crown, Milord?"

"It is strategic, Captain Hart. We are preparing for a thrust up the Hudson River. The revolutionaries are amassing there."

"If it is not general orders, Milord Admiral, then respectfully I must decline."

"You cannot decline a fleet order, Captain."

"*Courtesan* is not a fleet commission, Admiral. She is a warrant vessel. She is the property of myself and my sponsors. Unless you have general orders, Sir, then please tell your harbor guards to withdraw and allow me to dock. In addition to provision and fitting, I shall require approximately fifty replacement seamen. The hospital boats are bringing ashore thirty-seven wounded, and I have lost twelve."

Howe's eyes rounded. "Forty-nine casualties, Sir? What on earth did you encounter? Speak up, man. It will be in the reports, you know."

Hart flushed. "It was a schooner, Milord." He heard intakes of breath from aside, and flushed again, angering. "Fortune was with him, but it will not be the same again."

"A schooner? Surely not the *Faith*? You mean she still floats?"

"She does, but not for long."

From aside Jennings muttered, so all could hear, "Four guns against forty-four. Magnificent!" Hart shot him a glare of hatred.

Howe shook his head, his eyes wide. "That little

305

vessel decimated you, Captain Hart. And you propose to go after her again? I wonder why?"

Hart contained himself, white-faced. "Matter of honor, Milord."

"Well, I should think so! However, I cannot allow it, Captain. Warrant or not, I need your frigate to join escort on four ships-of-the-line. We have a campaign to wage, Sir."

"And as I said, Sir, I must decline. Now, may I . . ."

"Captain Hart, don't force me to read you the articles of command, Sir. You already have earned a severe reprimand for your conduct in Delaware Bay, but I would as soon postpone that. Now come, Sir. Accept fleet orders and we'll get about our business here. You may access the yards and all appurtenances just as soon as you have signed for this campaign. I can have it no other way, Sir. I am short of commission vessels. I am calling in all warrants."

"And I," Hart said stolidly, "decline."

Howe rounded on him, eyes blazing. "If you decline, Sir, I shall have you on report before the Court of King George."

"You have no grounds, Milord. *Courtesan* is on full warrant. It is my right to accept or decline any but general orders. Do you have them?"

"You know I do not. But I have my authority."

"Yes, Milord. But it does not apply to *Courtesan*."

"It applies to this fleet, to these yards, and to the wares stocked here, and by God, Sir, you shall have no access."

"You cannot do that, Milord."

"Captain Hart, you have put me to the test. I can, and I am. From this moment *Courtesan* is decommissioned from fleet service on bad report. The company of marines aboard her is hereby withdrawn for other service. We can do without her . . . and without you. Your present ship's compliment are under your articles, but you shall have no replacements. Sailors of the King do not serve aboard private vessels. Further, your vessel is blocking King's waters out there. I give you one hour to remove it. And hear me, Sir. If you attempt to enter provision dock, if you attempt to enter the yards, if you are still within the authority of this harbor an hour from now, I shall blow *Courtesan* right out of the water.

"I cannot revoke your commission, Sir. Would that I could. But I can and do remove you from the service of my Admiralty. Go about your damned piracy, Captain, but if you ever dare fly the flag of England or of this Admiralty you will be charged as a hostile and treated as such by any ship at hand. Now get out!"

The color had drained from Hart's face. Now it was replaced by livid fury. He gritted his teeth, turned and strode from the room. Behind him he heard muted exclamations and Howe's angry voice, "I'd stockade the man if I could. Just one charge under Crown authority and I'd have him in irons, by damn!"

When Hart had gone back to his launch, Roger Mercer entered the office. "Signal from the yards, Milord. They've spotted sailors from the *Courtesan* jumping ship. They ask what action, Sir."

307

"No action, Captain. No action whatever. They are *Courtesan's* problem, not ours."

"Oh, and Sir, there's a young officer waiting to see you. Commander Lewis Farrington, late of the sloop *Wolf*. He's lost his ship, Sir. He's here to report."

"He'll have to wait, Captain. I'll see him when we've finished here. Oh, what I would give for a legitimate charge against that captain! It's men like him who made the problems in the colonies."

Within the hour *Courtesan* had made sail and cleared the harbor, her crew depleted now to fewer than a hundred men. At the helm Mister Mace kept his eyes ahead and his thoughts to himself as he brought her south with a quartering wind. The man behind him, brooding and pacing, was in a state Mace had never before seen. It would not do to catch his attention.

XXI

It was a singular-appearing vessel that put into Delaware Bay on the night day of September, 1777. A schooner by design, it was high-railed fore and aft, with a shingled deck house amidships and odd double-braced davits carrying a heavy launch astern. Gaff-top sail blocks hung from both topmasts, and the snouts of long eight-pounders protruded from bulwarks at forepeak and stern. Despite its size, the ship had fighting tops on both masts.

Its name was *Gladys* and it had fought. Battle scars showed in the fothering of the hull, the myriad patches on its sails, the bright cording spliced into stays and shrouds. Its beams were smeared and streaked with patching tar. One of its catheads had been shot away. But it took the wind like a sweet lady and handled daintily as it beat up into the river.

"Indee trader," a bystander allowed as the schooner rounded off Dover. "I wager she's fought pirates."

"Trader? With them chasers?" Another shook his

head. "That there's one of Dale's privateers, sure as the world. She's been playin' hell with somebody."

"If she's one of Dale's privateers, what's she doing up here?"

"I don't know," the watcher said solemnly, "and I ain't about to ask."

She anchored in midchannel off the lower point docks and lowered her launch, and a company of seven put ashore, avoiding the areas where there was activity. Oarsmen returned the launch to the ship, where riflemen stood guard at the rails. Near Sutton's dock, where the sheered cutter *Triumph* was careened for repairs and refitting, Isaac Purdue and Shelby Jones sat on a roadhouse porch and watched curiously.

"Not overly friendly, are they, Cap'n?"

"Seems not." Purdue squinted and shaded his eyes, studying the schooner.

"Do you know her, Cap'n?"

"I don't know. Something about the silhouette . . . no, I suppose not." Yet through the waning day, Jones saw his captain pause several times to gaze out toward the anchored schooner. He seemed puzzled.

From lower point, the seven from the schooner walked to an inn, had supper there, and waited for a coach to Wilmington. They were a quiet group. They kept to themselves and none saw fit to approach them. Four of the five men had the look of sailors, but they carried rifles. The fifth, a tall man in a blue coat, wore a sword. Of the two boys, one carried a long rifle and one a pistol. They kept their baggage close about them.

It was an all-night journey to Wilmington, by

coach-and-four. They were the only passengers, and the driver and guard rested easy. Woe be to the highwayman who braced that lot sleeping below.

Sunlight was bright in the east parlor of John Singleton Ramsey's house when a wide-eyed servant interrupted the great man's breakfast. "There's folks here to see you, Sir. They waitin' in the entry."

"Who are they, Colly?"

"Well, they's a man an' two boys in an' four more outside, but one of the boys ain't a boy, sir, it's Miss Constance. Least, I think that's who it is. I don't . . ."

"Colly, will you get out of the way?" She burst through the door. "Papa, it's me. I'm home!"

His chair clattered to the floor behind him. They rushed together and locked in a misty-eyed embrace. Through the open doorway Patrick Dalton watched, seeing a plump, pleasant-looking man with the eyes of a trader.

Ramsey peeled Constance off him and held her at arm's length. "Look at you! Just look at you! Young lady, what have you done? Where have you been? I should take a strap to you. I should . . . look at those clothes! What in Heaven's name are you . . ."

"Oh, Papa, hush. Everything's fine. I have all your money."

"What money? What is going on, Constance?"

"Your money, Papa. We got *Faith* and took her up to Rhode Island and sold all the rum, and then we came back. Oh, Papa, it was so exciting, you'll never . . ."

Ramsey cast a dazed look around him and noticed the two strangers in the doorway beyond Colly. The young man was tall and slim, blue-coated, and stood spread-legged, his hands behind him, as a man might stand on a quarterdeck. The boy had an armload of ledgers.

"Hello? Constance, who are these people?"

"Oh, Papa, I want you to meet Mister Dalton. And this is Billy Caster. He has the accounts. We got an excellent price for the rum."

Still dazed, he put her aside. "Colly, bring chairs. And another pot of tea, please. Missy, I think we had best all sit down and see if we can get to the bottom of this."

Dalton and Billy judiciously chose chairs out of the line of fire and pushed them further back before sitting. They took tea, glanced at each other solemnly, and remained silent. It was going to be up to Constance to get this straightened out.

An hour later John Ramsey had the gist of it. He sprawled in his chair, looking drained, as Constance went off to bathe and change clothing. For a while Ramsey just sat, trying to let it all soak in. Then he squared his shoulders, hitched his chair around, and fixed Dalton with a gaze of pure, cold malevolence. "Young man, I simply don't know what I should do next. I don't know whether I should shake your hand or call my servants in and have you caned insensible. This is simply beyond belief!"

Dalton nodded soberly. "I quite agree, Sir."

"Not two weeks ago I spoke with your Admiral Lord Howe. He agreed my vessel would be returned to me intact. And now this. I gather *Faith* was gone even at the time we were speaking, and my daughter aboard her. And battles at sea, and a shipload of convicts, and my own daughter . . ." His voice trailed off, his words failing him.

For lack of a better opening Dalton said, "You seem quite well, sir. I had understood you were in poor health."

"It was nothing. A bout of the vapors. I am quite recovered. Don't change the subject. What has happened to my daughter?"

"I assure you, sir, Miss Constance is quite undamaged. She has, of course, been in some jeopardy, but there was nothing I could do about that save to protect her as best I could, which I have done. I regret the entire occurrence, sir, but it has ended happily."

"The devil it has! I do not expect to be happy again for quite some time to come, Mister Dalton. What then of *Faith?*"

"I presume your vessel was insured, sir?"

"Of course it was . . . is . . . and handsomely."

"Then I suggest you apply to your insurers, sir. *Faith* is gone."

"Gone? Gone where? How?"

Dalton dropped his eyes. "Just . . . gone. I'll say no more than that about the schooner."

Ramsey stared at him, then turned on Billy, an imperious finger thrust at him. "You, boy! Billy, is it? How do you say? What of my ship?"

Startled and embarrassed, Billy kept his eyes on the books in his lap. *"Faith* is gone, Sir. It's like Captain Dalton says. That's all."

Ramsey shook his head slowly, methodically. "Very well, then, I shall ask Constance. Now about the cargo. Constance says you sold it? By whose authority, sir?"

"By the authority of the owner's agent, sir. Miss Constance. It was sold at the port of Westerly, below Newport. Billy has all the accountings, and the men waiting outside are guarding the money."

"The men outside? Oh, yes. Colly, go get those men and send them in here. Mister Dalton, I am acquainted with the pirates at Westerly, and I dread to open those books. I had counted on getting top price for that cargo. It was important to me."

"Billy, give Mister Ramsey the cargo register, if you please."

Ramsey read the numbers, then read them again. "By the Lord, sir, how did you manage that?"

"It was Miss Constance's doing, sir. She held the man's warehouse in ransom. I believe it is quite a good price. As to the rest of *Faith's* cargo, we were forced to use it for various contingencies. But I believe the returns from the rum are adequate to cover all of it."

Guy Neely and the others entered then, carrying sacks of coin. They deposited them on the table, then stood back, looking sheepish. Ramsey goggled at them. "Neely? You? And Virgil? And . . . and . . ."

"Michael Romart, Sir. And this here is Jubal Foster. We've hauled for you, Sir, time and again."

"I know who you are. And was it you, then, who took my daughter up to New York, who got her into this mess?"

Dalton came to his feet. "Don't blame these men, Sir. They have no guilt in this."

"Sit down, Mister Dalton. Let them speak. You, Guy Neely. Explain yourself.

"Yes, Sir. We done that. Miss Constance came to

314

us—to me—and said she was going after the *Faith* and would we help her. We didn't have any choice, Sir. It was either that or let her go alone. We couldn't hardly abide that, Sir. And the Cranston boys, bless their souls . . . they're both dead now, Sir . . . they went along for the adventure, so to speak. That's how it was, Sir."

Ramsey was aghast. "Six grown men, and you couldn't stop one little girl from committing a horrible foolishness? I can't believe it."

Neely cocked his head, puzzled. "One little girl, Sir? We're talking about Miss Constance, Sir. How would you have proposed we stop her? She's your daughter."

"Yes," Ramsey sighed. "I know."

Colly reappeared at the door, followed by two more servants bringing tea and chairs.

Ramsey glared defeatedly at Dalton. "I don't suppose you would object if I counted the money."

When Constance returned they were all down on hands and knees on the parlor floor, stacking coin while Billy Caster entered sums into a ledger. At her entrance they all stood wide-eyed. The gown she wore was a froth of yellow crinoline and snow lace. Her hair was done up with combs and a puff cap. Slippered toes peeked from her hem. Neely and his men bowed gallantly, a tribute to beauty. Dalton and John Ramsey stood agape, frozen by their separate reactions. Dalton was dazzled, stunned. The girl who knelt to touch off cannon, who paced grime-faced and imperious about his midships deck, the pretty imp with skirt tied up between her knees, was gone. In her place stood a lady . . . a vision. Dalton felt his knees trembling and hastened to bow to recover his equilibrium.

John Singleton Ramsey saw his daughter, yet not somehow the daughter he knew. Pert smile, radiant hair, tilted eyes, and tilted nose were all in place, but somehow the totality had changed. He stood in the presence of a full woman, and knew he would not see his little girl, as she had been, again. Constance had grown up.

She caught his eye and smiled, but the smile she turned on Patrick Dalton was a far different thing. Ramsey saw it and felt a strange loneliness within. He looked at Dalton and saw the rest of it. He wished his wife could be here. She would have known what to say. Had this man . . . had they . . . no. He caught himself—they had not. But it really didn't matter. There would be no parting them now. "Mister Dalton, where will you go from here?"

"He's going back to sea, Papa. Maybe to New Spain. And I am going with him."

Dalton's eyes went round. "You will do no such thing!"

"And why not?"

"Because I will not allow it!"

"Just as you will not allow laxity aboard your ship? Hush, Patrick. I've decided."

Ramsey sighed. "Then you won't go because I won't allow it. Constance, where is *Faith*?"

She looked at him with a determination he had never seen before. "Didn't Patrick tell you, Papa? *Faith* is gone."

"By damn," he erupted, "will someone give me an answer? Gone where?"

"We had a fight with a frigate, Papa. *Faith* is gone. Please don't ask any more."

"Then how does your Mister Dalton, as you say, propose to go back to sea?"

"Oh, we have a ship, a very nice schooner. Her name is *Gladys.*"

He pursed his lips. "Ah. *Gladys*, is it?" His merchant's eyes studied them one by one. "And a schooner. How convenient. And *Faith* is gone."

"Yes, Papa—gone."

He sagged back into his chair. "Well, I suppose the insurance repayment will come to a tidy bit. And a man can always outfit another ship. But the insurers will want to know a few details, don't you think?"

"We salvaged her records, Sir. Mister Caster has brought you a copy of *Faith's* log, all scribed 'in fine.' All the details are, I trust, intact."

"Yes, Sir," Billy said. "Everything's just as we said."

"A schooner is, after all, no match for a man-of-war," Constance stressed. "Is it, Mister Dalton?"

"Oh, by no means, Miss Constance."

"Then *Faith* is sunk?"

"If I were an insurer, Papa, I would never doubt it for a moment."

Ramsey turned to Neely. "You four? You agree? *Faith* is gone?"

"Gone as ever I seen, Sir." The others nodded. "Poor little thing just couldn't have had a chance against a forty-four-gun frigate."

"Though she did," Jubal Foster chipped in, "manage to sink a brigantine, a brig, two gunboats and a coaster, an' cripple several others before th'

317

frigate caught up." Dalton scowled at him and he went silent. Ramsey stared at him, stared at his daughter, stared at Dalton, stared at his hands. "Sit down, all or you. Whatever the pretense turns out to be, I want to hear the real story, the whole story. And I want it now."

In the evening, Ramsey took Dalton aside. "I fear I have lost my daughter to you, Patrick."

"When I leave the bay, Sir, she will not go with me. I promise you."

Ramsey sighed. "You are a very young man, Patrick. I suspect you have much to learn about women."

Dalton flushed. "Nonetheless, I can't tolerate the idea of her aboard my ship, in jeopardy. Never again."

"No, of course not. What did she say to you after supper?"

"She told me if I did not take her with me, the schooner *Faith* would be resurrected and I'd find myself on the beach."

"Essentially the same tack she took with me. My cargo, since it was sold at Westerly, must be considered contraband. My daughter threatens to so testify if she doesn't get her own way. I am inclined to believe, I suppose, that a pleasant cruise down to New Spain might do no great harm to her—provided she was accompanied by a man of honor."

"I am a gentleman, Mister Ramsey."

"You are Irish, Mister Dalton."

"And you are a smuggler, Mister Ramsey."

Ramsey nodded. "We do see eye-to-eye. But as to

the cruise—it should be safe enough. And I've had in mind for some time to try to establish a trade base in New Spain. You see . . ." He tipped his head, looking more closely at Dalton. "You *do* intend to go to New Spain, don't you?"

There was distance about the younger man, suddenly, a deep melancholy that made him seem far away. He didn't answer.

Ramsey peered at him. "Ah. It's the frigate, isn't it? Your friends . . ."

"It's more than that, Sir. That same frigate—that same man—dishonored his flag a time before. There was a captain, his name was Furney. I sailed with him. He was a good man, Sir. He's dead, and so is his ship . . . and most of the good lads aboard her . . ."

"And it was the same frigate? I see. But Patrick, a schooner? *Faith* is no . . ."

"When I said *Faith* is gone, Sir, I meant it. Maybe you'd like to see for yourself."

"Maybe I would at that."

The two of them, with a pair of Ramsey's men as crew, set out early in the morning. Ramsey's sailing yawl was a fast boat, and they were at the anchorage by noon. The men on the deck of the schooner waved as they recognized Dalton. At sight of the lethal-looking armed ship riding the hull of *Faith*, Ramsey whistled. "I wouldn't have believed it." They hove alongside and boarded.

In Dalton's absence Charley Duncan had taken charge of final repairs. The shot-weakened foremast was splinted and bound with new rope. The blasted

319

cathead had been rebuilt, from rooftree timber. Spars and tackle were repaired and varnished. Permanent deadeyes set the cables that held the fighting tops. They had even trimmed the mounts under the long eights and given the guns sighting slides.

"It is a warship," Ramsey swore. "A jolly-be-damned warship!"

As Dalton trailed along, looking grim, a grinning Charley Duncan showed the merchant about the ship. Ramsey was intrigued. Again and again he shook his head and muttered, "I wouldn't have believed it."

Faith showed her battle scars, but they were neatly patched and mended. The schooner was fighting-fit and ready. Ramsey paused amidships, where dark stains splotched the scrubbed deck. Dalton came up beside him. "Clarence Kilreagh," he said. "A one-legged old Irishman and a friend. And there, Solamon Grimm, an habitual rapist, felon, and fine seaman. And Martin Smith, who couldn't navigate ashore."

Duncan's eyes were concerned. "We tried holy-stoning, Sir, but the stains wouldn't come up."

"No, Mister Duncan, I wouldn't expect they would. You see, Mister Ramsey, the ship has blood upon her, and it calls . . . it calls."

Ramsey was quiet as they headed back up the river in the yawl. He was deep in thought. They were back at his house in time for supper.

It was a silent meal. Ramsey, Dalton, Constance, and Billy Caster were at table. Neely and his men had gone off to see the Cranstons' mother, carrying a purse provided by Ramsey—wages for the two she had lost.

After the meal Ramsey got his daughter aside. "You love him, don't you, Constance?"

The stars were in her eyes. "Yes, Papa, I do. And I'll go with him."

"But he's a marked man, girl. Can't you see that?"

She understood. He was not talking about the charge of treason. "I have seen it. I've seen it all along. It's as though there's a wound in him that will not close. But I can mend it, Papa. I know I can."

He shook his head. "You can't mend it, Constance. It's a wound that requires cleaning by the same as made it. Your young captain is a fortunate man, more so than he knows. But unless he heals himself, the scar will always be there."

"I don't understand, Papa."

"You understand very well. You know what he needs to do, and you know he can't take you with him. Maybe he will come back, girl. And if he does, there are many things we can do to make things right again. But not while he still bleeds. He has a ship and a cause."

"Oh, the damned ship . . ." she stopped, and her eyes filled suddenly. "Oh, I didn't mean that. Oh, no. It truly is his ship, and I understand. Papa?"

"Yes?"

"A rough old man—a very *gentle* rough old man— told me something back there, when we were escaping . . . something about a man and his woman and his ship. He said a man can love both, and they don't conflict unless she makes it so. Was he right, Papa?"

Ramsey nodded. "Yes, dear, he was absolutely right."

"Oh, Papa . . ." she flung herself on him, buried her face in his vest. "I just don't know who will fire his cannons for him."

XXII

On a brisk, overcast morning, Patrick Dalton took the tiller from Charley Duncan as *Gladys* cleared the chop of Delaware Bay and slid into swelling sea. She was a trim ship with a trimmed crew. They had assembled on deck, and he had pared them down. Only those who volunteered, knowing where they were bound, remained aboard the schooner.

The two pressedmen, Tarkington and Moses, were left behind. They had coin in their purses and an offer of work at Ramsey's docks. Billy Caster, grasping a struggling Bernice in his arms, had gazed from the dock as they made sail. It was captain's orders. He could not go. Beside him, Constance and Ramsey watched silently.

Guy Neely had succumbed to the persuasion of Ramsey. He was, after all, a bit old to go adventuring again. And someone had to rebuild number three shed.

But now the rest—nine renegade King's Navy tars,

two Delaware sailors, and an Irish fugitive at the helm—manned a sleek fighting schooner past the protruding shoals and brought her north, full and by on a course upcoast in search of *Courtesan*. The mirth was gone from the former *Faith*. Instead, a grim *Gladys* set forth with great guns full-loaded and great sails trimmed, following the call of the bloodstains on her deck.

There was no laxity aboard this ship. She was going hunting.

Lethal long eights prodded the wind fore and aft. Hard-charged four-pounders sat at ports in her gunwales. A smart swivel gun from Ramsey's stores was mounted amidships, and the new deckhouse carried "cartouche" charges for the guns, as well as powder, shot, fuse, and swabs, and a dozen rifles. The rest were on their way inland. Dalton had carefully not inquired where.

Gladys was to sea and running a long tack when the cutter *Triumph* glided from the distant bay behind and raised its wings.

The seas ran strong. A steady wind bore from the west-northwest and scudded gray clouds beneath the solid overcast of sky.

"There's a cold wind blowing, Mister Duncan," Dalton told his first.

"Will we find her, Cap'n, do ye suppose?"

"We'll find her. Hart's not a man to take a humiliation. Put men in the tops, if you please. I suspect it will not be long."

He held on tack until the shore was out of sight, and a bell more. Then he brought her about cross-wind and tacked westward. Near the coast he came about again, north-northeast, and headed back out. Sharp eyes in the tops scanned the horizon. Below decks, Mister Arthur fired his stove and prepared the dog-watch meal. In midafternoon there was a sighting—far back, hard down on the horizon, a suit of sails. It was not their quarry.

The overcast held and the wind held steady. The schooner had completed another long port tack offshore and was coming about far at sea when Michael Romart squinted from his perch at the foretop and called, "On deck!"

"Aye, Mister Romart?"

"Sail off the starboard bow, Sir! Hard down but comin' on!"

Duncan looked at his captain and Dalton nodded. "It's him, Mister Duncan. The wind says it."

"Now what, Sir?"

"Continue on course, Mister Duncan. Tack for inshore to catch the wind. We should have sight of him soon. We'll just let him come to us."

There was a coldness in him as the schooner made west on short tack, aiming for the coastline. I could go to ground here, he thought, and no harm done. I could get inshore and let him pass. I could come about, get the wind on my beam, and make for the open sea. Chances are he has not even seen me yet. It would be so easy. Just put her on a beam reach east-southeast . . . at that angle to the wind no square-rigger alive could catch her. We could be long gone. We could fly. . . .

Fly? Or flee? Again in his mind he saw a sluggish boat under sail on choppy seas, a frightened boy at its tiller, going away. Safety ahead, fear behind. Fly away. Fly from Belfast. Fly from Ireland. Fly from the wrath of Fitzgerald's churls. Fly from the responsibility of captaincy . . . hide in subservience. Fly from Long Island. Flee . . . he closed his eyes tightly and let out a long-held breath. Not again. He had flown too much, fled too much. Even a poor fox, too long harried, must turn and bare its fangs. To die? Possibly. But to die then as a fighter in its full.

He held course with a firm hand on the tiller. To fly would be to never return to Constance, to live a fugitive knowing she had been there, waiting, and beyond hope.

Can a schooner destroy a frigate? Can the fox destroy the hunter? At what point does it no longer have a choice? And when it does not, what then? It goes for the throat.

He let his mind open to the voices around him— the grim voices of men out for blood. They trusted him. They were less frightened than he, because they had him to turn to. He was the captain. It rested with him.

Distant coastline was in sight, a bleak thread on the horizon. It was vaguely familiar.

"On deck!"

He roused himself. "Yes, Mister Grimm?"

"I can read her sails, Sir. It is a frigate."

He squinted into the distance to his right. Yes, there she was. A tiny dot at the edge of the world, still miles away. His gaze roved back to the shore ahead and the familiarity hit him. It was here *Herrett* had fought the snows. That was the same coastline he had seen beyond the fleeing schooner. It was here *Courtesan* had betrayed *Herrett*. It was here Captain Furney had died . . . and with him his ship.

The blooded deck of *Faith* had come back here.

She sang her wind song as she rode the swells, responsive to his hand, lithe and trim as a corsair, drumming sails spread full on a long beam reach, crooning easily at half hull-speed.

The dot was perceptibly closer when he read the shoreline. Out there, *Courtesan* sailed with the wind at her back, coming to meet him. On her present course the wind was square-rigger's wind. But out *there* . . . he looked back into the open sea . . . out there the wind was what you made of it. Set your course across it and it would be schooner's wind. Then no vessel could be her master.

"By the mark four, Sir. Shoaling."

There was no more time. Come left and flee, or come right and fight. When does the fox turn? When it decides to.

"Very well, Mister Duncan. Hands to the sheets. Bring her about for port tack. Trim and taut, Mister Duncan." As the sheets eased, he put the tiller over and the schooner came about, its lofty nose sweeping north, northeast, jib aligning on the speck of sail beyond, sweeping past. "Sheet home! Sheet home! Trim and find your battle stations, lads. All hands on deck!"

She took the wind on her hind quarter and leapt into the swells, climbing nose-high as she picked up way. Iron-gray water curled past her bow and broke into driving spray. North-northeast she ran, hull-up and singing, and men gathered at the port rails to peer ahead at the now-discernable frigate coming south.

"He hasn't turned, Sir. Do you suppose he's seen us?"

They watched. The frigate did not veer. Soon they would be past its course. It should have started angling to intercept. Duncan came aft. "Do you suppose, Sir, at this distance he doesn't recognize us?"

Dalton swore. Of course he didn't. Fighting tops, raised gunwales—the schooner's silhouette was greatly changed. "Go below to the sail locker, Mister Duncan. You'll find a red flag with white cross. Bring it up, run it to the masthead. He'll know that when he sees it."

The schooner ran up her battle flag. The white cross on a red field fluttered in the wind. It was a flag she had worn before. It was Captain Hart's own prize flag. Men on the foredeck gaped at it in wonder, then whooped and cheered as they recognized it.

"On deck!"

"Aye, Mister Grimm?"

"The frigate's changing course, Sir. She's . . . aye! She's coming to intercept!"

"Mister Duncan, do we still have our proper escutcheons?"

"Aye, Sir. They're stowed forward."

"Then break them out, Mister Duncan. We've been *Gladys* long enough. If *Faith* is going to glory, let it be by her own name."

"On deck! Another sail, Sir. Aft an' a quarter astarboard. I make her a cutter, Sir."

"How does she bear?"

"She flanks us, Sir. North-northeast the course."

Did Hart again have two ships? He remembered the fighting coaster in the funnel. No, there had not been time. This was another ship, then. An outsider. Hope, then, it doesn't get itself involved here.

"Keep an eye on her, tops. But the frigate's our concern."

They sounded bells as the distant coastline disappeared below the horizon. Dalton held steady on course and watched the frigate grow as it angled toward them from the northwest, closing. After a time he could see the dark shape of its hull. He judged distance, speeds. He needed to cross paths ahead of the frigate, avoid coming abeam of it.

Forty-four guns it carried, with its firepower amassed along its sides. Abeam of it was death. They were near now, and closing fast. "Up gafftops, Mister Duncan! Tops aloft!"

Faith heeled as the high laterals took wind, and her hull-keen rose in pitch. Bright water coursed in sheets from her driving bow.

"We can range him soon with the bow chaser, Captain. Shall we open fire?"

"Hold fire, Mister Duncan. One last time, we'll give the prizemaster the honor of the first shot."

Duncan grinned, understanding the subtlety. "Aye, Sir."

They closed to a half-mile, then a quarter. With all laterals flying, *Faith* was outpacing the frigate. She would reach their crossing barely ahead of her foe. At three chain lengths they stared across at each other, beam-to-bow, converging. Smoke blossomed from forward batteries of the frigate. A ball flew overhead, another scudded into the schooner's wake. Two more plowed water ahead and beyond. There was no question this time—Captain Hart was no longer trying to take the schooner. He was out to destroy. Dalton smiled tightly.

"Port guns and swivel, hold on her nose. Fire as she bears."

Faith closed on the big ship, took a swell, and dived ahead of it, almost under its looming bowsprit. The thunder of guns was a rolling avalanche of sound. A ball from *Courtesan's* bow chaser holed the schooner's spanker, and iron balls crashed into the frigate's forecastle deck. In an instant *Faith* was past, scooting under the warship's nose while it still rode in its own smoke. "Bow chaser, bear and fire!"

Behind Dalton the great long eight lurched and bellowed at *Faith's* stern rail. Gouts of splintered wood flew from *Courtesan's* fore hull. There was a gaping hole behind her spreader stays. Then they were away, and Dalton eased the schooner about, coming through the wind.

A quarter mile to the southeast, *Courtesan* put her nose to the wind and stood, dead still in the water, waiting. There was a cheer from *Faith's* foredeck. "First blood! First blood!"

"Don't let them get too assured, Mister Duncan. We've hardly hurt him. We've done barely more than made him angry."

The ships stood off, assessing each other. Dalton was content. The first strike was his, and the second

330

move was his advantage. He was dead upwind of the frigate. It had no choice but to wait his play.

"All reloaded, Sir."

"Very well, Mister Duncan. Please bring all the four-pounders to the starboard rail. I think this time we shall try to unload all seven guns in one pass."

Spanker and spencer were hauled full out a'starboard, and *Faith* took the sea on her cleaving breast—due downwind, rudder compensating for slanted sail. She drove head-on at the waiting giant. As they neared, *Courtesan's* spars turned and the big ship began easing to the right, bringing its beam batteries to play. Dalton gritted his teeth and held course. Smoke billowed from the frigate, a solid cloud of it blanketing the great port beam. *Faith* shivered as a pair of balls splintered wood high in her forward hull. Another clipped strands low on the port shroud. Others threw great spumes of spray across her deck, and there was a rending crash high in the tops. Debris rained on her deck. At a glance, Dalton saw half the fighting top on the mainmast dangling loose, fouling the bridle of the spanker sail. Then *Faith's* long bow chaser roared, and he heard a crash from the closing frigate. With hard hands he eased the tiller and let the sails take her. *Faith* heeled about, hard aport. The gun crews on her starboard rail were waiting. Four four-pounders opened fire as they hove past the frigate, close and deadly. The swivel gun barked, and Ishmael Bean shouted, "By God, I took out her bilge pumps!"

Faith continued her tight arc, cross-wind and back toward the wind, putting *Courtesan* close on her

331

dancing stern. The long-eight there spoke again, and a bow-chaser from *Courtesan* echoed it.

From above, a crash and a scream. Something plunged from the tops to splash alongside *Faith*, then was gone. He fought the tiller, through the wind and about, to stand again upwind of the frigate, a harried fox catching its breath.

In coming about, *Courtesan* had made way to the east. Now they stood as they had before, a quarter-mile apart, nose-on. "Damage, Mister Duncan?" he glanced at the pale face of his first.

"We've lost Mister Abernathy, Captain. He was in the main-top. We've got a hell of a snarl up there, you see . . ."

High in the mainmast was a shambles of broken spar, fluttering line, and bits of loose rigging. Men were swarming the shrouds to clear it away. Dalton assessed it. *Faith* was wounded now. She could maneuver, but some of the quickness would be gone. Abernathy . . . a bright, ferret-faced able seaman. God save you, Mister Abernathy, he thought.

Minutes passed as they cleared away in the tops. When they came down again *Faith* was in shape to sail, but short-rigged on the main. Some of her agility was gone. In the distance, *Courtesan* had described a great circle, swinging away with the wind, then circling back to stand starboard-on to the schooner. *Faith's* upwind pass had hurt her. Hart would not let him do that again. He was ready. The schooner could no longer sweep past without coming along the frigate's beam, exposed to a full broadside. Dalton got out his glass. The frigate's nose was a shambles of shattered timbers. Its staysail was down, the spreader wrecked on one side, and its martingale was halved. And he knew there were holes in its hull on the far side. Still the frigate remained ten times the ship *Faith* was—in size, in guns, in massed fire-power.

"Do you know if we holed him at waterline, Mister Duncan?"

"I think we did once, Sir. But I couldn't be sure."

Damn those port and starboard batteries! *Faith's* only chance was to sink the frigate. The schooner could not win a standup fight. And to sink her, they must hole her abeam enough times to flood her holds. But abeam was death. There were her teeth, her great gun batteries. He remembered the dark snow's bombards. Never again.

"We will attempt a feint, Mister Duncan. Hold our guns on the starboard. We will fire broadside from there again."

Sails took the wind and *Faith* charged down again at the waiting frigate. This would be the last dash from upwind, he knew. "Concentrate all guns on the waterline. Fire as she bears. Remember what our lady said, Mister Duncan? She said accuracy with a cannon is no mystery. You just point the bloody thing and fire."

Faith drove for the frigate's nose, closing hard into the range of her starboard guns. Dalton counted the seconds. He knew the knack of *Courtesan's* gunners. He counted on that. At a distance of four chain lengths he put her hard over aport, and even as she turned, the frigate's entire starboard rank of guns

333

erupted. The deck heaved below Dalton's feet as a ball holed the schooner from side to side directly below him. A foot astern and it would have smashed his rudder.

The sea behind the schooner boiled with scudding cannonballs. *Faith* raced toward the warship's stern. "Waterline, Mister Duncan! Fire as she bears." Again the four four-pounders thundered, a ragged synchronization of bedlam, and Dalton saw three gouts of water against the hull of the frigate. Another was high, holing her just above the water. Now he's hurt, he thought. Now he knows how it feels. *Faith* skidded past, under the frigate's stern. The swivel gun barked, shooting up through the quarterdeck, and a moment later the aft long eight put a ball through the warship's stern, just missing the rudder. That ball would travel half the length of the great ship before it was spent, he estimated. It would be hell in there.

He started to come about, and the world exploded. Something hit him a smashing blow between the shoulders, throwing him forward. There was a crash like a falling tree. He picked himself up, dazed and bloody from skidding along the deck. A large piece of ship's rail lay atop him.

"They've got our mainmast, Sir!" Duncan was hauling him to his feet. Even as he looked up the mainmast swayed drunkenly and stays sang and parted. *Faith* reeled. All about there was a crackling like gunshots. At its stump, the great mast was holed and parting. With a heavy shudder and screaming lines, it toppled to the right, overside, taking spanker

334

and gafftop down with it. *Faith* sat low and broken in the swelling sea, dragging her wings in the water. A pair of legs protruded from beneath the shattered stump. Their feet wore boots, not buckled shoes. Virgil Cowan was dead.

Dalton shook his head. He seemed to have no great damage himself, though his back was a solid bruise. "Hands to the main, Mister Duncan. Cut it away and look lively."

They set to with axes and knives. Broken shrouds, gnarled lumps of stayline, snarls of rigging went overboard. And finally, with boathooks and pries, they pushed the great stump off *Faith's* shuddering beam. *Courtesan* had come full about and was closing aft. "Man the foresheets! Spencer alee. Sheet home! Sheet home!"

Raggedly, as Dalton plied the sodden tiller, the schooner took wind on a single mast and headed east, plowing water like a scow, her balance gone. Astern, *Courtesan* also was limping. But the warship still rode high and came on.

"On deck ! On deck!"

"My God," Dalton jerked upright. "Mister Grimm, why are you still up there?"

In the foretop Brevis Grimm was pointing wildly. Dalton swung around. Angling in from upwind was a cutter, all sails full, guns run out and nose high. As he saw it it veered, made directly at the frigate and swept past, a dashing run under its nose with all guns firing. The thunder was deafening as it rolled across the water. Both ships were shrouded in smoke. Then the cutter was past and going about, tacking due west, going away. He caught a glimpse of the colors flying haughtily at its gafftop. It was the same cutter that had pursued *Faith* in Long Island Sound.

Desperately, they fought to gain way. *Faith* ran heavy, nose-down, creeping windward. Yet she moved, and as the waters whispered by she picked up a little speed. Slowly she left the staggering frigate behind. Hart was in no hurry now. He could bind his wounds and take his time. The schooner could no longer escape him in any wind.

A mile or more to the west, they saw the smart cutter putting over, turning upwind. Dalton envied him. He could no longer get upwind. Now he was vulnerable.

With a half-mile separating them, Dalton brought his schooner about a final time, nose-on toward the frigate. With her jibsails and spencer still intact, *Faith* regained a little of her spirit as she took the wind on her nose. Her bow rose slightly and waters whispered by her beam.

Dalton looked about him at his wrecked ship. Debris and wreckage were everywhere. Charley Duncan and Cadman Wise met him in the stern. Their faces were white. "Has he beaten us, Sir?" Wise asked. "Are we going to die?"

There's no flying now, Patrick Dalton, he told himself. You haven't the wings to fly.

As though reading his thoughts, Duncan said, "We still have teeth, Sir."

"Aye, we still have teeth." Out across the water, the frigate was binding its wounds. It would come when it was ready. Dalton's eyes widened. "Gentlemen, assemble all hands. There may be a way."

336

Muffled thunder came from the north. Smoke stood high out there. Like a gnat harrassing a war-horse, the cutter had run in and swept the frigate again. Now it was racing away. Dalton appreciated the assistance.

He assembled them and outlined his plan. Their faces were grim. Duncan breathed, "Audacious." The rest just looked at him and nodded. Then they went to work.

From the chain locker they retrieved the last four kegs of Constance Ramsey's Greek fire. "Ugly little bombs, aren't they?" Duncan asked, loading one of the tar-blackened casks aboard the hauled-up launch hanging from its stern davits. In the top of each cask was a touch-hole sealed with tar. They placed them carefully in the launch, then built a fire in a sand-tub on *Faith's* stern deck. Tar-clothed torches were placed ready to hand.

Hauling from the capstan, they drew the great long eight from the stern and drug it to the bow, where they mounted it alongside its mate. The four-pounders were ranked slide to slide at the starboard rail and the swivel gun trained a'starboard. All of these were quoined high, their snouts pointed up-ward at an impossible-seeming angle. They seemed almost to be standing on end. Seamen gaped at them and shook their heads.

Every boathook and fending pole aboard was laid out at the starboard rail. Every man aboard armed himself with pistol and cutlass, and Victory Locke came up from the hold with Claude Mallory and Purdy Fisk trailing behind him. Among them they carried ten primed rifles. They headed into the

337

shrouds, up toward the remaining mast's fighting top, Victory Lock chiding them as they went, "Look alive there, ye scutters, an' handle these things like Mister Caster taught ye. Shoot at them, not us."

Seven men remained on deck. They would need no sail-tending. Once her tattered few sails were set, *Faith* would not trim again. She was going only one direction.

Dalton looked about. There was nothing more to do. "Make sail, then, lads, one last time. Let's trim her up and make her run. Set our course to ram."

With white faces and frightened eyes they dressed Spencer and gafftop on the lonely foremast, and *Faith* shrugged her bows and crept forward, forty degrees into the wind, aligning her sprit on the dark tower of the frigate. Gradually, tiredly, she picked up speed.

"We'll take a beating going in," Duncan allowed. "He'll throw everything he has."

"Then we'll just take it," Dalton said. "There's no other way." Far out to the north, the little cutter had come about and was making again for the frigate.

Faith raised her nose like a tired and beaten lady. Her song was ragged, her helm unsure, but she took the wind on her remaining sails and began her run. By the time she had closed a quarter mile she was as hull-up as she could now be.

The frigate was scarred, but not mortally. Down in her bilges, they would be patching those waterline holes. She sat deep now, but rode steady. She had all her masts, all her sails, and all her guns, and as

Faith closed Dalton had a glimpse of Jonathan Hart at the quarterdeck rail, feet spread and hands behind him, contentedly watching them come. The man was mad, obviously. He was about to be rammed broadside, and he made no move to escape. Then his guns started speaking and Dalton understood. Hart did not expect *Faith* ever to reach him.

One after another the frigate's beam guns spat balls at the schooner's prow. Most of them scudded alongside, sheeting spray. The trim hull was a small target head-on. But now one took her below the bow, and bulkheads collapsed below deck. And again she shuddered as a ball sheared her martingale stay and her bowsprit wavered under its weight of sail. Again she was hulled, and yet again. But still she moved. She closed, fury raining around her, smoke rolling across her path. Hart was at the quarterrail again, but he did not look content now. He was pacing, shouting orders. Two chain lengths and *Faith* took a ball in her knees. Her foredeck sagged. Then the range was point blank. Duncan at one and Wise at the other, they touched fuse to the twin long eights, and panic erupted aboard *Courtesan*. Both guns were loaded to the breech with nails.

Faith closed. In the final yards she actually seemed to pick up speed. Dalton prayed as he hauled the tiller hard over. The rudder must carry her now. With an agility like her old self, *Faith* swung her bow. She was so close that her bowsprit raked the frigate's beam strakes as she hove in. Then her spreader shattered against a gunport. Lines screamed and parted in the fore. Her fife rails crumbled and deadeyes took the slack of fore shrouds as she sheered along the side of the great ship, her braced deckline collapsing its hull in a long, grinding gash along its side. When she ground to a shuddering halt the two ships were together, *Faith's* deck four feet below *Courtesan's* banked gunports. In unison the *Faith's* grime-streaked crew touched off all of the four-pounders and the swivel gun, shooting iron ball directly upward through hull and deck. Planking, tackle, decking, and gore erupted upward at five points along the frigate's starboard side. In a blind panic, gunners and deck hands fled from the gun-wales—those who still could flee.

"Rifles! Covering fire!" Dalton roared. "Mister Wise! Mister Romart! Cast off the launch! Torches alight!"

They raced for the stern. Lines sang as the heavy launch dropped from its davits into the water below *Faith's* tail, in the lee of the frigate's hull. Torches alight, they tossed them into the boat, then lit more. "The bedammed stuff isn't catchin', Sir," Wise screamed. "The torches are fallin' under it, not on it!"

Rifles barked from the fighting top. Victory Locke's crew was trying desperately to hold back the surging men on *Courtesan's* deck. Ten shots were all they would have. "More torches, Mister Wise!" Dalton ordered. He drew his sword. "We'll buy you some time. Hands to board! Over we go!"

With four men behind him he clambered up over the frigate's gunwale and into bedlam. The dead and injured were everywhere. The guns had done their work. The deck was a confusion of wreckage and scurrying men. Someone came at him with a boathook and he ducked, then took the man on his sword. He withdrew just in time to strike down another, then his crew were about him, pistols and cutlasses, defending the deck. Purdy Fisk held his cutlass in both hands, swinging it like a flail. Michael Romart carried a piece of cask as a shield, and his blade snaked from behind it, becoming redder with each stroke. Claude Mallory was defending his right, and Charley Duncan his left. Men charged them, then faded back. They had the circle of deck to themselves.

Victory Locke came scrambling down the frigate's shrouds, dropped to the deck and swung a long rifle into the face of a charging gunner. From behind and below Dalton heart shouts and glanced around. At *Faith's* stern rail Brevis Grimm had grabbed up a torch and was teetering on the rail. Even as Cadman Wise reached for him he jumped. As his body hit the edge of the launch he swung the flaming torch down on top of one of the Greek fire casks and it burst alight.

Something hit Dalton a glancing blow and he whirled to ward off a swinging boathook. "She's alight! *Faiths* to me! Over we go!"

As they pulled in about him he heard a shout, high and angry, above the turmoil. Beyond the seamen ringing them was one in officer's coat and cockaded hat, brandishing a sword. Twin epaulettes gleamed on his tailored shoulders and there was a madness in his eyes. Swinging his sword, he fought to clear through the crush of his own men, his eyes never leaving Dalton. But the press was too great. Men surged and Hart was pushed back and away. There was no more time.

Dalton shouted, "To the *Faith!* Over the side!"

They scrambled past him, fighting the crushing men behind them, and one by one dropped over the rail, back to *Faith's* deck. "Pikes and poles now," Dalton called. "Cast her off!"

With one final slash at a pin-wielding man, he jumped to the rail and over, rolling as he hit *Faith's* deck. He whirled to fend off a return boarding party, but there was none. Sweating and grunting, the men about him put their backs into the poles, pushing *Faith* away from *Courtesan's* looming hull. Slowly she edged away.

Cannons thundered somewhere, and there was the crash of splintering deck. The cutter had swept in again, attacking from the other side.

They pushed, putting all their might into it. Seven poles thrust against the battered hull before them and *Faith* crept away, sliding past the lee. Her nose emerged into the wind and limp jibsails filled. She tugged and moved, coming away.

The sounds of fighting erupted again on the deck above them, and Dalton looked up as the frigate's hull began to slide past. A great-shouldered, half-bearded figure appeared there, grinning down at him. Robert Arthur had a pike pole through him, protruding a foot from his chest. He also had a man in each hand, waving them like dolls. One of them wore epaulettes on both tailored shoulders. As blood gushed from his still-grinning mouth, Robert Arthur swung his arms together, cracking two last skulls.

Faith found her wind and slipped away, off the riding beam of the great ship. Dark smoke roiled behind her, and flames shot up the side of *Courtesan's* hull. The frigate had the wind behind her—a square-rigger's wind—and it pushed her relentlessly forward against the blazing launch snugged under her lee.

XXIII

What the cutter *Triumph* escorted into Delaware Bay on the fifteenth day of September, 1777, looked like nothing much at all. A battered hull, most of its bow and much of its beams shot away, a foremast carrying shred of sail and no mainmast at all, it crept, limped, and stumbled as it made its plodding way upchannel. But it came under its own power, on spencer and jibs, and there was no towline on it.

Isaac Purdue held *Triumph* back, letting the wrecked schooner lead the way in, as befitted a proud lady.

Slowly, inching along at a single knot to keep water from washing her bilges, she negotiated the lower bay and came to south point, where awed yardsmen put out in boats to bring her to the dock. No one asked her name and she traveled incognito. There were no escutcheons upon her, nor any aboard. She was just a battered warrior, and was due the honor of her rest.

Those who came down from her deck were equally

battered. They had washed away the grime of battle, but their wounds remained. And those who looked into their eyes turned away very quickly and did not look back. There were only eight of them, and the last one off was a tall young man in a tattered blue coat. Despite his limp, despite the bandages and bruises, he had the look of a captain.

After a time they were met, and taken away upriver. And those who had questions of Isaac Purdue, gazing thoughtfully after them, got little answer. "Some tales," he said, "will last awhile to the telling."

In the quiet study of John Singleton Ramsey's great house, Patrick Dalton sat in moody silence before the hearth. He had been fed, rested, tended, and clothed, and it seemed there was a finality about it. All the things that were done were done. He had run, then turned and fought, and he had lived. *Faith* might never sail again, but he had brought her home.

He would go somewhere, do something, he supposed. Maybe he still could make for New Spain. But right now he was drained. Oddly, the aftermath was cold and lonely.

Then a door opened and he turned.

"Put it right there, Colly," she said. The man lugged a keg into the room and set it on the floor beside Dalton. "Thank you, Colly. That will be all."

Dalton stared into the fire, disinterested . . . remote.

When the door had closed behind the servant,

Constance tugged a bench before the fire. "Patrick," she said, "come sit here. There's room for two."

He turned, started to shake his head, and stopped. She stood there in the firelight, her arms full of quilts and two tin mugs in her hands.

"And you might open that keg while you're at it," she told him. "You are a cold and irritating man, Patrick Dalton. But only when you're sober."

EPILOGUE

EPILOGUE

"Black Dick" Howe's advance up the Hudson had failed. "Gentleman Johnny" Burgoyne's advance down the lakes to unite with him ended in capitulation at Saratoga, and the Crown's best plan to strangle the young revolution ended in defeat. There would be other maneuvers, other strategies, but in the meantime the colonies gained strength. Where there had been smithies now there were foundries, casting great guns for the ships being readied in forty or more yards protected by American rifles.

In Philadelphia they were saying that the war being fought on land would be won at sea.

And where there were yards to build ships, there were men to sponsor them. Some would be warships. Some would not.

Mould lofts, keel blocks, mast ponds, and sliding ways crowded the waterfront at South Point. Before them was water for launching and behind was timber for building. Ropewalks and sail loft stood shoulder-to-shoulder with hewing pens and chandleries. Drone of saws and call of riggers blended with the ring of hammers and the chants of careening crews.

High on the point, drawn up on ways, a battered hulk was being stripped down for fittings, while nearby a new hull took shape. Fine-cured new keel sported a sturdy stern post. Treenails bound the knees of a ribwork of trim-curved futtocks. Cypress strakes, stringers, and wales were fitted under the eye of a master shipwright while great pine boles waited in the mast pond to be stepped into place.

The new vessel's design, drawn on the floor of the mould loft, had come from no designer's plans, but from measurement of the members and fits of the shattered hull nearby.

No skill was spared in the building of the new ship, for this would be John Singleton Ramsey's vessel and its accounts were paid as the work progressed.

Months would pass ere she stood to the stepping of masts and spars, the rigging of shrouds, and the dressing of her fine suit of new sails, but already those who worked her knew her by name.

She would take the water as a proud topsail schooner. She would make the music of the sea for a man who had ears to hear it. She would go where she would, with a master's hand at her tiller.

Her name would be *Faith*.

PINNACLE BRINGS YOU THE FINEST IN FICTION

THE HAND OF LAZARUS (17-100-2, $4.50)
by Warren Murphy & Molly Cochran

The IRA's most bloodthirsty and elusive murderer has chosen the small Irish village of Ardath as the site for a supreme act of terror destined to rock the world: the brutal assassination of the Pope! From the bestselling authors of GRANDMASTER!

LAST JUDGMENT (17-114-2, $4.50)
by Richard Hugo

Only former S.A.S. agent James Ross can prevent a centuries-old vision of the Apocalypse from becoming reality . . . as the malevolent instrument of Adolf Hitler's ultimate revenge falls into the hands of the most fiendish assassin on Earth!

> **"RIVETING...A VERY FINE BOOK"**
> *—NEW YORK TIMES*

TRUK LAGOON (17-121-5, $3.95)
Mitchell Sam Rossi

Two bizarre destinies inseparably linked over forty years unleash a savage storm of violence on a tropic island paradise—as the most incredible covert operation in military history is about to be uncovered at the bottom of TRUK LAGOON!

THE LINZ TESTAMENT (17-117-6, $4.50)
Lewis Perdue

An ex-cop's search for his missing wife traps him a terrifying secret war, as the deadliest organizations on Earth battle for possession of an ancient relic that could shatter the foundations of Western religion: the Shroud of Veronica, irrefutable evidence of a second Messiah!

Available wherever paperbacks are sold, or order direct from the Publisher. Send cover price plus 50¢ per copy for mailing and handling to Pinnacle Books, Dept. 17-204, 475 Park Avenue South, New York, N.Y. 10016. Residents of New York, New Jersey and Pennsylvania must include sales tax. DO NOT SEND CASH.